RISKY COWBOY

HOPE ETERNAL RANCH ROMANCE, BOOK 6

ELANA JOHNSON

ISBN-13: 978-1638760214

RISKY COWBOY

CHAPTER ONE

Spencer Rust buttoned up the red, white, and blue plaid shirt, not necessarily trying to be patriotic, though he knew it would probably help. He checked his belt to make sure it sat in the right place, and he reached for his boots.

These old things could stand to be replaced, but Spencer hated shopping with about as much intensity as the sun shone in Texas in June. The moment he stepped outside, he wondered why he lived here, and yet, he'd never lived anywhere else.

Memories started to stream through his head, and Spencer pressed against them. It would do no good to hash up the past, even if he was willingly stepping into that past this afternoon.

"She's not going to be there," he told himself. Sweet Water Falls wasn't a huge town, though it did bring in people from several little towns around it. All the shopping was in Sweet Water Falls, with ranches, farms, and other communities spreading out from it like spokes on a wheel—at least until the beach took over on the south and southeast.

Spencer loved Sweet Water Falls. He loved his job at Hope Eternal Ranch. He really did. Honestly, and truly did.

Something, however, seethed inside him. An animal that paced back and forth, demanding to be set free.

He'd been at Hope Eternal for thirteen years, and that was the longest Spencer had stayed anywhere. Even as a kid and then a teen, his life had been filled with constant turmoil. This new job in Cotton Creek could be "the one." That boss in Short Tail just didn't understand.

He boxed up the memories and shut the lid tightly. Tape went on the outside of the box, but Spencer knew it wouldn't last for long. He always thought about his family and his past in the summertime, when his mother had died.

With his well-worn boots on, Spencer stood. He'd told exactly one person about his interview today, but he didn't expect to see Nathaniel Mulbury on his way out. A ranch in the summer—especially a commercial ranch like Hope Eternal, where tourists came to visit, buy honey, watch live horse care demonstrations, and even stay in cabins out on the river—was extremely busy.

Nate had two kids now, and when school wasn't in

session, he'd have both his boys with him, slowing him down. If Nate could even go slow, which Spencer wasn't sure about.

He smiled to himself and left his bedroom. He shared the house where he lived with four other cowboys, which didn't bother him all that much. But at thirty-seven, Spencer was starting to wonder what it would be like to live on his own. He hadn't really done that in his life, though most of his memories only had himself or his parents in them.

Sure, he'd had a few girlfriends over the years, but Spencer...well, he hadn't had much luck with women.

His pulse rioted as he reached the front door, where he hung the nicer of his two hats. The other one always waited by the back door, as that was the exit he used to go to work on the ranch. If he was going to church or town, he used the front door, and thus, wore his nicer cowboy hat.

Out on the porch, in the shade, the Texas heat didn't hit him square in the face. No, that heat penetrated his lungs on the first breath, and Spencer dang near choked on the humidity. His body remembered how to behave in the heat quickly, and he was fine by the time he reached the sidewalk at the bottom of the steps.

At four o'clock in the afternoon, Spencer didn't expect to run into anyone leaving the ranch. He'd be lying if he said he hadn't planned it that way, so he didn't even think that.

"It's time," he told himself. "This is the right thing to do."   ·

While he wasn't entirely sure of that, he got behind the wheel of the truck and left Hope Eternal Ranch in his rearview mirror.

"It's not the last time," he said, keeping up the stream of talking to himself. He'd been doing that since his momma's death too, and old habits sure did die hard around these parts of Texas.

The highway leading north and then west took him to Sweet Water Falls Farm, and it only took fifteen minutes from one ranch to the other. They weren't the same at all, though Spencer's job wouldn't be too terribly different. At least on paper.

Hope Eternal ran a lot of horseback riding lessons. They were a working ranch, with agriculture, breeding, branding, and so many chickens, Spencer had lost count. But they were really a tourism ranch. The owner, Ginger Mulbury, made most of her money off families coming to the Coastal Bend of Texas for an authentic western vacation. And the horseback riding lessons.

Wayne Cooper owned the operation where Spencer was now turning off the asphalt and onto a dirt road. It was a dairy farm, not a cattle ranch, and not a tourism destination. He ran the place with his three sons, but all Spencer could think about was Wayne's youngest daughter.

"She's *not* going to be here," he told himself as he came

to a stop in front of the beautiful, sprawling farmhouse where Wayne lived with his wife. The rumor mill around Sweet Water Falls churned constantly, and just because Spencer was a man working at an outlying ranch didn't mean he hadn't heard about Clarissa Cooper's big exodus to San Antonio.

It was almost like she was a local celebrity just for going to culinary school, as if she was the first person to ever do so.

Spencer tried to box her up too, but Clarissa had a way of busting right through the confinements, tape, and resistance he put up against her. He supposed it was the fire of the redhead in her, and a smile touched his mouth.

Maybe he'd be ready to play with that fire this time.

"Don't be stupid," he told himself, and he sounded so much like his father it made him pause. He did not want to be like his father, not in any way, shape, or form. Not in how he acted. Not in the way he dressed. Not in how he spoke.

He took a deep breath and got out of his truck. Wayne had said to come by the house first, and they'd talk about the job, the farm, all of it. Spencer swallowed hard as he made his way over the gravel and onto the sidewalk. Then up the steps.

The front door opened before he reached it, and Wayne Cooper slipped outside. "Chrissy is sleeping," he said with a quick smile. "Don't want to wake her."

"Of course not," Spencer said, glad his voice had softened. He reached to shake Wayne's hand. He'd known the man for years, and a measure of relaxation moved through him as they shook hands and smiled at one another.

"Hoo boy," Wayne said, taking off his cowboy hat and running his hand through his hair. His was mostly white now, with only a hint of reddish-blond in there from days past. He wore a huge, white cowboy hat, a plain blue button-up shirt that went all the way to his wrists, and jeans. His belt looked as dusty as his boots, and he walked over to the west side of the porch and leaned into the railing, facing the farm.

"You haven't worked a dairy farm before, have you, son?"

Spencer bristled at the word *son*. "No, sir," he said anyway. "I'm at Hope Eternal right now. Not a lot of dairy cows there." Zero, in fact.

"Out at Sugar Hill before that," he drawled.

"Yes, sir," Spencer said, staying right where he was. The porch extended to both corners of the house, but it was narrow, and he'd just have to come back this way anyway. "Cattle there. I was only there for a few years."

He didn't say he'd left because he didn't like the way the boss treated his hired help. That too sounded like something his dad would've said.

Wayne nodded and turned back to him. "The job has changed a little," he said. "Due to some things shifting around here I wasn't aware of when I put it on the board."

"Okay," Spencer said. "I can handle anything. I've

been workin' with animals and people for decades." He offered Wayne a smile as he approached in a gait that looked like it had a hitch in it, like his right leg was a little shorter than his left.

"Let's go out on the farm and take a look-see around, should we?"

"Sure," Spencer said, glad Wayne had returned his smile. He seemed perfectly at-ease, and Spencer relaxed out under the blue sky, with the rolling fields, waving trees, and whispering breeze.

"There's farm chores," Wayne said after he'd gotten in Spencer's truck. "Just take the road back the way you came, but don't turn toward the highway. We'll go out to the barns first."

"Okay." Spencer did as he said as Wayne continued to talk.

"We've got horses to tend to. They have stalls and an arena that has to be kept clean."

"No problem." He glanced at Wayne. "Hope Eternal has over a hundred horses now. We do these massive horseback riding lessons in the afternoons. *Every* afternoon."

Wayne nodded and pointed to a deep, brick-red stable. "Right there, son."

Spencer pressed his teeth together and parked at the stable. He got out quick as a whip and hurried around to the passenger side to help Wayne down. The older man did fine, but Spencer really didn't want to be with him should he take a tumble.

"My sons run the milk side of the operation," he said, limp-walking toward the stable. "But we've got hay to harvest, barns to stock, horses to care for. We've got chickens galore, and my daddy has about ten dogs that circulate around him at any given time." He flashed Spencer a grin and opened the stable door.

Spencer held it for him so he could enter first, and he'd already moved on to talking about the work that had to be done around the ranch too—fences being restrung, watching for foxes in the chicken coops, and all the road maintenance.

None of that would be new for Spencer either, and he took a moment to gaze past the stable to the cowsheds where the dairy cows were milked. The milk parlor sat there too, with several other outbuildings related to their dairy operation here at Cooper & Co.

The farm itself was called Sweet Water Falls Farm, but the dairy side had been labeled Cooper & Co. Everyone knew that, but no one knew why.

His eyes landed on the retail shop here on the farm, and Spencer quickly tore his gaze from it and entered the stable. Clarissa ran the retail shop, and he told himself over and over and over again that she wasn't going to be there.

For one, they closed pretty early, though Spencer didn't have the hours memorized. Number two, he'd heard she'd be in San Antonio, training for her new job this week. By the time he put in notice at Hope Eternal and made the move over here, she'd be long gone.

His gut writhed at the thought of sitting down with Nate and Ginger and telling them he was leaving the ranch. Ginger would take it personally, and Nate would have questions about why Spencer felt like he needed a change. They wouldn't come at him in rapid-fire succession, but they'd still come. Nate was a thoughtful, meticulous man, and he could see deeper than a lot of other people. Spencer supposed his time in prison had fostered that inside him.

He wondered what he'd learned from all the bad things that had happened to him in his life. How not to snap at someone when he was angry, he'd learned that. He'd learned not to even get angry, especially about simple things like rain and animals that got stuck in fences. Those were just things that happened, not events to rage about.

"...over there," Wayne said, and Spencer realized they'd gone through the whole stable already.

"Okay," he said, though he hadn't been listening to the man he hoped would be his new boss soon.

"So we'll head over to the barn, and then I'll take you to the shoppe. Clarissa will go over that part of the job with you."

"O—what?" Spencer came to a full stop. "The shoppe?"

Wayne simply walked outside and held the door for Spencer. He better get a move on—and start paying attention to what Wayne said. "Yes, the shoppe," he said, indicating it where it sat across a small parking lot. "We sell cheese, milk, butter, and ice cream. I guess anything Clarissa makes, we sell it."

A single car sat out front, and Spencer could only blink at the quaintness of the place. The shoppe looked like it had come from an old western novel, complete with a white picket fence along the faux porch, dark brown boards as the walls, and a bright white roof. The sign even held the old-fashioned lettering, with an extra P and E on shoppe.

"We do a lot of business through the shoppe," Wayne said, continuing toward the barn. "Clarissa handles all the sales for the milk to the bakery in town. They make everything with our milk. We have trucks coming every day to the farm, but again, my sons handle most of that."

"So what will I handle?" Spencer asked, paying much closer attention now. He thought he saw the curtains in the shoppe flutter, but that couldn't be. Clarissa absolutely was not here.

His brain fired at him though, a bullet that Wayne had said only moments ago. Or maybe an hour. Everything in Spencer's head felt blended up at the moment.

Clarissa will go over that part of the job with you.

She was here, and he was going to have to talk to her soon. Very soon.

"All the local sales that do pick-up," Wayne said, and Spencer tore his gaze from the billowy curtains to follow the man. With his attention so complete on that blasted shoppe, he didn't see the barrels right outside the stable, and he went plowing right into two of them.

Water slopped inside them; pain shot through his thigh and stomach; pure humiliation hollowed him out.

He told himself not to look over to the shoppe to see if Clarissa had seen him get gutted by two benign barrels, but he couldn't help it. Sure enough, this time, the redhead stood in the doorway of the shoppe, her arms folded and her glare strong enough to cross the parking lot and pierce him in the heart.

"Come on, son," Wayne said from the barn. "You'll have work to do in here too."

Spencer tore his eyes from the stunning, disapproving woman across the parking lot. "Yes, sir," he said, hurrying now to get away from the woman he'd once dated and had thought he'd never see again.

CHAPTER TWO

Clarissa Cooper could only stare as she stood just outside the shoppe. "This can't be happening," she said, but she'd know that gait, those boots, and that pair of broad shoulders anywhere.

Just because she hadn't seen Spencer Rust face-to-face in a while didn't mean her memory had been wiped clean. The real question was: What in the name of everything buttery was he doing here?

"This has disaster written all over it." Just like that time she'd tried to make black licorice, cream, and sugar to play nicely together. Clarissa could usually get any flavor to marry well with the ice cream base she'd perfected at her family's dairy farm, but that concoction had been her one great failure.

At least in the kitchen.

She'd failed plenty of other times, in plenty of other

ways. She had a half-finished business degree, a culinary certificate she hadn't used yet, and four long gashes on her heart to prove it, almost like the claws of a tiger had taken a swipe at her for not mixing catnip into a creamy ice cream base.

Spencer Rust had almost been the cause of one of those gashes, and she wasn't going to let him have another chance to derail her future.

Her father had opened the barn door across the parking lot from the Cooper & Company Shoppe, which Clarissa had been running for the past eight years. He'd already gone inside, and Spencer brushed his hands down his torso as he hurried after him.

"Almost like he's seen Satan himself," Clarissa muttered, already disgusted with the man. Deep down, she knew that feeling extended to herself, because her heartbeat had gone haywire when she'd seen him exit the barn from inside the shoppe.

She wasn't even sure how she'd come to be standing outside.

Spencer went into the barn, and at that moment, Clarissa's heart started beating normally again. Stupid thing didn't realize it was supposed to do that all the time, and that it couldn't stall or freak out at the sight of every tall, dark, and delicious cowboy.

She turned away from the barn and went back inside. She brushed her hand along the window to fix the curtains she'd practically ripped down when she'd recognized

Spencer and continued over to the wall to retrieve the clipboard just inside the kitchen door. The store was closing in ten minutes, and she needed to do the inventory. Then she'd know what cheeses to make in the morning, and which products she needed to put on sale before they expired.

Cooper & Co didn't use any antibiotics or hormones, and that meant their completely organic milk and milk products couldn't sit in coolers forever. Pick-ups had to be made within the hour of her pulling the product from the refrigeration unit in the milk parlor. Almost everything she sold in the shoppe had a shelf-life of less than four days.

Yes, she was proud of her family's operation. They'd worked hard to build the dairy farm, and her great-granddaddy had settled here in Sweet Water Falls over a century ago. She'd filed for historic status for Cooper & Co a few months ago, but she hadn't heard if the state had approved it or not.

If they did, the farm would get a nice plaque to put on their sign out on the highway. She supposed Daddy could put the plaque anywhere he wanted, and she hoped the Texas Agriculture Board would get their act together before October. Daddy's birthday was at the beginning of that month, and she wanted to give him the plaque and the certificate as a gift.

He'd worked around the farm since he was old enough to walk. All Coopers did, even her older sister, Cherry, and even her.

She and Cherry had both left to go to college, as had Lee, her oldest brother. Her other two brothers hadn't, though, and she could see why not. They knew how to run the farm without certificates and math classes.

Clarissa sometimes felt like that about her culinary education. Some of her cooking ability had come as innate ability. Her palette could detect the subtlest of flavors. She loved creating recipes, and she'd started a document on her computer with all of her best ice creams, cakes, cookies, and brownies. She didn't dare call it a cookbook, though somewhere in the back of the part of her mind that still dreamed, she *was* writing a dessert cookbook.

Surprisingly, she didn't want to own a bakery or sweet shop. She had two really good friends in town who did that, and she saw how much they worked.

You'll work that much if you get the job at Overlook, she told herself. Excitement zinged through her at the thought of even stepping foot in the four-star restaurant in San Antonio as a professional chef. Her best friend from culinary school had landed a job there a few years ago, and Leslie had contacted Clarissa a couple of months back, saying that an opening might be coming up in the kitchen there.

Clarissa had thought she'd been happy in her family's small cheese kitchen here. She did get to mix up herby cheese spreads and make varieties of ice cream no one else got to experiment as freely with.

And she *had* been happy. She liked being near her

family, though her brothers were some of the grouchiest men on the planet. It didn't help that Mama kept after the three of them constantly to find someone to marry and start having babies with.

Lee, the oldest had been married before. He had a son he saw all the time, and who came to live on the farm constantly, as his ex-wife lived only a short twenty-minute drive away, and they shared custody of Ford.

Mama didn't keep her lectures about settling down and raising a family to just the boys either. Cherry and Clarissa heard it plenty, that was for sure. Even though her mother was sick and barely left the house anymore, Clarissa knew exactly how she felt on a variety of topics.

Her stomach flipped at the thought of leaving Sweet Water Falls. She'd only done so to learn new skills and get an education, and she couldn't imagine moving to San Antonio permanently.

Cherry had done it a decade ago, and while the two girls bookended the family, with Cherry the oldest and Clarissa the youngest, Clarissa did love her sister fiercely.

Guess who's on the farm today? she typed out and sent to her sister. When she and Spencer had broken up nine years ago, she'd promptly left town. She and Cherry had still talked about him for months, though, because he *had* put one of those gashes on her heart.

"Not an *almost*-gash," she told herself, and it felt like the wound was starting to reopen, and she'd only seen him. What would it be like if she had to speak to him?

Who? Cherry asked.

Spencer Rust.

You're kidding. Why?

Cherry worked as a college counselor, and she had busy times and not-busy times. The first week of June wasn't terribly chaotic in that she had to deal with students, but the counseling department did a lot of registration and setting up for fall semester over the summer. Not only that, but Cherry was well-known for disappearing in the middle of a conversation simply because she had the attention span of a goldfish.

I don't know, Clarissa said. *I just saw him and Daddy go into the barn from the stable.*

With horror, she realized why. Her fingers flew over the screen, but she hadn't finished her text before Cherry's came in.

Is he going to hire him? He put up a new job last week, didn't he?

Clarissa jammed her thumb against the backspace arrow to delete her message, which had said the same thing. *Yes,* she sent instead. *How can he hire him? Do you think he's forgotten that we used to date?*

In typical Cherry fashion, she didn't answer. Clarissa should be glad she'd gotten as many responses as she had. Cherry's super-hot boss had probably walked by, and her sister had been trying to get a date for six months now.

Clarissa didn't have the heart to tell her it wasn't going to happen. She certainly didn't have any wiggle room to speak when it came to relationships. After she'd dated Spencer, she'd poured herself into her culinary training and returned to the farm. He'd still been at Hope Eternal Ranch, but Clarissa knew how to revolve around the sun that was Spencer Rust without coming into contact with him.

She'd perfected it for the past eight years, in fact.

Now, though, it seemed as though he'd thrown his heavenly body out of orbit and was careening toward her.

She looked up from her phone when Cherry still didn't respond and kicked herself into action. She couldn't stand here and text her sister about Spencer. She had work to do, and then she needed to close up the shoppe and get on home.

Her résumé needed to be updated, as she'd need it to apply to any job in San Antonio, including the one that had just come open at Overlook. The restaurant sat on the top floor of a prestigious hotel that overlooked the river that wound right through the city.

Clarissa had been there once, to visit Leslie, over a year ago. That trip usually stayed buried deep in her gray matter, because her boyfriend at the time, another dark, dreamy, delicious cowboy named Russ Hatchell, had broken up with her on the drive home. All the romanticism of the sunset through floor-to-ceiling windows, and perfectly seared scallops, and the huge brownie sundae they'd shared with a single spoon had been soiled in less than five minutes.

Another of those gashes on her heart belonged to Russ, because Clarissa had genuinely loved him, and she'd thought they'd be married by now.

Sometimes life didn't understand her fantasies, and she'd almost stopped dreaming.

In the realm of men, she had. She held no more wondrous plans for her Cowboy in Shining Belt Buckle, who'd come rescue her from a life of dairy cows and crotchety brothers.

As far as her cooking career, though, Clarissa still held out some hope that she'd find somewhere where she could use her hard-fought-for and expensively-obtained baking skills. "And it's not your family's dairy farm in Nowhere, Texas," she muttered to herself, focusing on the clipboard in her hand.

Sweet Water Falls wasn't really Nowhere, and she criticized herself for being unfair. She was just ready for a change. Any change. *Please*, she prayed, the way her mama had always taught her. *Something has to change, or I'm going to lose my mind.*

As she'd done a thousand times before, she checked the refrigeration units and made checkmarks on her clipboard. She checked the fridge in the small kitchen attached to the shop and went through the ingredients there. She looked at the schedule for ice cream flavors, checked the levels in the big cardboard containers in the freezer case out front, and turned toward the menu board, which she hand lettered every time there was a change.

She'd taken a few design classes as part of her unfinished business major, and she did like expressing her creativity on the menu board and in her recipes. She turned away from the black chalkboard with flowery writing as the tinkling bell on the door sounded. She put a smile on her face, because if there was one thing Clarissa knew, it was that the customer was always right.

They didn't care if it was closing time, or if she'd just lost a boyfriend, or that yet another chef hadn't returned her inquisition for a job at their restaurant.

"Evening," she drawled before she could turn to see who it was. "Oh, hey, Daddy."

The smile faltered as her dad stepped aside and Spencer Rust himself filled the doorway. Those dark eyes had not changed, and they devoured her as easily as they ever had.

"Evenin', Clarissa," he said, touching the brim of that stunning cowboy hat. "What's the flavor of the day?"

Dark, dreamy cowboy, she thought. With her stupid heart tap dancing now, she turned toward the menu board, which she'd just been studying. She'd seen the flavor of the day, but her mind had blanked with one look from Spencer, and all she could hear was the racket her pulse made in her ears.

"Looks like it's Rocky Road," she said.

She probably needed to see a cardiologist. All they'd have to do to replicate her issues was flash a picture of

Spencer onto the wall. *Oh, yes,* they'd say. *This requires surgery. Complete heart transplant.*

She turned back to Spencer, and he hadn't taken his eyes from her. "Sounds amazing," he said, and Clarissa found herself agreeing with him.

Wait. She didn't agree with Spencer Rust, and the argumentative side of her almost said the ice cream would certainly be disgusting. Then she remembered she'd made it.

"Waffle cone?" she asked, and it sounded like she'd gargled with one. Perhaps she needed to see an ear, nose, and throat specialist. She'd just have a dozen procedures done to eliminate her husky voice, the tightness in her jaw, and the way her stomach swooped at the very idea of Spencer getting close to her again.

"Yes, please," he drawled in that sweet-as-honey Texas accent, making her heart kick out extra beats.

"Daddy?" she asked, glad the gargled tone had cleared.

"I want the butter pecan, baby."

"In a cup," they said together. Clarissa smiled at her father and got busy scooping their treats. He didn't like ice cream cones—or so he claimed. Clarissa thought it had more to do with the fact that Mama wanted him to cut back on the sugar, but he couldn't stay away from the ice cream.

He'd tried the sugar-free variety, and Clarissa had spent eight months trying to find a recipe that would give him the flavor he wanted without the sugar Mama didn't want. She hadn't found it, and Daddy had just gone back to regular ice cream, claiming that tofu had no place in his treats.

He now compromised by having his ice cream in a cup. He almost always chose butter pecan or maple nut, because he said the taste of the sweet milk came through in them better. Daddy loved everything about dairy, but nothing more than ice cream.

As she rounded the case to deliver the ice cream to the two tough cowboys, she asked, "What are you doin' here, Spencer?" She shot a quick look at Daddy but didn't let it linger for long, because the floor was uneven in the shop. She also congratulated herself for saying her ex-boyfriend's name without choking or talking like a Chipmunk.

"He's your replacement," Daddy said.

A strangled noise came from her mouth, and Clarissa's feet caught on the uneven titles. She yelped as she stumbled forward, managing to lift the cup with the butter pecan high enough to save it, but that required her to smash the waffle cone with all that delectable chocolate ice cream, nuts, and marshmallows right into Spencer Rust's patriotic plaid shirt.

He grunted as he kept her from falling with his body and then steadied her with his hands on her waist. Pure horror mingled with humiliation inside her, making her pulse positively panicked now.

"I'm sorry," she said as Daddy took his unscathed cup

of ice cream as if she hadn't just thrown herself into Spencer's arms and ruined his shirt. Spencer's cologne muddled her mind, the heat of his hands on her back absolutely delightful.

No, she told herself. *Absolutely unwanted.*

She looked at her father with round eyes, so many thoughts running through her mind. "I thought you said he was my replacement."

"I did." Daddy licked his spoon, too much enjoyment in his eyes for what had just happened. He knew she and Spencer had dated years ago. *Of course* he knew. Just because he was almost seventy didn't mean he'd lost his memories. Was this some trick to get them back together? There had to be dozens of cowboys applying for the job opening here at Cooper & Co, but she had the very real feeling Daddy would hire this one.

She narrowed her eyes at him, but Daddy just dug his spoon into his butter pecan and took a bite.

With his words ringing in her ears, Clarissa managed to step back, and Spencer's hands dropped from her body. She stared at the horrible chocolate stain on his chest. It seemed to spread, and when she blinked, the ice cream had covered his whole shirt and then started to melt into her life too.

"I can pay for that," she said, blinking to get the image of that ice cream to stop spreading. It wasn't doing that, and she was just so horrified and electrified and terrified-thrilled that her imagination had run wild.

With a jolt, she realized she was still staring at his chest. Maybe that was why she couldn't look away from the ice cream stain. That chest...

He looked down at his shirt for several long moments too, finally lifting those glittering eyes to hers.

Then he started laughing.

CHAPTER THREE

S pencer accepted the invitation to clean up in the sink in the kitchen. It sat right next to the door leading back out into the customer area of the shop, and he listened to Clarissa talk in rapid-fire words to her daddy about the tiles in this shop and how they needed to be replaced.

He scrubbed at his shirt, finally tossing the rag into the sink. The shirt was ruined anyway. He sighed as he looked up to the ceiling. "What am I doin' here?"

He didn't have a good answer, other than he didn't want to be at Hope Eternal Ranch anymore. His hope *had* been eternal, and he still hadn't found someone to spend his life with.

He had healed, though, to the point where he'd actually wanted a relationship that lasted longer than a few months. The problem was, every time he tried, he ended up left in the dust.

Women always chose someone else over him. Always.

Luck had never been on Spencer's side. If it had been, he certainly hadn't known it when his mother died when he was only thirteen. Or when his daddy had drank so much, night after night, that the farm where he'd grown up had been run into dust and weeds. A teenager can only do so much and go to school.

When his granddaddy had found out, he'd taken back the farm Spencer loved, and he'd been in the wind since. Basically.

He supposed finding the job at Hope Eternal had involved a fair bit of luck, but he knew his hard work had been what kept him there. That, and his connection to the owner, Ginger. She hadn't owned the ranch at the time of his hiring, but they were close to the same age and both determined to prove something to the world.

In many ways, he'd grown up with Ginger Talbot. She was married now, with a baby and a step-son, and Spencer had seen her heal, grow, and change in the ways he wanted to. He just didn't know *how*.

He felt like he'd gotten as far as he could go at Hope Eternal, and he simply needed a change. He had to take a chance. Take a risk. So he'd put out some interest in a new job at a new ranch. He'd been working at Hope Eternal for thirteen years, and he had the chops to handle almost anything.

When the Good Lord didn't answer his question, he left the kitchen and came face-to-face with Clarissa Cooper. *Almost* anything.

He wasn't prepared for this woman, and he should've been.

"I'm really sorry about your shirt," she said through nearly clenched teeth. "Please do send the bill to the farm."

"It's fine," he said, barely able to meet those dark green eyes of hers. They'd always made him want to lean closer and look deeper, and he knew if he did that, he'd fall in love with her all over again. "I'll just throw it away."

"All right," Wayne said from the door of the shoppe. He opened it, setting the bell into motion. "You two have fun tonight."

"What?" Spencer and Clarissa asked at the same time. She spun toward her father, and Wayne simply grinned.

"I thought you were going to show me the house," Spencer said. He'd come for the final interview, but Wayne hadn't asked him a single question. He'd shown Spencer the stable and the barn, talked about the milking part of the dairy farm, and then brought him to the shoppe, claiming they needed an evening pick-me-up in the form of ice cream before he took Spencer over to the house where he'd live if he got the job.

Spencer didn't much care what the house looked like. It would be a private residence, and that felt like a step up to him, even if he didn't own it and pay the mortgage. He wasn't exactly tired of living with other cowboys, because he liked the company at night. But he almost relished the idea of having a place all to himself, where he could leave the radio on all night and not disturb someone else's sleep, or walk around the house in his underwear on Sunday mornings before he put on his shirt, tie, and slacks and went to church.

"I said you'd get shown around," Wayne said. "You're going to be taking Rissa's place, and she's the expert. She'll get you up to speed with the shoppe, and she knows which house you'll be in." He grinned widely at the pair of them, and Spencer didn't like the twinkle in his eyes.

"It's right next-door to hers." With that, Wayne tipped his hat and walked out.

"Daddy," Clarissa said, practically running across the shop after him. She yanked the door open. "I'm busy tonight."

Wayne called something back to her, and her shoulders drooped. She hung onto the door for another few seconds, and then she closed it and pressed her forehead against it.

Spencer wanted to tell her she didn't have to show him the shoppe. He'd seen the hours on the door, and they were closed. She likely did have plans for tonight, and they hadn't included him for almost a decade.

That's your fault, he thought. *You should apologize.*

Was nine years too long to go without apologizing? Spencer didn't think so, because if his daddy showed up on his doorstep with his hat in his hand and an "I'm sorry, son," dripping from his lips, Spencer would take it.

And it had been *two* decades of silence between him and his father. His throat suddenly turned to sawdust, and that had nothing to do with the cold ice cream stain on his shirt or the way Clarissa clung to that door like it was Captain America's shield and she needed it to protect herself from Spencer.

"Listen," he said. "I'm starving, and I'll just go grab something and get out of your hair." He wasn't even sure if he'd gotten the job or not. Wayne had said he'd be taking "Rissa's" place, but...had he gotten the job?

She drew in a breath and turned back to him, displeasure sparking in those dark green eyes that he'd once seen drift closed just before he kissed her.

A long, long time ago, he told himself. He couldn't go get excited about the possibility of kissing her again.

"Do you know how to make cheese, Spencer?"

"No, ma'am."

"Ice cream?"

"No, ma'am." Discomfort started to seep into him. He'd thought he'd be working with the horses here. The stables he knew. A barn he was comfortable in. Sweet Water Falls Farm had two arms of operation, and the job listing hadn't said anything about working the dairy aspect of it.

Wayne himself had said his three sons would handle the dairy side. He knew Cooper & Co did all of their own processing, and he'd known they had a retail store. He'd been impressed with the cleanliness of the shoppe and how complete it was, with refrigeration units full of cheese, cream, butter, and milk. All organic, of course, as the sign on the door had proclaimed.

His brain whirred as two pieces got put together. "You make all the ice cream here."

"Yes," she said.

He looked to his left, where a refrigeration unit stood holding cheese, butter, and spreads. "And all of this." Wayne had said she made it all; she'd gone to culinary school; the hand-lettered signs on the shelves and menu board screamed Clarissa.

"Yes," she said with a sigh. "He didn't tell you the job included the shoppe, did he?"

Spencer looked back to her, and he thought he saw a moment of understanding in her gaze before she darted her eyes away from his. "No," he said slowly. "That was not in the job description."

"Then we have a lot to do in a short amount of time," she said. "Here's how this is going to go." Those eyes flashed dangerously. She reached up and slid the elastic out of her strawberry blonde hair, the long locks falling over her shoulders in waves. "You're going to *take* me to dinner, and we're going to go over all of your duties here in the shoppe."

His eyebrows drove toward the sky. "You're going to teach me?"

"I'm going to try to talk some sense into my father."
She sighed and shook her head. "But in the meantime, yes.
I'm going to teach you."

Spencer narrowed his eyes at her. She didn't want him
here, that much was obvious. "Aren't you leaving Cooper
and Co?"

Clarissa raised her chin, almost defying him. "Yes."

"Where are you going?"

"San Antonio."

"Some big wig job at a restaurant, I heard." He cocked
his one eyebrow, the question clear.

But Clarissa's façade and bluster fell, and she looked
at the ground. "I'm still working on the 'big wig job' part of
that."

"I'm sorry, could you repeat that?"

She lifted her eyes to his, and he grinned at her.
Slowly, a smile crawled across her face too. "Stop it," she
said.

"Stop what?"

"Looking at me."

"So we're going to go to dinner, but I can't look at
you?"

"Yes," she said, but she didn't stop looking at—or
smiling at—him. She even took a step toward him, and
Spencer felt the temperature in the store raise a few
degrees. Dozens of memories ran through his mind, all of
them with her delicate hand in his, her laugh filling his
ears, the touch of her lips against his.

They'd had a good summer together, once.

"Why are you leaving the farm?" he asked.

"Oh, you know," she said, stepping past him and going around to the other side of the ice cream counter. "First lesson, the store has to be cleaned and left precisely how you want it the following day. You won't have time to do it before you open."

"I don't know," he said, putting his elbows on top of the ice cream case and leaning into them. "Tell me."

Clarissa looked up from the chore of wiping the counter where she'd scooped their treats. Her eyes held fear and hope at the same time, and it sent Spencer's male side into overdrive.

"I'm leaving," she said slowly. "Because it feels like I'm never going to get what I want here."

"Mm," Spencer said, connecting to her in a whole new way. "I know what that feels like."

"Do you?"

"Yep." He smiled at her, and a blush crept into her cheeks, accentuating her beauty and making a few freckles stand out. She really was beautiful, and the way her daddy had gobbled down his ice cream, she had talent in the dessert-making department.

Spencer would like her even if she didn't. Clarissa was a strong woman, with a good head on her shoulders. She knew what she wanted, and she took actionable steps to get those things.

"I'm surprised you haven't gotten what you want," he

said. "You were always so good at that." She'd left Sweet Water Falls—and him—to go to culinary school. He'd lost track of her then, as he had his own life to live and she was just one more regret hanging in the back of his mind.

He'd dated a lot of women since then, making new mistakes with each and every one of them. He'd learned from those mistakes, and he really thought he was ready to try again. Maybe he didn't need to leave his comfort zone at Hope Eternal Ranch, not if he could go to dinner with Clarissa. Perhaps she could be the risk he took, the change in his life that he needed.

As proof that he'd learned something, he simply waited for Clarissa to say something. She shrugged and said, "I know what I want, but I don't know how to get it. Not here, at least."

He'd rather not talk about what he wanted and all the ways he'd failed spectacularly to get them, but he nodded. "Makes sense." He cleared his throat. "Before we do anything else, I need to apologize for what I said before you went to culinary school."

Her eyebrows went up, and she swallowed. Spencer's own chest tightened, making his heartbeat seem so big inside the smaller cavity. So much stuck in his throat, and he hated that. He didn't want any awkwardness between the two of them, especially if they had to live next-door to one another.

She's leaving, he told himself, though she had just admitted she didn't actually have a job in San Antonio yet.

Spencer knew how long a person could look for a job, because his father had been looking for twenty years.

"Anyway, you don't have to say anything," he said, swallowing away the bitterness in his throat. Not a day passed where he didn't think about his dad, but he seemed pretty prevalent today for some reason. "I just wanted you to know my insensitivity and stupidity have been weighing on my mind all these years, and I'm sorry."

He nodded, feeling lighter now that the apology was out. If she wanted to talk more about it, she could certainly say something. He'd never known her to stand there and stare, but he hadn't seen her or spoken to her in a while.

She said nothing. Moved not an inch. Blinked some more.

Feeling like he'd suddenly lost his clothes and stood in front of her naked, he stepped away from the ice cream case. "This is a pretty nice place." He took in the open-beam rafters in the ceiling. The black floor tiles were a bit uneven, but nothing that would cause a major problem for someone not completely taken off-guard, rushing around the counter, and holding two servings of ice cream.

The walls sported light gray paint, and the curtains screamed country-chic with a hint of the red-checkered pattern than Spencer thought every proper farm had somewhere on the property. A little table for two sat in the corner, with a sign that read *Every day is a good day for a sundae.*

He smiled at it, noted the door had been painted a

bright, bright blue and faced Clarissa again. "Did you paint the door?"

"Yes," she said, a frog in her throat.

Spencer nodded, because he could've told anyone that. Clarissa liked bright colors, because she herself was so bright and lively. During their single summer together, she'd told him of her "dream house" and how it would have a bright blue door with a window in it. This one didn't have a window, but he supposed this wasn't her house either.

His stomach growled, and he told himself he should leave. He couldn't make himself do it though, and he decided to employ another strategy he'd learned after a painful break-up with a woman named Pippa.

Ask me about myself from time to time, Spence, she'd said as she'd gone around her house and boxed up the things he'd left there over the months they'd been together. *You never ask me about myself, my day, none of it. It's you, you, you all the time.*

He didn't want to talk about himself right now, or possibly ever again. So he asked, "What is it that you want, Clarissa?"

CHAPTER FOUR

Clarissa couldn't believe the audacity of the man standing in front of her. At the same time, Spencer had always been a sweet guy. He'd encouraged her to apply to culinary school, claiming they could continue their relationship from a distance easily.

When she'd been accepted, she'd fully intended to do that—until he'd said, *I never expected you to get in.*

In all honesty, she'd used that single statement to spur her on during the difficult times in the kitchen. She was going to show Spencer Rust—she was going to show the world—that she'd not only gotten into the best culinary institute in the state, she was the best one in her class.

"What do I want?" She spread her arms wide, as if she could grow wings and fly. "What I've always wanted," she said, letting her arms drop back to her sides. "I told you once." Her pulse pounded, because the things she hadn't gotten yet made her anxious and upset.

"Husband," he said, holding up one finger. A second one popped up beside it. "Family."

It was amazing how two words could hold so much information and be so devastating. Not only that, but she couldn't believe she was standing here talking about husbands and families with a cowboy who'd once had a shot at being involved in those things.

She nodded, swallowing. "I can't keep doing the same things I've always done and expect different results. So I'm going to San Antonio. I have résumés out with several restaurants. I have a friend there, working in the industry, and she feeds me a lot of information." Clarissa needed to go call Leslie right now, in fact. "And I have enough money to live there for a month or two before I must have a job."

Pressing her lips together helped her stop talking, and Clarissa mentally told herself not to say another word. She didn't *know* Spencer just because they'd dated once, years ago. She didn't have to defend herself to him, and she didn't have to show him every detail of the shoppe today either.

Her shoppe meant a lot to her, and that was the only reason she'd show him how to do anything at all. She couldn't stand the thought of Mrs. Burnett coming to get her dill and parsley spread and not having it for her. Or having Tenley Barker, a good friend who ran the bakery, come to get her milk and not having it crated and ready for her.

No, when Clarissa left Sweet Water Falls Farm, she would do so with a replacement in her spot that could do everything precisely as it was meant to be done. That was why she'd asked Daddy to put the job up so early.

"That's why I'm leaving Hope Eternal too," Spencer said, but Clarissa had forgotten what she'd said.

"To do something different?"

He shrugged one shoulder though she suspected he should've kept nodding. "I want something different. So yes."

"What do you want?" she asked.

He held up that one finger again. "Wife." Another finger. "Family."

Clarissa dang near swooned on the spot. She swallowed and picked up her washcloth again. The counter in front of her sat spot-free, but she started wiping anyway. Anything to keep herself from looking at Spencer.

"You didn't want those things last time." It had been a wedge between them, actually. Spence had been a fun-loving guy, always ready for the next adventure. He'd liked holding her hand and kissing her, and she'd had no objections to that either.

But he hadn't been to college, and he hadn't been serious about anything. He had a job at Hope Eternal Ranch that he'd seemed dedicated to, but when she'd asked him what he wanted his life to be, he'd actually drawn a blank.

Cherry had told her that not everyone had their whole life planned out by age fourteen. That statement still burned Clarissa when she thought about it, because she hadn't had her life planned that early either. She had goals, sure. She knew what she liked; lots of people did. But planned out?

No, Clarissa hadn't planned out her life by age fourteen. Even now, the plan ebbed and flowed, because her goals never seemed to get any closer to where she stood.

"I'm not the same person I was ten years ago," he said.

No, he wasn't. He was more confident. Better-looking. Sporting bigger muscles. His eyes still glinted with desire when he looked at her, and the electric zing he'd always produced in her zipped through her bloodstream.

Maybe she needed a blood transfusion.

"Let's go over the cleaning procedures," she said. "And the inventory. I don't think I have time for dinner." She raised her eyebrows to see if that was okay with him. "There's lots of time for everything else."

He nodded and shoved his hands in his pockets. "I best be getting back to Hope Eternal myself. But I don't even know if I got the job. Your dad never did say."

"I'll talk to him," she said, though she was going to do her darndest to get Daddy *not* to hire Spencer.

"Just to talk him out of hiring me?" Spence quirked

one eyebrow into a sexy glare, and Clarissa couldn't help smiling.

"I'm very particular about this shoppe and the kitchen," she said. "You might want to reconsider anyway."

"I know what you're particular about," he said, clearly flirting with her.

"Uh, no you don't," she said firmly. "You don't know me at all, Spencer."

His face blanked and he straightened from where he'd been leaning against the case. "I'm sorry. That was...arrogant. You're right. I don't know you very well."

She nodded, glad she'd established this professional boundary between them. "I am going to talk to Daddy about the job. I can text you if you give me your number."

"Okay." He prattled it off for her, and she put it in her phone.

"Daddy's not super-hands-on with the new hires. He'll probably dump you onto me, and I'll be the one showing you around and training you about everything anyway."

"Whatever works for you guys," he said from the other side of the case.

Clarissa had half a mind to text her father in all caps right now. *WHAT WERE YOU THINKING? DOES HE REALLY ALREADY HAVE THE JOB?* would work nicely. Maybe with a double-question mark for emphasis.

She sighed as she looked up and shoved her phone in her back pocket, the demanding, shouting text unsent.

"Well, come on over here, cowboy. The cleanliness of an ice cream parlor isn't something you learn at arm's length."

———

CLARISSA SMELLED THE CHARRED CORN BEFORE SHE came to a stop in front of the farmhouse where her parents lived. That meant Lee was cooking, and since it was a Wednesday, that made sense. With Cherry as the exception, as she lived in San Antonio, they each came to the homestead to make dinner one night per week. Between the four siblings, Daddy, and leftovers, there was always plenty of food at the farmhouse.

Mama was too ill to cook much anymore, but she needed good nutrition. Now that June was in full swing, they'd be bringing in a lot of fresh ingredients from the farmer's markets and the farm's agriculture side itself.

Summer was Clarissa's favorite time to eat, and her mouth watered at the thought of a good chicken and charred corn taco. Lee excelled in his cooking skills too, as did her other two brothers. They'd had to fend for themselves a lot growing up, and now with their additional responsibilities in the kitchen, every Cooper could certainly put out food worth eating.

She found her eldest brother in the kitchen, scooping the corn from the grill pan and into a bowl. "Evenin', Lee," she said, taking a seat at the bar and surveying what he'd prepared.

"Evenin'," he said, his perma-frown between his eyes already deep tonight. "Will you go get Daddy and Mama? They went out onto the deck with Queenie."

"Okay." Clarissa got to her feet and walked past the dining room table and built-in breakfast nook to the double-wide back doors. She stepped back outside to find her parents sitting in the swing on the edge of the deck. It wasn't shaded out there, but when Mama had complained that she couldn't see the farm from the swing's former spot up against the house, Daddy had moved it.

Daddy would move heaven and earth for Mama.

He'd been holding on to her for five years now, and Clarissa sometimes thought the only reason her mama hadn't passed yet was because of guilt that then Daddy would be left alone. Mama clung to the last threads of her life too, with her therapy dog, Queen Elizabeth, at her side

"Hey, you two," Clarissa said as she approached them. Mama turned her head to look up at her, and her skin looked almost translucent today. "Enjoying the sunshine?"

"It's glorious," Mama said with a smile. Her papery hand covered Clarissa's. "I heard your boyfriend came to the farm today."

Clarissa shot a look toward Daddy, but he just kept stroking Queenie's head and jowls.

"No, Mama," she said sternly. "He didn't. Daddy's not even going to hire him. Are you, Daddy?"

"Of course I'm going to hire him," Daddy said. "He's the most qualified, Rissa."

"I'm sure that's not true," she said through clenched teeth. She often gave her brothers a hard time for being so grouchy, but she had the fiery vein of a redhead flowing plenty hot inside her too. She could go from hot to cold in less time than it took Texas weather to change, and that was saying something.

"It's mucking out stalls and exercising horses," she said. "Every man, woman, and child in Texas can do that."

"It's so much more than that." Daddy got to his feet and glared at her before switching his gaze to one of love and concern for his wife. "Come on, my love. I'm sure dinner is ready if Clarissa is out here."

"Yes," she said, regretting the argument already, and it had just begun. "Lee sent me out to get you." She turned back to the house to find her brother opening the door.

"Did you decide to have a jaw instead?" he called, clearly not happy about the ten-second conversation they'd had about Spencer. "It's ready and getting cold."

"They're coming," she called back, plenty of bite in her tone too. Lee had zero patience, and she suspected that had something to do with his inability to get a woman to go on a second date with him.

Mama finally made it to her feet on the second try. Soon, even Daddy wouldn't be able to get her up and out of bed. In fact, Clarissa knew that Travis had been by twice this week to do just that. She was closest to her younger brother, who elbowed the ever-griping Lee out of his way as he came out onto the deck.

"Daddy," he said, smiling for all he was worth. *Oh, boy*, Clarissa thought. Something huge must have happened.

She smiled at her mother as she went by, but the gesture wasn't real and didn't last long.

"We got the Greenwood contract," Travis said, practically dancing over to Daddy. "It's in the dairy office, signed, sealed, and done."

Daddy started to laugh, and he released Mama to hug Travis and pound him on the back. Clarissa jumped to Mama's side to steady her, and they kept moving toward the house. Thankfully, Mr. Bossy had gone back inside.

When she arrived, Clarissa found Will had arrived as well. He growled something at his phone, his fingers flying over the screen. He had the fastest fingers in the west—for real. He'd won an award at some stupid cell phone store a couple of years ago for being able to send the most accurate texts the fastest.

"What's with you?" Clarissa asked, standing close to her mother as she sank into a chair at the dining room table.

"The fertilizer company wants to push us back a week," he said without looking up. "They did that last time too, and our crops aren't doing as well. They can't keep doing that. Our money is as good as someone else's."

"You tell them," Clarissa said, because sometimes it was fun to encourage her brothers' bad moods. They were going to have them no matter what she said or did, and she'd learned how to swim in the shark-infested waters a long time ago.

"No Ford tonight?" Mama asked.

Lee moved the tortillas and the charred sweet corn to the table. "No, Mama. He's got swimming lessons on Wednesdays now, just for the next couple of weeks, remember?"

Clarissa remembered Lee telling them all that, but Mama obviously didn't. She turned away from her confusion to help her brother get dinner on the table. She caught his look of gratitude, though no words were said, and finally Daddy and Travis came in the house, their chat about the contracts with a huge grocery chain out of New Orleans done for now.

Daddy didn't like talking business at the dinner table, but he'd do it any other time of day. Clarissa put the bowl of guacamole on the table and sat down beside Mama. Daddy braced himself against the empty chair on her other side and looked around at his sons, who all still stood around.

"Come sit down, boys," he said, and all three of them did. They had varying shades of red hair, with Lee's being the darkest. Everything about her oldest brother was the darkest, including the green in his eyes, and the way his skin tanned more than the others. His mood and attitude too, in Clarissa's opinion.

Travis sat next to her, and since he'd sold a huge contract today, he alone wore a look of glee. "How was your day, Rissy?" he asked just as Daddy said, "We have so much to be thankful for. Let's pray, and then we'll eat and talk about those things."

He met Clarissa's eyes, and since she didn't wear a cowboy hat and Daddy hadn't taken his off yet, he took a moment to do that. Lee too, as he'd obviously hustled through the house to share his news without removing his hat.

Otherwise, hats came off at one of the doors. Mama's rules. She wanted to see a person's face when talking to them, and she claimed cowboy hats gave men an unfair advantage in a conversation.

Clarissa happened to agree, but the unfair advantage came when flirting with a cowboy. Mm hm, a man who could duck that head with that hat on it, whether he was embarrassed or just shy, really got her pulse pounding. Oh, yes it did.

She bowed her head and closed her eyes, but she barely heard her daddy's prayer. The image of Spencer in his dark brown cowboy hat filled her mind and stole her focus.

When her brothers chorused, "Amen," she did too.

Daddy took his seat, and said, "All right, Trav. You start. Two things you're grateful for today."

Clarissa stayed out of the way while her brothers dove for the food, and then she took her own taco and loaded plenty of grilled chicken, corn, and guac into the tortilla. Her mind spun around what she could say she was grateful for, and when it came her turn, she said, "I'm grateful we have this time together to say what we're grateful for."

"Cop out," Will coughed into his third taco. Maybe his fourth.

She ignored him and took another bite of her taco. With that swallowed, she said, "I'm grateful for the chance to spread my wings and fly."

Mama grinned at her. "To have faith is to have wings," she said in her raspy voice, and Clarissa simply smiled back at her.

It would do no good to admit that flying actually scared Clarissa. That she actually didn't know if she'd take off or fall flat on her face.

What she did know was that she had to *try*, and she supposed that it did take a bit of faith to even take that first step toward trying.

CHAPTER FIVE

Spencer knocked on the front door of Ginger's and Nate's house, then opened it. "Ginger?" he called.

"In the kitchen," she said, and she sounded stressed. Spencer didn't want to add to that, but he had to talk to her today. After he'd left Clarissa at the shoppe two days ago, he'd called Wayne to confirm that he'd actually gotten the job.

With that confirmed, Spencer had set the first day he could start at Sweet Water Falls Ranch, and now...now he just had to go talk to Ginger.

She'd need to replace him, and he hated the situation more than anything as he stepped inside and closed the door behind him to seal out the Texas summer heat.

"Hey, Spence." She smiled at him as she wiped her hands on a dishtowel. Behind her in the kitchen, Connor stood on a stool at the counter, mixing something in a bowl. "We're making oatmeal chocolate chip cookies. Come sit down."

He had to get back out to the stables in an hour to start getting the horses ready for their first round of riding lessons, which he'd assist with until eight o'clock that night.

He reached up and removed his hat, turned to set it on top of the upright piano next to the door, and then joined her and the kids in the kitchen.

"Uncle Spence, look," Connor said, always so excited about everything. Spencer also liked how he called all the cowboys at Hope Eternal Ranch "uncle."

"What am I lookin' at, bud?"

"I made this all by myself. Cracked the eggs and everything."

"That's great," Spencer said, smiling at the boy. He'd be turning nine this fall, and Spencer hoped he'd get an invite to the boy's birthday party. His chest pinched, and he sighed.

"What's goin' on?" Ginger drawled, and Spencer looked away from the dough. "Con, you use the scoop now, remember?" She pointed to it on the counter and swung her two-year-old up onto her hip. She set Ward on the kitchen counter and added, "Just watch, baby. Conny's gonna make the cookies."

"Can I give him some dough?" Connor asked, looking at Ginger.

"Yep," she said. "I want some too." She held out her

palm, and Spencer added his to the fray as well. Connor grinned as he used the scoop to deliver perfect little cookie dough balls to Ginger and Spencer.

Ginger took a bite of hers, a moan coming out of her mouth. "Mm, this is great."

Spencer put his whole cookie dough ball into his mouth, the cinnamon and sugar a beautiful combination with the oats and chocolate. "So good," he said around the mouthful of dough.

He really wanted this life Ginger had. She'd come so far while he'd been standing still. "Where's Nate this afternoon?"

"He, Ted, and Dallas went to the house in White Lake." She met Spencer's gaze, a whole conversation happening between them. Connor's father had lived in White Lake and worked as a ranch auditor. There'd been an accident a few years ago that had taken Ward from this earth, and he'd left Connor to Nate's care.

Nathaniel Mulbury had been in prison at the time, and he'd been released into the Residential Reentry program, of which Hope Eternal Ranch was a certified center. Ginger had fallen in love with him, and they'd named their first child together after Nate's brother —Ward.

From time to time, Nate took his buddies from prison —all of whom now lived at the ranch or in nearby Sweet Water Falls—up to the house in White Lake to check on things. Nate would sell a few things, check the buildings, make sure the land was being taken care of properly, all of it.

He'd asked Spencer to go with him a few times, and Spencer had. He liked Nate a whole lot, because the man didn't say anything that didn't need to be said. That would be Ted, another man from the prison that had come to the ranch after his sentence had ended. He was a big bear of a man, with the darkest hair and eyes of any human being Spencer had ever met.

"Jess is bringing her kids for cookies and ice cream while she does the lessons."

"Right," Spencer said, taking the hint that he better get talking. "Listen, Ginger, I hate to do this. I really do, but I've found another job at another ranch, and I'm going to take it."

Her eyes widened, and Spencer should've anticipated that. The words had seared his throat, and he couldn't say anything else.

"Why?" she gasped out. She looked at the boys and moved away from them, indicating that Spencer should too. "Did we do something wrong here?"

"No," Spencer said, his throat so dry and scratchy. "Nothing like that. I just—" He didn't want to have to explain it all in such detail. "Remember when I started here?"

"Of course I do," she said. "I'd just decided to make this my full-time career too, and my daddy told me I had to train you." She smiled at him, but the happiness didn't reach all the way to her eyes.

Spencer grinned at her. "We both worked really hard that first few months."

"We did," she said, her smile fading. "Spencer, you can't leave."

"I can't stay."

"Is this about your dad?"

He shook his head, though Ginger knew more about Spencer's past than anyone else. "I mean, I've been thinking about him a lot lately, but this move isn't about him."

"What's it about? I didn't think you were unhappy here."

"I'm not unhappy here." He reached up and ran his hand through his hair. "Ginge, I just...I thought I'd have found what I was looking for here, the way you have. I mean, look around you. You've got this amazing, brand-new house. A husband who loves you. Two amazing kids." I gesture toward my cowboy hat on the piano, indicating the house beyond the front door, where I live. "I still live in the Annex. I'm still sharing my space with a bunch of other men. I haven't dated anyone with any level of seriousness in what? Four years?"

At least four years, he thought. "I need a change, that's all."

Ginger's dark green eyes shone with compassion and displeasure, but at least she took a few moments to consider all that had come spewing out of his mouth. "Where are you going?"

"Sweet Water Falls Ranch," he said, already holding up one hand. "I don't want you to say a word about Clarissa Cooper."

"I wasn't going to."

"Yes, you were. Your eyes turned into moons." He grinned at her. "I'm not going to Sweet Water Falls because of her. She's leaving for a job in San Antonio anyway. She won't be there."

Ginger turned back to the boys as Connor said he'd just finished scooping the cookies. "What do you think will be different there?" she asked. She picked up the tray and put it in the oven before facing him again.

Spencer honestly didn't know how to answer her question. He'd had the same one so many times over the years as his father had moved the two of them from place to place, always searching for the greenest grass.

They never had found it, and Spencer had left home the very day he'd graduated from high school. He hadn't even been an adult yet, but he'd lied to his first foreman, and he'd worked all over the Texas Hill Country for over six years before permanently landing at Hope Eternal Ranch, further east in the Coastal Bend.

He'd liked the beach feel of the town, while still having a horse-focused job on a ranch.

"I don't know what will be different there," Spencer said. "I just know I can't stay here anymore."

"It's because all the ladies are gone, isn't it?" She smiled as she looked at him. "I need another account manager. You can sit in on the interviews."

He grinned at her and shook his head. "No, I'm done dating people I work with." That had never worked out for him, and yes, he'd sat on the sidelines while every new man that had come to the ranch in the past few years had married women he'd tried relationships with.

In that moment, he realized what had changed. "I've changed, Ginger. I think I'm finally ready."

Her eyebrows went up. "Really?"

"Really," he said. "I'm not angry at every woman I see anymore, and I've seen how happy you are with Nate, and Emma with Ted." He stopped there, because he'd tried a relationship with Jess, but she'd felt like his little sister. Then she'd gone and fallen in love with Dallas Dreyer, become a mom to his two kids, and they had one of their own now too. Even they were a good example of the fact that marriage could work.

"I'm starting to believe in marriage," he said. "I'm not afraid to commit anymore. I'm not."

Ginger's face softened and started to crumple as she stepped over to him. "I'm so happy for you," she said.

"Don't cry," he said, hugging her. "I'm going to miss you so much."

"Yeah," she said, pulling away and wiping her eyes. She sniffled and tried to smile through it. "I hear Old Man Wayne Cooper is no softie."

Spencer chuckled, because Wayne Cooper did have a reputation around Sweet Water Falls and the surrounding area. He remembered how fast the man talked, even if his legs limped a little bit. "No, he's not."

"How's Chrissy?"

"You know, I don't know." Spencer sat down at the bar and accepted another dough ball from Connor. "Wayne didn't let me in the house."

"She's been battling that cancer for a long time," Ginger said, and Spencer recognized the look in her eye.

"What are you thinking?" he asked.

"Nothing."

"It's something," Spencer said, frowning. When she still wouldn't say, he added, "Ginger."

"Fine, I was thinking it would be nice to take them some cookies."

"Yeah, so you can talk him out of hiring me."

"No," she said, but her voice sounded so false. "No one talks Wayne Cooper out of anything."

Spencer said nothing, but he thought about Clarissa saying she was going to talk to her daddy about the job. He didn't think she'd get her way, even if she was the youngest and a woman. Daddy's little girl and all that.

"I don't want you to go makin' trouble for him," Spencer said. "It's me who'd made this decision."

Ginger met his eyes, and Spencer pleaded with her silently. "Fine," she said. "But you could take them some cookies from us and just say hello. Maybe they'd like to swap cowboys."

"Cowboy swap," Spencer said with a smile. "I doubt it, Ginger, but I will take them some cookies."

So it was that Spencer carried a paper plate full of oatmeal chocolate chip cookies up to the front door of the farmhouse at the Cooper's farm the very next morning. Honestly, they were lucky they'd gotten any at all, because Connor had done an amazing job, and Spencer had eaten exclusively cookies for the past two meals.

He knocked on the door, bypassing the doorbell in case Chrissy Cooper was asleep again. He didn't hear anyone coming to get the door, though someone should be expecting him. "Not here," he muttered to himself. He didn't want to carry cookies around the farm like Betty Crocker, so he set them on the porch and went back down the steps.

His truck trundled down the dirt road and to the right side of the farm. Wayne had shown him a ranch office off the milkshed, and he parked beside a red truck, which sat beside a white one.

"Hello?" he called, his paperwork clutched in his hand.

A man stuck his head out of a doorway only a few feet inside the building, and a smile popped onto Lee Cooper's face. "Spencer Rust." He stepped out into the hall and shook Spencer's hand. "This your paperwork?"

"Yes, sir," Spencer said, though Lee was only a few years older than him. Maybe five or six. He glanced down as a boy came into the hall too. "This your son?"

"Yep, this is Ford." Lee looked at the child with reddish-blond hair. All the Cooper's had some shade of red hair, with Lee's being some of the darkest. Clarissa's was more a strawberry-blonde, and Ford's barely had any red at all.

"Say hello to the man," Lee instructed. "Shake his hand, son."

"Good to meet you," Spencer said, smiling at him as they shook hands. "How old are you now?"

"Eight, sir," Ford said, glancing at his daddy.

"One of my very best friends has an eight-year-old," Spencer said. "Connor Mulbury? Maybe you guys are in the same class?"

"He's in second grade," Ford said. "But not my class. He has Mrs. Bear."

Spencer nodded, but he didn't know one teacher from the next.

"I'll take your papers," Lee said, and he did, looking at them. "Daddy said you have a start date of June twentieth?"

"Yeah," Spencer said. "I have to finish out at Hope Eternal first. Is he around? He said he'd show me the house where I'll be staying, and then I can order things I might need before I move over here."

"Sure, he's right in here." Lee indicated the office, and the three of them went into the office. Sure enough, Wayne sat on a small loveseat under the single window in the office, a bag of shelled pistachios in his hand.

"Spencer," he said, leaning forward to shake Spencer's hand without getting off the couch.

"Sir." Spencer didn't want to sit. He had work to do, and he'd only come by for a quick minute to drop off the paperwork and see the house. But Lee sat behind the desk, and Wayne certainly wasn't going anywhere in the near future.

"Daddy."

Spencer turned toward the man and recognized the second Cooper son—Will.

"We've got cows out." He knocked on the wall just inside the office, and that single statement got Lee and Wayne up in a hurry.

"Sorry, Spencer," Lee said as he followed his daddy into the hall. "Oh, look, here's Riss. She'll show you the house, okay?" He didn't wait for anyone to say okay, and Spencer did not see Clarissa. His heart pounded like he had, and that she'd dolled herself all up for a dinner-date with him.

Slinky black dress. Heels. Makeup. Curled hair.

He stepped into the hallway to find her wearing a black plastic apron over her jeans, rubber boots, and a bright red tank top. She peeled yellow rubber gloves off her hand and said, "What's he talkin' about? Where are they rushin' off to like the devil has lit their pants on fire?"

She was just as sexy in the apron, jeans, and gloves as she would be in the black dress, and Spencer's brain misfired at him. Clarissa looked at him, and he gathered his wits so he wouldn't turn into a dummy in front of her.

"Something about some cows being out," he said. "I came by to drop off my paperwork, and your daddy was going to show me the place where I get to stay, so I can get whatever I need before I move here."

Her frown deepened with every word he said. "So I'm the real estate agent now, is that it?"

He shrugged but couldn't help smiling. "I guess so." He couldn't lie and say he was upset by the switch, because he did like Clarissa. He'd always liked her, and he thought they'd never really had a chance all those years ago.

Maybe they did now.

CHAPTER SIX

C larissa wasn't exactly sure what she'd find in the little cabin next to her house. No one had lived in it for several months now, and Daddy had taken care of the place. She distinctly remembered people going in and out of it, but she couldn't remember if they'd been a construction team or a housekeeping crew, as she'd refused to pay much attention to what went on next door.

"Daddy expects you to take care of the place," she said as she reached to the top of the steps. "It's not extravagant, but most of our cowboys share a cabin. This one is a little farther out, and it's not as nice. It's also smaller, as there's no loft and only one bathroom. So he puts just one man out here."

Spencer joined her on the porch, and claustrophobia immediately set in. He smiled as she turned toward the door. The roof covered the porch, but there was standing room only otherwise, and she couldn't stomach being that close to him. The near proximity of him meddled with her mind, making her think all kinds of things she simply couldn't think.

She remembered how much fun they'd had together once. She thought of his black and white dog, Boots, and how the dog would lick her face while she laughed in the cornfields. How Spencer would join her and the pup on the ground, and they'd look up into the blue, blue Texas sky and talk about anything and everything.

He'd kissed her for the first time in a cornfield, as those tall stalks could really provide a lot of privacy. Her blood heated as she entered the very non-cornfield interior of the cabin and looked around. It at least looked like it had been cleaned.

The scent of powerful cleaner mingled with pine— Daddy's favorite disinfectant always brought the outside in.

"Kitchen in the back," she said, waving her arm in that general direction as if Spencer couldn't see it. He pressed in behind her, and Clarissa kept moving. "Only one couch, but it's just you."

"Yes," he finally said after several moments of silence. They'd driven over to the cabins separately, because he wasn't staying long. She expected him to take a quick inventory and then get out of her hair.

Her stomach flipped, and she wasn't sure why. Maybe

she needed some sort of antacid or perhaps a stomach transplant. Then it wouldn't do weird things that made no sense. No matter what, every time she thought about Spencer, her dang stomach vibrated just a little bit, and now it had decided to play pancake and flip all over the place.

Spencer sat down on the couch. "This is nice," he said, grinning up at her. He put his arm along the back of it, and Clarissa could see herself sitting in the blank space next to him. She blinked, and she remained there, her own face glowing with happiness.

"There's a washer and dryer," she said, tearing her attention from him. If he wasn't so good-looking and so confident, Clarissa would have a much easier time defending her heart from him.

She crossed through the living room to the mouth of the hallway. The cabin on this side of the house was a box with four quadrants. "Two bedrooms, one in each corner," she said. "Laundry room here, on the left. Bathroom on the right. One closet at the end of the hall."

Spencer groaned as he got off the couch, and Clarissa retreated to the kitchen while he went to explore his house. The last thing she needed was to be caught with him in the narrow hallway or present while he chose a bedroom. She could only imagine the way her vital organs would react then, and she didn't think there was any surgeon in the world who could replace everything so that it was Spencer-proof.

He returned to the kitchen, and she noted he still had on his cowboy hat. "There are hooks by both doors," she said. "For your hat, jackets, whatever." She indicated the back door. "This cabin backs up to the range, and it's pretty quiet and peaceful here."

"Is that why you live out a little farther from the rest of the farm?" he asked, meeting her gaze.

"Possibly," she said, not wanting to give him anything. She'd have to work with him in close contact in the kitchen, and the walls she'd built to keep him out had already started to crumble.

She cleared her throat and turned back to the kitchen. "Go on and open the cupboards and see what's here. I don't really know much about it."

"The bed was comfortable," he said. "The extra room has a set of weights in it." His eyebrows went up in a question. "I can use those?"

"I'm sure you can," she said, her pulse quickening at the thought of him sweaty as he curled a barbell up to his chest. She backed up a couple of steps and opened the fridge. The stale air of the unused appliance hit her in the nose, and she flinched away from it. "Everything works, as far as I know."

Spencer proceeded to open the cupboards like she'd suggested. He turned on the stove, the fire lighting quickly, and the oven, and yes, they both worked. The water sputtered for a moment in the kitchen sink, but then flowed nicely.

By the time he got to the fridge, Clarissa had wandered back into the living room. Someone had put up navy blue curtains with the Texas star on them, and she did give those a cursory smile. The couch faced the front door, with the TV directly beside it on the left, in the small space there before the wall jutted out. On the right, a large window took up that wall, and a small table had been placed against the wall perpendicular to that.

"This is nice," Spencer finally said. "The carpet looks new, and it runs through the whole cabin. All the tile matches in the laundry room, the bathroom, and the kitchen."

Clarissa could only nod. Daddy did like things to match. He'd probably redone the floors after the last cowboy had left.

"Who lived here before?"

"Clyde," Clarissa said, her throat somewhat narrow. She'd been purposely avoiding thinking his name.

Spencer's gaze flew straight to hers. "You sound like you didn't like him."

"I...liked him fine," Clarissa said, her voice too high and too false.

Spencer's dark eyes searched and searched, and Clarissa's irritation with herself—and him—grew and grew. "I sense a story there," he finally said.

"It's not story time," she said, folding her arms. "Are you done? I have to get back to work." She had two clients coming that afternoon for their milk pick-ups, and she'd only gotten out one order.

"I just want to check out the back," he said. "Two minutes. You can go. I know the way out."

Clarissa nodded, but for a reason she couldn't name, she didn't leave as Spencer moved quickly through the house to the back door. She wanted to see his reaction. She loved sitting on her back porch, and while her house was twice as big as Spencer's cabin and she had room for a rocking chair, a little cupboard where she stored her cookbooks and a bag of cookies, his barely had room for a chair.

Clyde had put one back there, and he'd sat in it every morning and every evening. They'd first started talking across the space between their houses from the back porch. Then he'd started coming to sit on her steps for a few minutes in the evening. Then she'd invited him to dinner.

One thing had led to another, until Clarissa had been starting every morning with a kiss from Clyde and ending every evening the same way. His departure from Sweet Water Falls Farm and her life had left a gash on her heart that she'd been hoping a new chef job in San Antonio would heal.

She'd put in her application for the job at Overlook, but she hadn't heard anything yet. When she'd checked the listing that morning, the job had still been open. Unfilled. She still had a chance.

Something niggled in the back of her mind though. If

they'd been impressed by her application, wouldn't they call right away? Set up an interview, at least over the phone? Since the job remained open, she suspected they hadn't had any applicants they were all that excited about...including her.

She followed Spencer out onto the back porch, the wonder of the farm opening up before her and erasing all of her self-doubt and worries about the job in another city. Standing in the shade, with the warmth of summer on her skin and going down into her lungs, Clarissa sighed.

"Isn't it beautiful?" she asked before she could censor herself. Yes, she'd miss mornings on the farm. Lazy afternoons. Easy evenings and starry, starry nights.

The grass back here was a little wild, because Daddy didn't get out here all that much. He tamed everything else on the farm, from the horses to the cows to the patch of emerald green grass around the farmhouse.

But here...everything out this way was a little more wild. A fence separated the lawn from the first field, which was alfalfa. It had just been cut, and huge rolls of hay sat in the field to cure. One of their agriculture cowboys would be around to pick them up and take them to storage soon enough.

To their left, a cornfield, one of many on the farm, stretched toward the sky. Clarissa grinned at it, because she did love a cornfield with straight, neat rows and all those waving silks and leaves.

"Is that sweet corn or field corn?" Spencer asked.

"Field," Clarissa said. "All of our sweet corn is around the farmhouse." She glanced at him as he leaned against the railing. Clyde had taken his rocking chair with him, she noted. "Everybody on the farm eats corn for months out of the year. We plant it in rotations, starting in February. Our first harvest was last week, and we'll harvest somewhere every week from now until October."

Sometimes later, but Clarissa didn't say that. So much of the dairy farm life revolved around corn. Field corn increased the weight in cattle quickly, and it produced higher yields of milk for their dairy cows.

"Seems like I remember you sayin' you were going to do a Texas corn cookbook," he said without looking at her. "Whatever happened with that?"

"I've still got the beginnings of it," she said. "Somewhere on my computer." Truth be told, she'd forgotten about it completely. She had started a corn cookbook before she'd met Spencer, but just like most things in her life, it had taken a back seat while she'd gone to culinary school and then returned to the farm.

"I make a mean corn chowder," she said. "And a very good sweet corn ice cream."

He looked up at her, a light in his eyes. "Is that right?" he straightened, that sparkled of desire in his gaze meant only for her.

"Which part?" she asked, pressing herself into the far corner of the porch. "The chowder or the ice cream?"

"Both," he said, and while he didn't move physically toward her, Clarissa felt him get closer.

"Yes to both," she said.

He nodded and turned away, looking to the right. A big, red barn sat in the distance, and when the hay was down and the corn turned into silage, Clarissa could sometimes see people working around the barn from her back porch.

"And you live right there," he said, not asking a question but simply making a statement.

"Yes," she said. *Right there*, she added mentally.

"Great," he said, but she couldn't tell if he meant that from his flat tone. "Well, I best be goin'. I have work to do back at Hope Eternal." He knocked a couple of times on the railing, and they went back through the house together. She followed him back down the lane toward the milking operation, where he kept going, and she pulled off.

"Dear Lord," she whispered. "Help me continue down this path I've chosen." The one that led her to San Antonio and a big break in her career. One that didn't include Spencer Rust, even if standing on the porch with him and soaking in the farm atmosphere had been...nice.

———

THE NEXT MORNING FOUND CLARISSA BACK IN THE milk parlor, pulling bottles from the huge, walk-in refrigeration unit and putting them in the white crates. Daddy insisted the crates have the Cooper & Co logo on them properly, and once it started wearing off, he sent the crates out to be re-stamped.

Clarissa had to make sure every crate was exactly right for her customers, and she stacked two crates and headed for the door. It opened before she got there, though she could've kicked it open.

"Oh, hey," Travis said, giving her a quick smile. He was definitely the least grouchy brother, but Clarissa thought she might be the only one who thought so. He was closest to her in age, and they'd always gotten along really well. "Is that for Spike?"

"Yes," she said. "Is he here?"

"Just pulled up." Travis took the crates from her. "You get the other two, and I'll take these."

"Okay." Clarissa turned back to quickly pack the nine milk bottles into two more crates. She was running a little late this morning, but with Travis's help, no one would know. She lumbered along under the weight of the crates, once again passing them to Travis in a doorway to load into the back of Spike Gulliver's truck.

"Morning, Spike," Clarissa said with a smile. She paused and reached for her clipboard. She prepared this each Sunday evening with the week's orders so she didn't ever have to search for anything. Once a customer signed for their milk, she moved the paper to the back of the pile. Every week, the signed invoices got filed, she printed new ones, and the clipboard hung by the door for anyone to use.

Ninety-nine-percent of the time, she interacted with her milk pick-up customers, but someone else could if necessary. The system was flawless, and Clarissa's pride grew as she handed the clipboard to Travis.

"Morning, Rissa," Spike said, and she grinned at him as he reached for the pen Travis extended toward him. "Remember I'm going to need a double order on Thursday?"

"Yes," she said. "I've got it noted." She moved toward them and took the clipboard from him. She flipped several pages, as today was only Monday. "See? Right here." She showed him the order form, which had a seventy-two circled, indicating twice as many bottles as he normally picked up.

"Great," he said.

"Making something special?" she asked, letting the pages flip back into position. She started to move his signed invoice to the back of the pile, being careful not to let the breeze steal away any of the pages while they were untethered.

"I'm doing a demo and tasting on Friday," he said. "For the parenting fair in town."

Clarissa looked up. "Oh, of course. You said that. I just forgot."

He smiled, and she found the tall, tough, bearded man about the opposite of who should be making organic baby food and then demonstrating his products at a parenting fair. He wore a plaid shirt and jean shorts to pick up his milk every Monday and Thursday, and his boots probably weighed as much as one of his tires.

"Good luck at the fair," she said.

He saluted and got behind the wheel of his truck. As he rumbled away, Clarissa checked her next pick-up.

"Need some help?" Travis asked.

She eyed him for a moment. "Why? Don't you have something to do?" Travis was their cleanliness expert in the milkshed. He made sure the stalls were ready for the milk cows, as they milked in four time slots throughout the day. He cleaned machines and tubes. He made sure their operation ran as sanitarily as possible—and that was a dirty job.

"Yes," he said, his eyes turning a bit harder. "I have plenty to do. But I wanted to ask you about Belinda." He reached up and scrubbed the back of his neck. "I texted her like you said, and she hasn't responded."

She slapped the clipboard against his chest and said, "Trade me, Trav. You take this and give me your phone so I can see what you said."

He took the clipboard, but he didn't immediately hand over his phone. "I said what you said to say."

"Did you?" she challenged. "Then let me see."

Travis turned away from her, his stride long and some-what of a march. He definitely hadn't told Belinda what Clarissa had advised him to. When would he learn? If he wanted the woman to go out with him, he had to play the game. No one knew the game better than Clarissa, and she hurried after him with, "Come on, Trav. It can't be that bad."

Inside the parlor, he hung the clipboard and pulled out his phone. He gave it to her, a glower in those bright green eyes that practically glowed in the dimmer light inside.

Clarissa swiped open his phone and went to his texts. Belinda's name sat a few down, underneath messages from Lee and Will and Daddy, all of which made sense. The four of them communicated constantly to run this place.

Hey, Belinda. I've been thinking about you. I was wondering if you wanted to go to the classic car parade next weekend.

Clarissa looked up. "It's not bad, Trav."

"Then why hasn't she answered?"

She checked the timestamp. Last night, just after dinner. Plenty of time to answer on a Sunday evening. Belinda Felton worked as a teacher, and school had just gotten out. "Maybe she's on vacation." Clarissa handed his phone back. "You started out good, Trav. Women like being told they're being thought about."

"But?" he prompted, shoving his phone in his pocket.

"But she's not interested in classic cars. *You* are. You need to entice her with something else."

"I forgot the name of that restaurant you wanted me to mention," he said. "I figured she could bring it up."

Clarissa shook her head and smiled though Travis's frown grew. "No, honey. She wants *you* to know what she likes. It's The Bluebell Café. Text her right now and see what happens."

As she packed more bottles into more crates, Travis sent the text. Clarissa had just filled the second one when his phone bleeped.

"Saddles alive," he whispered. "It worked." He held up his phone, his face glowing as bright as the screen. "Thanks, Rissy." He hugged her, and Clarissa laughed.

"You're welcome," she said. "Now help me get these orders packed. You owe me that much."

Her brother stayed and helped her pack the crates, but he also gave her a distraction from stewing over Spencer. Thankfully. Clarissa had already lost too much sleep over the idea of the man moving in next door to her, and she needed a break.

The problem was, the moment the orders were packed and she stepped foot in the shoppe to get it up and open for the day, Spencer crept right back into her mind, where she didn't want him.

CHAPTER SEVEN

Spencer spotted Nate as he lifted the weight away from his chest. The other man grunted, but the movement was smooth. He got it all the way up, held it, and started to lower it. Spencer kept his hands right there, because the last thing he wanted was Nate to drop the buck-fifty weight onto his chest.

Ginger would never forgive him.

"Got it," Nate said, and Spencer took hold of the bar between Nate's hands and helped get the weight back to the rack. Nate slid out from under it and sat up, grinning. "That was one-fifty."

Spencer held up his hand and gave Nate a high-five. "Nice one, man." He enjoyed working out with Nate in the mornings. Ted joined them almost every day, but he hadn't arrived yet this morning. "Ted's gonna be mad he missed it."

As if summoned by his spoken name, the door opened, and Ted Burrows walked in. He looked about the way he always did—happy to see another day, and Spencer braced himself for Ted to say something about the glorious sunshine.

"It's a beautiful day," Ted said. "I ran out to Sunset Point and back, so I'm late." He took in the bench press and Nate sitting on the weight bench. "I missed it, didn't I?"

"One-fifty," Nate said, getting up to clap his best friend on the back. They were really like brothers, and while they'd included Spencer in their camaraderie, he knew he'd never have what they had.

Nate and Ted had shared much more personal things, and they'd been in a terrible situation together, that Spencer would simply never understand. He still smiled at their brotherhood, and he still loved them. He didn't want to go to prison to find the kind of relationship they had, but he would like someone he felt absolutely safe with. Safe to be his worst self, and safe to try to be the best self he could be. Fail, and try again.

An image of a certain strawberry blonde, with blazing green eyes full of trouble, filled his mind. He hadn't been back to Sweet Water Falls Farm in a week now, and he was moving there this weekend. Nerves skittered through his body, and he turned away from Ted and Nate.

Luke came into the shed, his phone at his ear. "...I have to go, Ma. Yes, I'm here. She's fine. I'll call you later." He hung up and grinned at his friend. Lucas Holt had been released from prison last, and he'd married Hannah Otto a few years ago. They had a baby boy now, and Spencer had seen all of the men who'd come from the River Bay Correctional Facility turn into completely new men.

He wanted to do the same.

They'd had big changes in their lives, and they'd made the best of bad situations. They'd become different people, and he found nothing but inspiration in the men he'd grown to know and love.

"Where's Dallas?" Luke asked, glancing around though there was nowhere to hide. "He said he'd come this morning."

"He texted to say he might not make it," Nate said, stepping over to hug Luke too.

Ted, the big teddy bear that he was, embraced Spencer and said, "Morning, bro. I can't believe you're leaving."

Ginger had just told everyone yesterday at their Sunday afternoon picnic. They set one up every Sabbath afternoon on the deck at the Annex, and since Hannah and Emma were both great cooks, everyone on the ranch ate like kings at least once a week. At least in the summertime.

"Yeah," Spencer said.

"This is a good move for you?" Ted asked, pulling back and looking at Spencer. He'd been there yesterday, but his toddler had been crying, and he hadn't had a chance to come talk to Spencer yet.

Which was fine. Everyone else had mobbed him, and Spencer almost wished he'd been able to sneak away from Hope Eternal Ranch like a thief in the night. *No*, he told himself. He wasn't going to be like his dad in any way, and slinking away in the middle of the night was something he would never, ever do.

Spencer knew what it was like to wake up in the morning and have no indication of where his parents were. The panic that something bad had happened. The pure fury that he'd been left behind. The hurtful realization that he—even as someone's child—wasn't good enough to be told what was going on.

He would absolutely never, ever do that to someone.

"This is a good thing for me," he confirmed to Ted. At least he hoped the move to Sweet Water Falls Farm would be good for him. He had high hopes, and every time he thought about it, the change felt right.

"Good," Ted said. "Slate says y'all are goin' to the beach tonight."

"Yeah," Spencer said. "Anyone's invited. I could take Missy and Frannie for you if you want."

"Maybe," Ted said, stepping back over to the door to open it. His four ranch dogs, whom he'd named after the original judges on *American Idol*, came trotting into the weight shed. When he'd first started letting them in, Nate and Luke had complained. But Ted had set up a little area for them between the wall and the sink, and the four blue heelers trotted over there without any direction from Ted.

He refilled their water bowls and tossed in their bones and balls before caging them inside with a baby gate. Spencer smiled through it all, and he wondered if he could get a dog when he moved to the farm.

He'd gotten a few texts from Clarissa over the past week, mostly about his culinary skills, of which he had very few. He was thirty-seven years old and still alive, so he could definitely do a few things in the kitchen. The feel of a wooden spoon wasn't foreign to him by any means. He'd much rather use a spatula for the meals he made, which included a lot of pancakes, fried eggs, and grilled cheese sandwiches. No wooden spoon required.

She'd told him she'd outlined a schedule for their training, which would begin bright and early next Monday morning, and Spencer had simply agreed with whatever she'd said. She'd been unsuccessful—obviously—in talking her father out of hiring Spencer, and he found himself with excited nerves to move into his own cabin now.

His fingers flew over his phone as Luke said he was going to jump rope if anyone wanted to join him. Spencer did, so he better get this text sent quickly.

Wondering what the rules are for personal pets. Could I bring a dog with me, for example? He sent the text to Clarissa, hoping six-thirty in the morning wasn't too early for her. She'd used the words "bright and early" herself, but Spencer knew that meant different things for different people.

"Spence, you in?" Luke asked.

"Yes," he said, glancing up from his phone to take the jump rope from his friend.

"How's Clarissa this morning?" Luke grinned at Spence, who quickly put his phone on the shelf where they had a Bluetooth speaker, water bottles, and weight gloves.

"I don't know," Spencer said, not trying to hide his irritation with the woman. He'd told Luke and the others all about his past with her, and yes, maybe he'd admitted that he could maybe try asking her out again. "She's so formal with me."

"You just gotta get to know her again," Luke said.

"I'm trying," Spencer said. Every time he'd tried to ask her about herself—how she liked her corn if everybody around the farm ate it, what she made for dinner on Tuesday nights for her family, what her favorite color was, how the cookbook was coming—she shut him down.

Really, she just stopped talking, which was the same thing. He hated her sudden text-silence more than anything, and he decided he would simply try to jump rope it all away.

"All right," Luke said. "We're going to do one-minute increments, with a thirty-second break for the first seven and a half minutes. Then we'll do two-minute—"

"Wait," Slate said as he opened the door and came in. "I want to jump rope."

"Get ready, man," Luke said, frowning at him. "What

took you so long this morning? I waited on your porch for ten minutes."

"Yeah, sorry." Slate deposited his keys and phone on the shelf too, glancing around at everyone. He wore a look of delight in his thundercloud gray eyes, and Spencer couldn't help smiling back at him.

"Jill's decided we can find out if we're having a girl or a boy."

Everyone started congratulating Slate, though they'd all known Jill was pregnant. Spencer had been out with Jill a few times, and she was a fun-loving, if a bit eccentric, woman.

"Yeah, finally," Slate said, accepting all their hand-shakes and hugs. "Now, I just have to work on her about the name. I mean, I don't want a son named Blueberry or anything."

Spencer burst out laughing with the others. Jill did like somewhat odd names, though she'd done just fine with their daughter, who they'd named Savannah. Totally normal.

"All right," Luke said again, before the laughter had truly started to die. "Let's go, guys. Daylight's burning."

And in the summer in Texas, if the work didn't get done in the cooler parts of the day, it had to be done while the sun beat down and burned up.

Spencer wasn't great at jumping rope, but he did what Luke drove him to do. The man had worked in a gym and trained as a boxer for years, so he knew how to get and stay in shape. Spencer wasn't out of shape in any way, but jumping rope really got his heart rate going.

Thinking about Clarissa while he did it nearly put him in cardiac arrest. Finally, the twenty minute circuit completed, and Spencer reached for his water bottle and his phone at the same time.

Thinking about Clarissa fueled him to do a lot of things, which was as frustrating as it was commendable.

Orderly pets are acceptable, she'd said, and that only made Spencer roll his eyes so hard that he feared they might get permanently stuck up in his head.

"JUST THAT DRESSER," HE SAID, POINTING TO IT. NATE and Ted stepped over to the drawer-less piece of furniture and lifted it easily. Spencer's bedroom was now empty of his personal belongings. He followed his friends out into the hall, but he turned back to survey the space.

It needed to be vacuumed and the shelves wiped down, but other than that, he'd left the bed all made up with sheets and blankets from the community linen closet. A few empty hangers hung in the closet, which seemed so huge and so gaping now that there was nothing in it.

"Spence?" Slate called, and he turned around.

"Yep, right here."

"Just these boxes in the kitchen?"

"Yes." Spencer arrived there and in one trip, Slate,

Jack, Nick, and Luke took the kitchen items and food Spencer had packed the night before.

In all, they'd been working for about ten minutes. That was all the time it took for him to move his life out of the Annex where he'd lived for thirteen years, and he ignored the narrowing of his throat and the pounding of his heart.

He wanted to go. He did. This was the right thing.

"Let's go, brother," Nate said, appearing in the front doorway of the Annex with Ursula, his wife's German shepherd. "We've got breakfast out here, and then we'll head out."

"The truck's packed?"

"All packed," Nate said. "One trip, like you said." He smiled as he stepped inside. "Stay, Ursula." He shoved the dog back out with his leg, glanced over his shoulder, and then closed the door behind him.

Spencer was the same age as Nate, and yet the other man felt so much wiser than Spencer did. "I want to do this," Spencer said.

"Change is hard," Nate said back. "You're not far away at all, Spence. Fifteen minutes in the car. That's five songs." He grinned, and Spencer shook his head, though a chuckle escaped from his mouth.

He'd once told Nate he could get through any task by figuring out how many of his country songs he "got" to listen to while he did it. Mucking out a really dirty stall, where a horse had been sick all night? Twenty minutes.

Six or seven of the best country music songs in the world, and the job was done.

"I'm going to miss working out with you guys in the morning," he said.

"Then come," Nate said. "Dallas does."

Dallas lived in town, not on the ranch, and yes, he came to the morning workouts sometimes. *Sometimes*, Spencer told himself. Nate, Ted, Slate, and Luke, who all lived on-site, were there every day.

Spencer had been too, and now he wouldn't be.

"I know you'll be welcome on Sundays," Nate said. "Ginger said just this morning that she was going to have you for dinner any time you wanted to come."

"So about like she does now," Spencer said with a smile.

"Yes," Nate said. "About like now. You're not losing us here, Nate. You're gaining everyone there."

He nodded and drew in a deep breath through his nose. His resolve strengthened. "There's something for me there, Nate. I can feel it."

"I hope so, brother." Nate took him into a tight hug. "I know you want this change, and I hope you find what you're looking for."

"Thank you," Spencer whispered, holding his friend tightly in return.

Nate stepped back and adjusted his cowboy hat. "Now come on, I'm sure Miss Emma's having a fit about melting frosting about now." He led the way outside, and the moment Spencer's boot touched the wood on the porch, applause filled the air.

He went to the top of the steps while Nate went down them and took in the crowd that had gathered to say good-bye. His heart filled with love for all the good men and women he'd worked with for so long. So many of them had shaped him and re-shaped him into the man he was, pinching off a corner there, and smoothing out a rough spot on his back.

He lifted his hand in an acknowledgement wave as Ted let loose with an ear-splitting whistle. At the bottom of the steps, Ginger met him with tears in her eyes.

"I'm going to miss you so much," she whispered. "We've been here so long together, Spence. Hope Eternal won't be Hope Eternal without you."

"Thank you for saying so," he said, though he didn't believe it. He'd seen plenty of cowboys and cowgirls come and go, and life on the ranch simply marched on. Hearts might be heavier for a few days or weeks, but time and distance healed things. A new normal was established—this time it would be without him.

He moved to the next person, who was Emma. "I packed a basket of food in the back seat," she said, holding him tightly. "It's got enough for lunch today and dinner, and maybe lunch and dinner tomorrow."

Spencer smiled down at her. "Em, knowing you, it has enough food for breakfast, lunch, and dinner from now until next week." They laughed together, though tears flowed down Emma's face. She turned away quickly and lifted her daughter into her arms. "Say good-bye to Uncle Spence. He has to go."

Spencer hugged the dark-haired girl, who gave him a sweet kiss on the cheek. He said good-bye to everyone, accepted their well-wishes, and ate too many doughnuts on such a rickety stomach.

Then, he made the fifteen-minute drive to Sweet Water Falls Farm, a truckload of men behind him. They got everything moved into the cabin in the same amount of time they'd taken to move it out of the Annex, and then Spence was left alone.

He stood in the house, looking around at the boxes, the basket of food from Emma, and his blanket on the back of the couch.

"This is your house now," he told himself, just as he had many times in the past. Before landing at Hope Eternal, Spencer had moved every few months for seven years. That was a lot of moving, and a lot of new houses. A lot of boxes packed and unpacked, and a lot of trying to find himself.

The walls felt too close, and Spencer stepped onto the front porch. Clarissa's house sat to his left, his being the last destination on this road, and about level with his. He saw the curtains flutter in her window, and he suspected she'd been spying on him during the move. So she'd seen his friends, and she'd seen how little he had to his name.

Since he had nothing to do between now and Monday

morning but unpack and settle in, he decided he had a few minutes to spare. Plus, he wanted to see the woman who'd been haunting him in his dreams and his waking thoughts for the past seventeen days, since first seeing her standing outside that shoppe, her arms folded.

He went down the steps, across their two lawns, and right up to her front door. Someone had painted it a blinding white, and Clarissa had hung a beautiful wreath of sunflowers on it, giving it a brightness boost.

He knocked, stepped back, and waited.

CHAPTER EIGHT

Clarissa knew who stood at her front door, and she didn't even have to peek through the curtains. She'd been lurking at her front window for the past hour, though the show hadn't really started until the past twenty minutes. Then, oh my. There'd been belt buckles, broad shoulders, and cowboy hats galore.

No less than five muscled cowboys had helped Spencer unload, and then they'd gone right back down the dirt lane they'd used to get to this tiny neighborhood at the farm. The other cowboy cabins sat on the agriculture side of the farm, and the half-dozen of those made another little community.

Her brothers shared two other homes that stood with a third, much smaller house that hadn't been inhabited for a long time. Travis and Lee shared a place right now, with the intention that Lee would move into the main farmhouse once Mama passed away. Clarissa pushed against the thought, though she'd had plenty of time to prepare for it.

"And it hasn't happened yet," she mumbled to herself just as the doorbell pealed through the house.

Oh, right. Spencer was standing on the front porch. Clarissa grabbed the binder she'd been working on since she'd realized her daddy was in fact going to hire Spencer. It had taken all the way until the day he'd come by to drop off his paperwork and she'd shown him the house. Clarissa could work quickly under pressure, and she couldn't stand the thought of leaving the farm without her recipes in someone else's hands.

At the same time, she didn't want to give her recipes to anyone else. Period.

"Think of the clients," she told herself.

"Clarissa," Spencer called. "I know you're in there."

His voice got her moving, and she held the binder like a shield as she yanked open the door. Spencer looked up from the ground, his hands tucked into his jeans pockets and that cowboy hat far too sexy for her health.

She definitely had a hole in one of her lungs, if the wheezing that happened when she breathed was any indication. "Spencer," she said, so at least her voice still worked. "Did you get moved in?" She looked to the right, where his house sat, as if she hadn't even noticed any activity on the farm that morning.

"Yep," he said. "Thought I'd come say hi. See if you needed any help today, since I have nothing to do until Monday."

"My weekend deliveries pick up really early," she said. "So they're done."

"Oh." He didn't back up or offer anything else. He nodded to the binder. "What's that?"

"This is going to be your shoppe Bible for the next couple of weeks." She put a smile on her face, because she was proud of the binder and what it contained.

"Couple of weeks?" he asked. "I thought you were leaving on Saturday."

Clarissa cleared her throat and stepped out onto the porch so he couldn't see that she hadn't packed a single box yet. Why should she when she had no job and nowhere to stay in San Antonio?

"I'm still waiting...I'm still waiting to see what happens," she said. "If you have a few minutes, we can go through a few things here." She pulled the door closed behind her and settled on the top step, Spencer doing the same. Her memory blipped, and Clarissa got transported back in time about nine years.

Precisely nine years, to a porch very much like this one. The farmhouse had a walk-out basement, with a few steps that went down to the garden area. They'd sat there several times over the summer they'd dated, and while Clarissa couldn't remember the exact topics they'd discussed, she did remember the scent of his cologne and the way he made her feel like a strong, sexy woman.

He looked at her, something dancing in those dark eyes, and she felt exactly the same way right now. "What are we talkin' in that thing? Recipes? Procedures?"

Clarissa flipped it open, took a deep breath of his earthy, musky, clean cologne, and moved half of the binder to his lap. He edged a little closer to her, and Clarissa's heartbeat pounced through her whole body. That thing definitely needed to be monitored.

The first page listed the shoppe's hours. "We're open six days a week," she said. "The doors open at ten, and we close at five. Saturdays, I'm done by three." She glanced at him. "You could work the store with me today, if you want."

"Sure," he said. "I only have a few boxes to unpack."

"Yeah," she said. "It didn't look like you had a whole lot."

Spencer grinned at her, and Clarissa realized what she'd just admitted to. "I mean...there were so many cowboys here to help."

Now she was just digging a deeper hole for herself. She pressed her eyes closed and flipped the page in the binder. When she opened her eyes again, she saw the delivery schedule. Before she could say a word, Spencer said, "Do you get a lunch hour?"

She looked at him. "Like, in the shoppe?"

"Yeah, like when you work the shoppe," he said. "And

am I really working seven straight hours there, and in the barns and stable? And I make the ice cream and the cheese and sleep and eat?" He flipped the colored tabs on the side she'd labeled *ice cream recipes* and *cheese spreads*.

Clarissa looked at him. "I guess you'll have to ask Daddy about that."

"I'm used to working a lot," he said. "I know a farm never sleeps. But this feels like a lot." He tapped the binder on his knee, but Clarissa felt the vibration in her legs too. "And there's deliveries to prep and deliver."

"They come pick-up," Clarissa said.

"Right, I know, but I have to have them ready for that. This says deliveries are from eight to nine in the morning."

"But only three days a week," she said, looking at her Monday-Thursday-Saturday schedule of who came, what time, and what their usual order was.

"How long does it take you to prep this?" He tapped the schedule again, his finger staying on Monday's deliveries.

With those six orders, Clarissa moved over one hundred gallons of milk on Monday morning. "An hour," she admitted.

"So I'm out in the milk parlor at seven a.m. three days a week," he said. "I work with the pick-up people for an hour. Then I have an hour to make whatever the shoppe needs, then I tend to the shoppe, then I have farm chores after that? Or before?" He shook his head, and he didn't seem too happy. "This feels like two jobs."

"You'll have to talk to the boss about that," Clarissa said.

"I don't know how to make cheese," he said.

"Some of the stuff I do while the shoppe is open," she said, ignoring his attitude. "We're not like the grocery store, Spence. There are long stretches where no one comes in."

"Great," he said. "So I'll be bored out of my mind." He sighed and ran his hand up his face to his hair. He took off his hat and inhaled again. "I'm not sure this is the job that was advertised."

"Again, that's something you'll have to take up with the boss." She snapped her binder closed, because she didn't want to explain anything else to him.

"So no lunch hour in the shoppe."

"I never struggle to find a time to sit down and eat," she said. "It's not a problem, but no, there's not a sched-uled, close-the-door-and-lock-it time for lunch."

"What about today?" he asked. "Would you close the door and lock it and go to lunch with me?" She resettled his cowboy hat on his head and looked at her, no shame or anxiety in his expression at all. After a few seconds passed where Clarissa couldn't formulate a response, he grinned. "We never did get to go to dinner a couple of weeks ago."

"I can't close the store on a Saturday," she said. "I'm not going to tell you that you can't bring lunch into the shoppe. It's a free country, after all."

"Mm, that it is." He smiled at her and retrieved his

phone from his back pocket. "It's almost ten now. How about I come by with lunch later, and then I can stay and help in the shoppe?"

Clarissa had just told him she wouldn't object to him bringing lunch, but that didn't feel like telling him yes to a date. "All right," she said, which wasn't a yes either. At least not the word "yes."

It meant the same thing, though, and Spencer's grin turned a bit arrogant. Still handsome as ever, and Clarissa got to her feet. "I have to go. You know where the shoppe is."

"Yes, ma'am," he said. "I sure do."

He'd dragged out his words and added that Texan drawl on purpose, but Clarissa didn't roll her eyes this time. She'd just accepted a date with the man, and she really needed to get her head checked before she opened the shoppe and had to deal with Mrs. Peay, a woman who came every Saturday for the homemade pimento Clarissa stocked the refrigeration units with every weekend.

THE BELL RANG ON THE OUTSIDE DOOR, AND CLARISSA finished packing the spreadable cheese into the tub, snapped the lid on, and tapped the screen of her tablet to get the label to print. She then stepped over to the door and said, "I'll be two seconds."

"No problem," a woman said, and Clarissa returned to

the stainless steel counters in the kitchen and stuck the label to the top of the lid, which proclaimed what this spreadable cheese was—garlic and dill cheese spread.

She loved putting savory flavors together, and she wanted the freedom to spread her wings and fly, fly, fly in a real restaurant. She wanted to work with proteins and vegetables—and cheese. *Anything* more than cheese.

She bustled out to the front of the shoppe and opened the fridge next to the door. "Hey, there," she said. "I've got some fresh spreads here. Can I help you find what you're looking for?"

"I bought some pepper jack cheese here a couple of weeks ago." The woman turned from the other fridge along the wall with the table, and Clarissa recognized her.

"Oh, hey, Bea." Clarissa hesitated to go hug the woman, but her Texas roots wouldn't allow her not to. So the result was a strange, awkward half-hug that left her smiling like a fool. "There's some pepper jack in the back if there's none out here."

"I don't see any."

Clarissa stepped past her and peered into the fridge. There wasn't any white cheese in the fridge at all. "I probably sold it all this morning. Give me two shakes." She bumped through the black plastic door to the back of the shoppe again, and pulled open the freezer.

After turning to get a wire basket, she filled it with more shredded cheese and took it out front. "It's frozen," she said, "But by the time you get home, it'll be ready to use." She reserved a bag of pepper jack and handed it to Bea Matthews.

"Thank you, dear," she said, tucking it into her red plastic shopping basket. She continued to browse around the store for a few more minutes, and then Clarissa checked her out. Her smile had just fallen when the door dinged again. Three teens entered the shoppe, and Clarissa reached for her gloves. She knew what they wanted—ice cream.

"Hey, guys," she said, her professional smile in place. "What can I get y'all?" She scooped and cleaned up while they lingered at the table, laughing and talking about something she didn't care about. She just wanted them to clear out so when Spencer arrived with lunch, they had somewhere to sit.

Noon came and went, and Spencer didn't.

Clarissa wiped up the table, checked the inventory, and realized she forgot to tell Spencer that the last hour on Saturdays was clearance time. The regulars knew that, and they'd come during those sixty minutes to get the almost-expired goods for half-price.

She'd just pulled out her phone to text Spencer that if he didn't come in the next few minutes, she'd be too busy helping customers. Not only that, but he hadn't helped in the shoppe at all that day.

"He's not on the clock," she reminded herself, and she turned from her unsent text when the bell on the door rang.

Spencer walked in, and she expected to see him carrying some brown bags he'd gotten from a drive-through somewhere. Instead, he carried a tray with a cloche on it. A legit cloche.

Surprise dove through her, and she said, "What in the world is that?" as he slid the tray onto the little table.

"Sorry I'm a little late," he said. "I may or may not have had to start this meal a few times."

Clarissa wasn't sure if she wanted to eat whatever was under that cloche, but at the same time, she couldn't wait to see what it was. "Look at you."

"You didn't think I could cook, did you?" He gave her a half-smile, and she couldn't believe she'd forgotten about this sexy smirk. Her blood warmed, and she sank into the chair he'd pulled out for her.

"I don't know what to think about you," she admitted.

"I barely believe I made this, so don't worry." He chuckled and reached for the cloche. "I give you roasted tomato bisque with grilled cheese croutons."

Clarissa's mind blanked as he lifted the cloche with a flourish. Two bowls of soup sat there, as did a container of perfectly square, perfectly golden grilled cheese squares. "Let me finish it," he said.

He dropped a few of the croutons into her bowl and offered her a squeeze bottle of sour cream. "All done." He sat down next to her and put a couple of dots of sour cream in his soup.

"Where did you even get that?" she asked, indicating the bottle.

"I went to talk to your daddy about the job," he said, passing her a spoon. "Your mama gave it to me." He smiled at her, but Clarissa's heart tapped out a strange rhythm with the idea of him talking to Mama.

She dipped her spoon into the soup, her mind racing. "What did you decide about the job?"

"He didn't have much time to talk about it," Spencer said. "So I'm coming to dinner at the farmhouse tonight."

Clarissa had just lifted her spoon to her mouth, but she dropped it, the clatter of metal against bowl deafening in the shoppe.

"What?" she demanded. Spencer couldn't come to dinner at the farmhouse tonight. It was Travis's turn to cook, which meant they'd probably have some form of pizza or flatbread and a salad. Trav was a whiz with salads.

She just didn't want Spencer to know that.

CHAPTER NINE

S pencer didn't like Clarissa's reaction to him coming to dinner, and he stewed over what to say to her. Anything? Let it slide? Deal with her family tonight?

In all honesty, he could stay home too. Just send a couple of texts about how he couldn't make it, and he'd drop by and talk to Wayne whenever.

"Why does that bother you?" he asked, dipping his spoon into the soup and picking up a grilled cheese square. He ate the bite as Clarissa started cleaning up her splattered soup. That probably made him a jerk, but he figured she didn't want him staring at her while she composed herself.

"It doesn't," she said.

"Liar." He set down his spoon and leaned away from the table.

Her eyes flew to his. "I am not a liar."

"Liar, liar, pants on fire," he said, hoping to make this serious moment light. But she *had* just lied to him. "I'm just going to ask a simple yes-or-no question. Whatever you say is fine with me." It wasn't really, but he'd at least have his answer.

"Oh, someone else is lying now," she said, and Spencer could've categorized it as flirting.

He folded his arms and quirked his eyebrows at her. "Would it so terrible if we got to know each other again?" He held up one hand. "Yes or no. That's all I need."

He'd like a lot more, but Spencer knew better than most that all of his wants weren't always granted.

"Yes," she said.

"Yes, it would be terrible if we got to know each other?" He started nodding. "All right. I can—"

"I mean, no," she said over him, almost yelling it. They sat there and looked at one another, and Spencer's pulse hammered in his chest.

"No," Clarissa said, some of the panic in her expression starting to calm. "It wouldn't be the worst thing that happened if we got to know each other again."

Spencer nodded, his throat suddenly so dry. He didn't know what to add to the conversation, so he picked up his spoon and took another bite of soup. "My mom taught me how to make this soup when I was just twelve," he said, and that was about as personal as he could get. He didn't talk about his mom, to anyone, hardly ever.

Ginger was the only one who knew much about Melody Rust at all.

"She did?" Clarissa asked, taking up her first bite of soup. Spencer watched her put it in her mouth, and he saw the moment she tasted it. "Spence, this is fantastic."

He grinned at her. "You weren't expecting it to taste good."

"I'm a little surprised," she admitted. She took a bite with a crouton. "Very good."

"Thank you," he said.

"You said you had 'very few' skills in the kitchen," she said. "I distinctly remember those words in the text."

"I put a piece of sliced cheese on the bread," he said. "I didn't make the cheese from raw milk."

She giggled and took another bite. "It's not too hard, I swear."

"Oh, I think your mama frowns on cursing," he teased, and he was definitely flirting with her.

Clarissa tipped her head back and laughed, and Spencer didn't think she did that all too often. He was glad he could prompt such a thing, and he grinned at her.

"Tell me about your mom," she said as she quieted. "I don't think you talked about her before."

"I'm sure I didn't," he said. "I, uh, don't talk about her much at all."

"Bad times?"

"No," he said. "I mean, kind of, but not because of her. Because of my dad."

Clarissa trained those pretty green eyes on him, and Spencer wanted to tell her everything. "I'll give you the short version." After all, she was still planning on leaving Sweet Water Falls, and he was probably a huge fool for even bringing up the idea of getting to know one another again. She'd just leave again.

Hopefully not because of something he said this time, but leaving nonetheless. Maybe this time, they could do that long-distance thing he'd mentioned last time. San Antonio wasn't that far away. A couple of hours north, and he knew Dallas and Slate drove north to see Slate's parents in Austin all the time. Spencer could easily hitch a ride with them, have them drop him off in San Antonio and pick him up on the way back.

"The short version?" Clarissa said. "I think I need more than that. I mean, you're going to come to dinner with my family. That's about as up-close and personal as you can get."

Spencer smiled at her. "I already know your dad and brothers. It's just your mom I don't know that well."

"Trust me, you don't know my brothers either," Clarissa said. "If you did, you'd eat before you came tonight, and then you'd be able to escape without regret."

Spencer looked at her, more than happy to have her talk. "Why's that?"

"They're always so grumpy," she said. "About every-thing. So judgmental about everyone and everything. Last night, we had a shouting match between Lee and Trav about how long it takes to move cattle from one pasture to another. Lee thought the cowboys were taking too long, and Trav was like, 'dude, Lee, they need time to get animals to move.'" She shook her head and grinned. "It's intense, dinnertime at the Cooper's table."

She gave him a smile, and Spencer sure did like it. It felt real, like he was getting the real Clarissa Cooper as she was today, not one from his memory, and not one she *wanted* him to see.

"I can't wait," he said. "I've been dining with Me, Myself, and I for a long time."

Clarissa looked up again, more surprise in her eyes. "I remember you being an only-child."

"Yeah," he said with a nod. "Yep." He quickly took another bite of soup.

"And your mother taught you to cook." She gave him an encouraging smile.

"Yes," he said. "Before she died."

Clarissa did the spoon-dropping again, and Spencer should've warned her he supposed. "I'm so sorry, Spence. When did she pass away?"

"Years ago," he said, clearing his throat. "I just miss her from time to time." He lifted another spoonful of soup as if toasting Clarissa. "Like when I make this soup to impress a pretty woman."

"Oh, wow," she said, giggling again. "I do remember the bad pick-up lines."

"Come on," Spencer said, chuckling. "That was a good one."

"Well, the soup is delicious, and I am impressed."

"Thank you, Momma," Spencer said, lifting one hand to his lips to kiss it and then raising it toward the ceiling.

Clarissa laughed again, and Spencer decided today was a huge win so far. He'd moved, and while he missed his friends already, he did love his little house. He'd seen Clarissa twice now, and he'd made her laugh a couple of times too. Both huge wins in his book.

He finished his soup and said, "My mother died when I was only thirteen, so she didn't get to teach me a whole lot of different meals. I haven't starved to death yet, so I figure it's okay."

She reached across the table and covered his hand with hers. "Thirteen, Spence? I'm so sorry." She swiped at her eyes with her free hand. "And here I was feeling all sorry for myself, because my mama will probably pass in the next year or so."

"It's always hard, no matter when it is," Spencer said, turning his hand over and sliding his fingers through Clarissa's. He was done spilling secrets from years gone by, and he smiled at her. "My daddy was a mean old cuss, Riss. I think I can handle your brothers."

Fine, maybe he hadn't finished his confessions yet.

She simply watched him for a few moments, and Spencer swore he could see pieces moving around inside her head, forming a whole new picture of him. At least he hoped that was what was happening.

The bells on the door chimed, and Clarissa flinched. They both turned toward the sound and a woman walking in with her son. "Oh, Miss Tungston. I have that herb and cheddar spread on clearance." With that, Clarissa got up from the table and headed for the refrigeration unit, and Spencer lost her attention to the shoppe.

THAT EVENING, SPENCER HAD UNPACKED ALL OF HIS kitchen boxes. His clothes hung in the closet—well at least his shirts did. His jeans and shorts were all folded and sitting neatly in the dresser he'd made in the year he'd studied with a master carpenter. He'd decided that cabinetry wasn't for him, and he'd searched for something else. Spencer had no formal education, and he was lucky to have a high school diploma.

Since he'd been at Hope Eternal Ranch for so long, and Ginger had been a partner with the Bureau of Prisons for years and years, Spencer had plenty of experience with people turning their lives around. He knew men who'd come out of the low-security prison and gotten their GED while they worked at the ranch. He'd seen them go on to college and then advanced degrees.

He didn't want to go on to those things. He wanted to graduate from single to not-single. He thought of the feel of Clarissa's hand in his. Although it had only happened for a couple of seconds that afternoon, it had opened about a dozen doors in Spencer's life. Doors that hadn't been open for him in a long time.

He pulled up to the farmhouse and peered at the cheery lights shining through the front windows. It wasn't dark yet, but somehow the whole house seemed lit up from the inside. It pulsed with energy, and it drew Spencer toward it. Honestly, that vibrating, familial pulse of the place had called to him from Hope Eternal Ranch too. Being around people was something he craved, and finding a spot to belong among other men and women something he must have in order to feel complete.

So he found himself smiling as he crossed the lawn and climbed the steps to the front porch. Wayne had said to come right in, but Spencer couldn't do that. He knocked and Clarissa opened the door a moment later, so she had to be standing there waiting for him.

"Hey," she said, and she actually smiled at him.

"Hey, yourself." He stepped forward and brushed his lips against her cheek. "How's your mama tonight?"

"She's doing really well." Clarissa backpedaled away from him, and he realized he shouldn't have greeted her like a true Texan. "C'mon in. You're lucky, because Will had a pretty good day."

"Did he now?" Spencer gave her a smile and faced the kitchen, as that was definitely the heart of the farm. He saw Wayne moving around the kitchen, and he even saw

Travis carrying a big bowl to the table. The cowboy turned and came into the living room, a huge smile on his space.

"Good to see you, Spence. How did the moving go this morning?"

"Just fine." Spencer grinned at him and shook his hand. Grumpy? Spencer had no idea what Clarissa was talking about.

"Don't loiter out there," Wayne practically growled, and Clarissa turned toward the kitchen. Spencer followed her, with Travis coming in last.

"Will," he immediately bellowed. "There's smoke pouring out of the oven!" He ran toward it and yanked open the door. "I asked you to watch it."

"I was watching it."

"You were watching it?" Travis demanded. "How is this watching it?" He tossed the pan of pizza on the stovetop, and all Spencer could do was stare.

"Chris texted me, and he seriously asked for tomorrow off." Will glared back at Travis. "It's not even burnt. Something just dripped onto the bottom of the oven. My word."

"What about Chris?" Wayne asked.

"He can't have every Sunday off," Will said, whirling to his father. "You have to say something to him. He doesn't listen to me."

"It's your job to make him listen to you, son," Wayne said. "Everyone has to work two Sundays a month."

"I know that, Daddy," Will said, and Spencer saw what Clarissa meant by grouchy. He had no idea where to look next. Travis practically had his head down inside the hot oven, and Will and Wayne now stood toe-to-toe, as if they might come to blows. Clarissa massaged the bridge of her nose, and Chrissy sat at the dining room table like this shouting and smoke was normal near-dinner behavior.

Then Lee came in through the garage, and his hands looked liked he'd dipped them in tar. "Well, the mower is a complete bust," he yelled. Spencer was starting to think yelling was a normal indoor voice for these men.

"What?" Wayne asked. "That thing has a warranty."

"Then call it in," Lee griped at him as he turned on the sink with his elbow. "Because it literally just spewed oil everywhere."

"Don't wash your hands here," Travis said. "There's food in that sink, Lee."

"Calm—what?" Lee looked at his brother as nearly black water streamed from his hands and into the sink.

"Do you not have eyes?" Travis yelled as the back door opened again. This time, Ford came through it, and he had a dog with him that looked like it had enjoyed a great roll in the mud.

"Dad, Queenie got into that swampy spot. Should I just hose 'er off in the back yard?"

Before anyone could answer him, the canine shook all over, and everyone—including Spencer and Clarissa—went into an uproar.

CHAPTER TEN

C larissa rode with Spencer, though she was fairly certain she still had mud clinging to her clothes. She'd seen splatter like that before, and there was no way the men in her family would be able to clean it all. Once, months ago, the strawberry white chocolate ice cream base she'd been whipping up had suffered a mixer mishap. The appliance had gone on the fritz, and Clarissa still found droplets of dried, pink ice cream in various places around the kitchen.

The tension in the truck could've choked a man. It was definitely choking a woman, and Clarissa glanced over at Spencer. "They're insane," she said quietly, feeling slightly crazy herself. "I'm sorry."

She had a strong suspicion her brothers' loud mouths, quick tempers, and crotchety attitudes would prevent her from ever getting married. Those things had stopped them from finding someone to settle down with. She couldn't even imagine Belinda Felton in that situation. She'd run silently from the house, and she'd never text Trav again. He was smart to take her out first, that was for sure.

Clarissa hadn't had that option, and she glanced at Spencer as he took a peek at her. "It's fine," he said. "It was just a bad moment."

"The whole night is filled with moments like that," she said. "You watch, when we get back, the farmhouse will be stuffed from top to bottom with awkwardness and silence. Lee will have apologized, but Trav really hates it when he doesn't look first. This is *not* the first time that discussion has happened."

She sighed and closed her eyes for a moment. "Will's always on his phone. Always dealing with a problem he doesn't want to deal with. Lee's managing a lot, and he's under constant stress. Ford's just a kid, and Queenie... well, Queenie likes mud and always has." She opened her eyes and took a deep breath. "I hate to say it, but I think they do the best they can." She gestured across the dashboard. "And that was it. That was the best they have."

Spencer chuckled and shook his head. "Honestly, Clarissa, it's okay."

"You can call me Riss," she said. He had earlier that day, and she'd liked it. Daddy called her Rissa, as did a few of her closest clients and friends. Travis called her Rissy, and Lee used Riss. It has sounded intimate and kind when Spencer had used it earlier.

"Okay," he said, and the drive continued in silence.

Clarissa watched the world go by her window, wondering when she'd started letting that happen in her life. It was amazing to her how days could fold into weeks, then months, and then years. The time slipped by just like the trees did along the side of the road, and the next thing she knew, eight years had passed with her making herb and cheddar cheese spread for housewives in Sweet Water Falls.

Anger bloomed inside her. This was not the life she'd envisioned for herself. It wasn't even the life Mama had told her she'd have, which was one filled with love and amazing things. Joy and happiness. A husband, kids, a little dog running around.

She'd had one of those—a little white poodle she'd named Gemma. But when she'd left to go to culinary school, she'd re-homed the dog with an elderly couple in town. She wasn't sure if they still had Gemma or not. She wasn't sure if they were still alive or not. Her whole life had been wrapped up in trying out a new flavor of ice cream, experimenting with savory items in spreads, packing milk crates, and checking expiration dates on dairy products.

"My friends are going to bring my horse tomorrow," Spencer said, his voice quiet and soothing. Some of the tightness in Clarissa's body reacted to that almost lulling sound, and she began to relax. "Would you like to go riding with me? Do you ride still?"

Clarissa's chest pinched. "Not for a while," she admitted. She knew she suffered from tunnel vision, and she wondered if an optometrist could fix that for her. When she focused on something, it was like everything else just fell away. It didn't matter that she'd once had dreams to be the best chef in the state. She had a black licorice ice cream recipe to tame. Friendships didn't matter; relationships didn't matter; heck, sometimes Clarissa would go all day without eating, because her focus was so razor-sharp on some aspect of the shoppe.

"It's horseback riding," Spencer said, a hint of teasing in his voice. "It's like riding a bike. You don't forget how."

"What's your horse's name?" she asked, knowing she hadn't committed to going riding with him. There was something about that pesky "yes" that she couldn't quite say out loud.

"Mighty Mouse," he said, and Clarissa looked at him to see if he was joking. Apparently, he wasn't. She burst out laughing, and that felt so cleansing and so good.

He chuckled too, and with their laughter mingling, he reached over and took her hand in his. He drew it to his lips and kissed the back of it. "Don't worry about dinner, Riss." He spoke with so much strength and yet so much care too. "It's just food. We'll pick up pizza and go back, and it'll be like Travis made it himself."

"Yeah," she said, because she didn't know what else to say. She sighed as she sank further into her seat, finally relaxing all the way with the laughter, the sound of his bass voice, and the warmth from his hand in hers.

About the time they got back to the farmhouse with the pizza, Clarissa realized how much trouble she was in with Spencer Rust. Their eyes met, the scent of marinara and meats filling the space between them.

"So...," he said. "Horseback riding tomorrow?" He was a persistent cowboy, she'd give him that. She wasn't sure why she wanted to spur the relationship forward in one moment and then yank on the reins the next. That certainly wasn't fair to Spencer. She thought about her big plans to take over the world one restaurant at a time, starting in San Antonio.

Too bad none of her applications had resulted in an interview, not even the one at Overlook, where she had Leslie vouching for her.

"Okay," she said, still not giving him a yes. "But I work in the shoppe after church, so you'll have to come find me."

"Deal," he said. Then he slid from the truck and opened the back door to collect the pizzas they'd gone to pick up. Clarissa didn't move and instead, looked out the windshield at the farmhouse. It looked so serene and so peaceful, but she knew better.

"Dear Lord," she whispered. "Can we have one hour where someone doesn't get a horrible text, someone doesn't yell, and someone doesn't worry about the tractors?

Please. One hour. In the grand scheme of things, I think that's a very short time."

Her door opened, and she turned toward Spencer. "Ready, Riss?" he asked, concern in those dark eyes.

"Ready as I'll ever be."

"IT'S OKAY," CLARISSA SAID THE NEXT DAY, HER HEELS almost clicking against the berber carpet as she hurried across the lobby of the church. "Honestly, Leslie, it is."

"I just don't know what he's waiting for. I asked him about the applicants, because you would not *believe* what service was like last night." She exhaled like her boss was the most exasperating man on the planet. Clarissa knew he wasn't; that honor went to Lee, who had *not* apologized to Trav last night for motor-oiling up his cucumbers.

Clarissa pushed outside, free from the church now. She could breathe out here, and she paused at the top of the steps to do just that. "And?"

"And he said nothing had come in that impressed him," Leslie said. "I'm so sorry, Rissa. Really. He's just so particular, and even when I said I knew you could do it, that you were better than me, he said you have no experience."

Clarissa gazed out at the parking lot, the trees that lined it, and the blue sky beyond. The world felt still here in this part of Texas, with only the slight rustling to leaves and tree branches from the breeze, and the distant sound of a dog barking somewhere. Even that quieted, and Clarissa felt the moment freeze in time and infuse into her soul.

She did love small-town Texas. She loved the way she knew almost everyone inside the church behind her. She loved the way she could go inside any shop and receive a smile and a howdy from whoever worked there. She loved the water towers that gave every town personality, and she loved the way life just moved slower.

"He's right," she finally said. "Thank you for asking, Leslie."

"What are you going to do?"

Clarissa went down the steps and headed for her SUV. She wasn't going to sit in church for another minute, praying for something that wasn't going to come true. "Well," she said, exhaling. "There are plenty of restaurants in San Antonio. I just need one to take a chance on me."

"I can put out some feelers," Leslie offered.

"No, it's okay," Clarissa said. "I know how to look for openings online. I'll just apply to more places." There were plenty more places. If she had to start at the bottom and work her way up, so be it. She could. She *would*. She absolutely would.

"Let me know if I can help," Leslie said, and Clarissa smiled to herself. Her friend was so kind and so good. "I have a couch you can sleep on if you need to come pound the pavement."

"Thank you," Clarissa said, but she wouldn't be going to San Antonio quite yet. "I'll talk to you soon."

"Love you, Rissa."

"Love you too, Les." She ended the call and slid into her SUV before her emotions could spill out. They teemed inside her, and she sat in the deafening silence, trying to get her mind to settle down.

She'd set a departure date for June thirtieth, but that was next week—only ten days away—and there was no way she could go to San Antonio then. She didn't have anywhere to stay, and it took longer than a week and a half to get an apartment. She didn't want to pack up everything she owned if she wasn't moving, and she still hadn't taped together a box.

She didn't want to go to the city with only a suitcase, because that felt like a vacation, not a permanent move.

Spencer's handsome face flashed through her mind, and she sighed. He seemed determined to spend time with her, and she liked that. She'd spoken true when she'd told her brother women liked feeling thought about, and it was clear Spencer thought about her.

She just didn't know where her life was leading her, and she didn't want a matching gash on her heart from Spencer Rust. "Why did he have to show up now?" she asked the silence, the sky, the very state of Texas itself.

Nothing and no one answered, and Clarissa started

the vehicle and drove back to her house in the clearing that overlooked the farm. If she was going to go horseback riding with the hot cowboy, she needed to look her best. But maybe if she didn't, he wouldn't be as interested in her.

She dismissed the thought, because Spencer wouldn't care what she wore to go horseback riding. He liked her for more than her physical appearance, and that thought made her wonder if she didn't need a heart transplant, nor an ENT to check her throat, nor anyone to do anything about her swoopy stomach.

Maybe those were all normal conditions for a woman falling in love with a cowboy.

CHAPTER ELEVEN

Spencer opened the door to the stable, his gut tight. He'd had a little heart-to-heart with Wayne, wherein he'd told the man that nowhere in the job description that had been posted did it say he'd be making cheese, ice cream, or milk deliveries. Wayne Cooper had agreed, and they'd chatted about what really needed to be done around the farm on both sides—the agricultural and animal side, and the milking operation.

They'd agreed that Spencer would work in both; Wayne did need another cowboy in the stables and fields, and he also needed someone to start learning what Clarissa did to run the shoppe. "Would that work for you?" he'd asked Spencer. "Part-time doing both? Then we can decide where to put you permanently if Rissa ends up leaving."

That if had kept Spencer awake most of last night

after their chat. Or maybe starting at seven a.m. in the stables with a few cowboys he'd never met had done that.

"Mornin'," someone drawled, and Spencer tore himself out of his thoughts. A tall, broad-shouldered man stood in the open end of the stable, where the equipment was neatly kept.

"Good morning," Spencer said, putting a smile on his face. He'd started so many jobs over the years, and he could get along with anyone. "I'm Spencer Rust. You must be Gary."

"Gary Boyle," he drawled, shaking Spencer's hand. He had bright blue eyes and plenty of curly hair coming out from underneath his cowboy hat. Spencer didn't know how he handled all the itching from that hair, but he said nothing. "This here's Chris Bargrove. He's from Alabama, and he's like our resident horse whisperer."

"Pleased to meet you," Spencer said, the name Chris tickling something in his memory. Something about him not wanting to work Sundays.

"You too." Chris had a nice, firm handshake, and Spencer didn't get any attitude from him. His hair was all buzzed up the sides and back like Spencer's, and it looked brown to him. He had a warm pair of brown eyes that seemed to truly be pleased to meet Spencer. He didn't need to be making judgments about men before he knew them, so he dismissed what Will and Wayne had said about him.

"And then Mack Parker. He manages all the fields.

When they get planted, fertilized, watered, harvested, all of it."

The third man tipped his white hat at Spencer, who did the same to him. He had dark hair and dark eyes, and that contrasted with the white.

"You'll be with me today," Gary said. "We're doin' stalls this mornin'. Then I check on the enclosures for the horses and dairy cows. We have equipment to fix, though there's a whole crew for that, and property to keep up. There's always something to do." He gave Spencer a smile.

"I came from Hope Eternal," Spencer said. "I know how true that is."

"Oh, did you?" Mack asked. "My sister does riding lessons there. Noelle Parker."

"Sure, I know Noelle," Spencer said, his smile hitching in place now. He could never breathe a word to Mack that he'd once considered asking Noelle to dinner. Then he'd found out she had a boyfriend, and that had been that. Story of Spencer's life, really.

"All right," Gary drawled. "Gloves on the shelf there. We'll open up the back part of the stable to let the babies out, and then we'll get cleanin'."

Spencer didn't need gloves, because he'd brought his own. There was something about putting on a pair of gloves someone else had used, like wearing someone's dirty socks, and it made his skin crawl. He picked up a pitchfork and a shovel, and he learned real quick that Gary called all horses "babies."

His admiration and love for the animals came through just as fast, and Spencer could understand why. He loved watching a horse trot out of his or her stall first thing in the morning, almost like they'd been given wings and permission to fly.

With all the "babies" out in the pasture, the real work began. Spencer didn't mind work. His arms and back knew the motions, and it wasn't horribly physically exhausting. His mind had time to work, and that was the real problem.

Clarissa had disappeared from church about halfway through, and when Spencer had caught up with her in the afternoon to go riding, she'd said her friend from San Antonio had called. She wasn't going to get the job at Overlook, and she might be delaying her departure from the farm.

He didn't want to be happy about that, but he'd be lying if he said he wasn't. Since his momma hadn't raised a liar, he'd kept his thoughts to himself, where they'd swirled and swirled and kept him awake.

He'd crash tonight, that was for sure, as Gary set a blistering pace to get the stalls cleaned out and refilled with fresh straw and sawdust. Once that was done, Spencer felt sure it would be time for him to head over to the shoppe. But nope, the sun only hung about a quarter of the way through the sky, so though his stomach roared at him for something to eat, it wasn't even lunchtime yet.

Gary offered him a granola bar from an assortment of

boxes inside a cupboard in the barn, and Spencer took three of them. He also shoved a shiny silver package of Pop Tarts in his back pocket like it was his wallet.

"The dairy cows are huge," Gary explained as they walked from the stables toward the milking operation on the east side of the farm. "They don't know their own strength, and they can lean into a fence and knock it down." He glanced at Spencer, who nodded. "Especially around an old farm like this."

"How old?" Spencer asked, though Clarissa had told him Sweet Water Falls had been in her family for generations.

"Oh, a hundred and sixty years," he said. "Give or take a decade." He gave Spencer a rare smile and said, "There they are. We call 'em black gold."

"So horses are babies and dairy cows are black gold."

Gary chuckled and said, "That's about it. The milking operation is very profitable. Wayne and his sons run it with a tight fist, and they do a great job. Every cow is important."

"And the agriculture side makes sure the black gold keeps producing."

"That it does," Gary said. "So both arms of the farm are important."

Spencer nodded, and he went around with Gary, checking fences and gates and making notes of weak spots they'd need to address in the next couple of weeks.

"Around and around the farm like that," Gary said. "We assess, then fix. Assess again. Fix some more."

"How long have you been here?" Spencer asked, as he didn't remember Gary from last time he and Clarissa had dated. Of course, he'd gone to pick her up at the farm-house and taken her to dinner, or dancing, or star-gazing in the cornfields. He hadn't concerned himself with the hired help at the farm.

"Oh, seven or eight years," Gary said with a sigh. "Right about the time my wife filed for divorce." He cast Spencer a small smile.

"I'm sorry," Spencer said quickly. "I hope I didn't drum up any bad memories."

"Not for me," Gary said, and that was all. "All right, there's Mack. We check with him to see what's goin' on in the fields. He's got a crew of four he works real tight with, but he always needs more help."

"Right," Spencer said. "And Chris might have work for us in the maintenance shed."

"He might," Gary said, tipping his hat to Mack. "What's she like out there today?"

"We found that fox burrow," Mack said. "We're getting shovels and heading out to dig it up and clear it out."

"Perfect," Gary said, but Spencer didn't think more shoveling sounded anywhere near perfect. "Then we can tell the missus that her chickens are safe again." He grinned at Spencer. "Chrissy's lost three in the last month, and we've been tryin' to find these blasted foxes for weeks."

Spencer just smiled, took the shovel someone handed to him, and determined to dig until someone told him he could stop.

THE MOMENT SPENCER STEPPED INTO THE AIR-conditioned shoppe, he realized what a grave mistake he'd made in arguing with Wayne about his duties on the ranch.

"There you are," Clarissa said, turning from the refrigeration unit, where she'd obviously just put something. "Why are you covered in dirt?"

"Because until five minutes ago, I was standing chest high in a fox den," he said, taking off his hat and letting the cold air hit his face and scalp better. "Hades, it's hot out there." He closed his eyes and breathed in the air-conditioning, imagining it to frost his lungs and cool him from the inside out.

Clarissa giggled, and he opened his eyes to see her smile. He loved her smile, as it always made him smile too. "Bet you're wishing you'd given up the regular chores to learn to make ice cream about now."

"Rub it in, why don't you?" He grinned at her and took a couple of steps into the shoppe. "I'm still going to learn how to make ice cream, right?"

"That's right, cowboy," she said. "You didn't really get out of anything." She closed the door on the fridge and gestured for him to follow her. She went through the black plastic door to the back room, and Spencer followed her, feeling a little bit like he was doing something he shouldn't. Going somewhere forbidden.

The kitchen spread before him, and while he'd scrubbed his shirt at the sink just inside the doorway, he hadn't really examined the rest of the room. The wall to his left held the appliances—a huge, commercial refrigerator, a six-burner stove-top, and a dishwasher.

A stainless steel counter ran down the middle of the space, with shelves below it holding various bowls and utensils. The wall to the right housed the large sink he'd used previously, and then racks and racks of ingredients, more bowls and utensils, big cardboard containers, and plastic containers in a variety of shapes and sizes.

A machine sat on the counter, and Clarissa picked it up and moved it to the pantry area. "We don't need that today."

"What is that?" he asked.

"A label maker," she said, picking up a tablet. "I can put in what I've made and the weight, and then it prints me a label for the container. Then I can just scan the dill and Swiss spread and done." She flashed him a smile, and Spencer caught it somewhere inside his chest.

Label makers and spreads. He was so out of his league.

"We're going to start with ice cream," she said,

producing another binder, this one in blue, with plenty of wear and tear along the plastic edges. Spencer eyed it like it might contain a contagious disease if he opened the front cover.

Clarissa did that, and plastic sleeves held the recipes while she flipped through them. "I usually do a flavor-of-the-month. Like the Rocky Road."

"Do you not sell a lot of ice cream?"

"We're twenty minutes outside of town," she said. "Not exactly the most popular retail location."

"How long does the ice cream last?"

"Frozen? A couple of months," she said, glancing up at him. "It starts to get frostbite after that. I take it to Daddy at that point. The man thinks it's a crime to let ice cream go to waste." She smiled at Spencer, who returned it.

She straightened, suddenly serious. Her beautiful green eyes widened and she leaned her hip into the counter. "You look like you're about to bolt."

"I don't know how to do any of this stuff," he said, frustrated and already gesturing with his hands. "I know that, out there. I've already been at work today for five hours, but it's familiar. Sure, a different barn, with new locations for things. A new kind of shower head in the wash stalls. But I understand it." He heaved a sigh, realizing how tight his chest had gotten. "This? I don't understand this."

Clarissa blinked a couple of times, and Spencer could admit he hadn't strung together so many words in a long time. He usually went with the flow, but this felt like swimming through sharks.

"I understand," she said quietly. "It's new. Whoever Daddy hires to run the shoppe in the morning might do all of this." She turned and put both palms on the counter, her own frustrated sigh leaking out of her mouth. "This is important to me, and I know you'll keep the integrity of my recipes. I just...I just want to show you, so someone knows."

She wouldn't look at him again, and Spencer understood perfectly what she was trying to say. He stepped to the counter beside her, lifting his arm with a bit of hesitation. Then he slid it around her waist and brought her flush against him. "Okay," he whispered.

Clarissa leaned her head against his shoulder, making him feel stronger than he actually was. "Which flavor do we need to make today?" he asked, praying it was vanilla but knowing it would be something complicated like huckleberry cheesecake.

CHAPTER TWELVE

S tanding in the kitchen with Spencer made Clarissa's thoughts scatter. No one had ever invaded her space like this, and she wasn't sure she liked it. Then the weight of his hand on her hip told her how much she did.

She didn't want to be alone forever. She wanted someone she could trust explicitly, who understood what made her tick, and who respected her dreams and goals. She wanted to trust and love a cowboy the same way. She wanted to "get" him, and she wanted to support his dreams and goals.

In all honesty, the reason she was moving to San Antonio was because she was giving up on that kind of relationship. She couldn't admit that out loud, and the fact that she still hadn't received a single call for an interview despite the handful of new applications she'd put out at the end of last week made her gut writhe.

It was just last week, she told herself. *They haven't even had time to look at them.*

With that thought cemented fully in her brain, she began to flip the pages in the binder. "It's summertime," she said. "I can put on our social media that we have new flavors. Mint sells well in the summer." She continued to muse as she looked for the perfect recipe. They usually jumped off the page, striking her in the heart, when they needed to be made.

"Banana pudding," she said, landing on the recipe. "This is a good seller in the summer. We can make pops too, and those sell out fast." She looked at Spencer, but he had that wary look in his eye again. At least he wasn't turning paler by the moment, as he had been a few minutes ago. He really had looked like he was about to throw up or pass out, and Clarissa didn't want to deal with either.

She didn't know how to deal with the emotions storming through her chest, and she didn't know how to tell Spencer that since she'd seen him run into those barrels a few weeks ago, she'd started to doubt everything about her decisions.

She did know how to get out milk, cream, sugar, and vanilla. She knew how to boss someone around in the kitchen. She did both of those things until they had assembled the ingredients on the countertop.

"Okay," she said, pushing her hair back. "You cook an ice cream base until it's nice and thick. It's not hard. It just requires delicate heat. There are eggs in there, and they require a bit of special attention."

The bell chimed on the door, and Clarissa turned that way. "A customer." She immediately wiped her hands on her apron, though they hadn't started cooking yet. "You have to go help the customers when they come," she said over her shoulder, already moving toward the front of the building, "Then we'll come right back to where we left off."

He followed her into the front of the shoppe, where Clarissa asked if the woman there needed any help. Since it was Mrs. Sharpe, and she'd been coming to the shoppe for years, she sure didn't. She picked out her milk—chocolate for the kids—cheese, and butter, paid, and left.

"The tablet is a life-saver," Clarissa said. "We take all major credit and debit cards. It emails the receipt if they want one. Done."

"And you move it back and forth, from out here to in there."

"It's usually out here," she said. "I only had it back there to make the spreads this morning." She pointed to the refrigeration unit. "We should be stocked for a couple of days now. You don't have to make everything everyday."

"We don't make everything everyday. Got it."

She smiled to herself as she pushed back into the kitchen. "In fact, I wouldn't even be making ice cream today if you weren't here. We don't need it, but you need to learn." She looked at the ingredients on the counter and blew out her breath. "All right, we're going to start by steeping the vanilla wafers in the cream and milk."

As she went along, showing him how to steep, strain, and season, she realized she should've chosen an easier ice cream to make. Vanilla would've been best, because then she could've told him how he could make it into chocolate. Or add some candy and coloring to make it the rainbow bright flavor the kids loved when they came. Or she could've added strawberries to it, or cookies to make cookies and cream.

Mistake, she told herself, but she refused to let that word come out of her mouth. She'd be here next week, and she could make a very small batch of vanilla to teach him all of that.

"And then you just pour it into the machine." Clarissa supervised as Spencer picked up the huge bowl and began pouring it into the industrial ice cream machine.

Spencer did great, just as he always had. He may not have any degrees or certifications, but he picked up on things quickly. She'd made the spreadable cheeses that morning, and she'd wait until Wednesday or Thursday to make more. They were easy, because it was just mixing together ingredients, weighing out the product, and labeling it. She had recipes for everything too. Easy peasy.

"All right," Spencer said, setting the big bowl in the

even bigger sink. "How long does that go?" He peered at the binder. "Twelve minutes." Meeting her eyes, he asked, "It only takes twelve minutes?"

"Then it takes six hours in the freezer," she said. "So if you're out of the flavor you want in the morning, you're not serving it that day."

He moved his focus back to the binder and studied it. "And you really only do this once or twice a month."

"Really," she said. "It's not Baskin Robbins, Spence." She laughed lightly, thrilled when he did too. He looked much more relaxed now, and she felt brave enough to reach for his hand. "Hey, I realize I should've started with vanilla."

Their eyes met, and his fingers curled around hers and squeezed. "You like to make things a little more complicated than they need to be." He grinned at her, and he seemed so much like himself again.

"The cheeses are more often. They're also really easy."

"For you," he quipped, those dreamy eyes dropping to her mouth. He pulled them back to hers and blinked. "When will we do that?"

"Thursday," she said. "Then we'll have fresh product going into the weekend."

"And your brothers bring everything else over from the milk parlor?" he asked. "The milk, the butter, that kind of stuff?"

"Most things, yes," she said, pushing her hair off her

forehead with her free hand. "We can make the hard cheese on Friday or Saturday."

"Hard cheese," he said, flipping a page in the binder without releasing her hand. "How often do you do that?"

"Depends on demand, but usually only a couple of times each week," she said. "It's easy and fast."

Spencer looked up from the binder, where he'd now entered the spreadable cheese recipes. "You developed all of these recipes," he said, no question mark in sight.

"Yes."

He looked at her with sparks of interest. "Why are you—?"

"I can't make cheese forever," she said, already hearing his unspoken question. *Why are you leaving the farm? Why isn't running this shop good enough for you?* The questions bounced around in her ears, vibrating from one drum to the other.

"It's *spreadable cheese,* Spencer. I have a culinary degree from the best institute in the country." She looked around the industrial kitchen that had too much silver and always smelled a little too much like warm milk about to go sour.

She released his hand and stepped away from him, suddenly so claustrophobic in this huge room. "Do you remember what you said to me when I got accepted to the Culinary Institute of America?"

He hung his head. "How could I forget? You ended

everything with me because of what I said." He looked up again, his dark eyes so bright. "I apologize for saying I didn't think you'd get in. Really, Clarissa." He tapped the binder but kept his gaze on her. "*You* came up with all of these recipes. You're an amazing chef."

"Thank you," she said, but the unrest in her soul rose within her. "I'm better than cheese. I want to do more than make cheese and ice cream on a dairy farm in a Texas town no one's heard of."

Spencer studied her for another moment before resignation and understanding entered his expression. "All right," he drawled, though she suspected he didn't truly understand her need to be more than Sweet Water Falls Farm and Cooper & Co would allow.

She didn't really understand it either. Maybe she should get her head examined by someone who could iron thoughts and feelings flat and make sense of them.

Thankfully, the bell on the door out front chimed, and Clarissa spun in that direction, her the-customer-is-always-right smile on her face. "Excuse me."

THE NEXT NIGHT, CLARISSA MOVED AROUND THE kitchen in the farmhouse with ease. She already had a row of brightly colored bowls on the island, with lettuce, tomatoes, cheese, olives, black beans, and corn. She'd put out the condiments—salsa, sour cream, guacamole, and ranch dressing.

The tortillas were wrapped in tin foil and sitting on the burner, warmed and ready to go.

Lee came into the kitchen, saying something to Will, who followed him.

"Wash up," Clarissa said. "I've got three meats ready to go."

The doorbell chimed, and Daddy got up from the table, where he'd been studying the books for the farm. "I'll get it."

"It's Spencer," Clarissa said. "I invited him tonight." That brought the activity in the kitchen to a halt. Literally, all three men who'd been moving froze. Conversations died. It took Clarissa a couple of seconds to realize it, and she rolled her eyes. "It's nothing," she said. "Go let him in."

She picked up the pan with the steak in it and poured it onto the waiting plate. She repeated the action with the taco-seasoned chicken, and then the ground beef. By then, Travis had come inside through the back door, and Spencer arrived from the front one.

She'd given him a firehose of information this afternoon, and he'd just taken it all like a champ. He now wore a dark blue shirt with tiny white boxes to make a tight plaid pattern, a pair of jeans, and those sexy cowboy boots, all of which made her heart thump out several errant beats, the silly thing.

Everyone converged, and Clarissa smiled at all of them, even Mama still seated at the dining room table. Daddy would serve her, as she had some pretty big circles under her eyes today.

"It's a soft taco bar," she said. "Or burritos. Whatever you want to call it to be able to eat it." She smiled around at everyone, letting it slip a little bit. "There will be no fighting tonight. No complaining about things on the farm or the milk side." She straightened and folded her arms. "Travis is going to tell us about Belinda, and Lee will update us on Ford. Daddy's going to talk about his horse, and I'm going to give you an update on how things are going with Spencer in the kitchen, and the applications I've put out. That's it."

"Yes, ma'am," Travis said, his voice somewhat resigned. "But I don't want to talk about Belinda." He swept his hat off his head and moved to hang it by the back door. "I'll pray, and then I'll tell you about Queenie's newest trick."

An hour later, Spencer got to his feet, his smile still in place. Clarissa's speech had worked, and no one had grumped a single time. Fine, Lee had tried once, but Clarissa had glared him into silence mid-sentence.

"Thanks for dinner," he said, reaching to tip his hat that wasn't on his head. "I should be gettin' home. I walked over, so it'll take a few minutes."

Clarissa stood too, her heart pounding. She wanted to walk with him, but the kitchen still sat in disarray. She picked up her plate, as well as Travis's and Daddy's as she walked by.

"I'll clean up," Daddy said, getting up and collecting a few more plates.

She put the plates in the sink and met her father's eye. She hadn't been happy when he'd hired Spencer, but she'd had some time to get used to the idea. She'd enjoyed having him around, and it had actually been really nice getting to know him again.

"I'll walk with you," she said, stepping into her dad and giving him a hug. "Thanks, Daddy."

"Dinner was delicious, as always," he said. With that, he turned on the sink and got rinsing while Clarissa gathered her nerves and her wits and held them tightly.

She joined Spencer on the front porch, both of them just standing on the top step and looking out toward the road. The house sat back about two hundred yards from the highway, and they couldn't actually see the asphalt. If a truck went by, she could hear it.

"Thanks for having me," he said. "That was so much better than a microwavable bowl of mac and cheese." He chuckled as he went down the steps, and Clarissa hastened to follow him. She didn't have much to say, but Spencer took her hand, and that seemed to say a lot.

She smiled into the evening sunshine, the golden rays of it peeking over the tops of the trees in the west. The air felt very still tonight, and it went down like wet cotton.

"I haven't spoken to my dad in twenty years," Spencer

said. "I've been thinking about him a lot since I decided to leave Hope Eternal." He spoke in a quiet, reverent way, and while what he'd said surprised Clarissa, she didn't want to shatter the atmosphere he'd created.

"Why's that?" she asked, keeping her voice as muted as his.

"After my momma died, he turned mean. Well." He lifted one shoulder. "He's always been mean. He was mean to momma and mean to me, but we could handle him. After she died, though, no one could. He drank a lot, and he stopped working the ranch we lived on."

"Where was this?" Clarissa looked at him, feeling hopeful for some reason. Like maybe she could help Spencer work through this problem.

"A little town in the Hill Country," he said. "Just outside of New Braunfels." He looked off into the distance, obviously somewhere inside his own mind.

"I did the best I could, but it was a thirty-minute drive to school, and I had to ride the bus for a few years. That took over an hour. I tried to keep the house up, the barns, the horses…" He sighed. "In the end, we lost it all."

"I'm so sorry."

"My granddaddy found out, and see it was my momma's farm. His daughter. So he took it back when I was seventeen. Kicked me and my dad off the land, and Dad just sort of drifted then. I managed to finish high school, and I left him somewhere in Hondo. Maybe. Might've been D'Hanis. It was this little hovel of a house between the two towns. I just got in my truck and drove away."

Clarissa didn't know what to say. Her mind spun through such a sad tale, and compared to her own family, she couldn't even fathom not talking to her parents and siblings.

"I drifted a little too," he said. "Moved from ranch to ranch, learning things. I studied with a master carpenter for a while before I decided that wasn't for me. I met a woman and we got engaged. I was twenty-two."

She drew in a sharp breath. "Really?"

He gave her a sad smile, his focus not really in his eyes. "In no way were we ready to be married. I had no job at the time, as her daddy had just fired me for, uh, kissing her in the barn. She was only eighteen."

Clarissa just kept putting one foot in front of the other, as this was obviously Spencer's time to talk.

"She pulled out in the end," he said. "Made me feel so worthless. I already felt like that, because I'd failed my momma. I'd failed on the farm. I had no one. Nothing." His voice sounded haunted and hitched up in his chest at the same time.

"I finally landed at Hope Eternal Ranch, and that place—and Ginger—saved me. When I met you a few years later, I was still healing. I wasn't ready for us." His hand around hers tightened, and their pair of houses came into view. He remained quiet for the last few minutes of their walk, and since her house came before his, he took her up the steps to the front porch.

She turned back to him, wanting to hug him and reassure him that he was worth something to her. "Spencer," she started.

"I'm ready now," he said quietly. "That's what this quiet seething has been inside me. It's telling me that I'm healed now. I'm ready to leave all of that negativity in the past and move forward into the future with someone."

She searched his face, but the light was dimmer under the eaves, as the sun had continued its arc in the west.

He cupped her face in his hand, and oh, Clarissa liked his touch. She leaned into it and let her eyes drift closed.

The charge between her and Spencer couldn't be denied, and Clarissa was trying to fight it. While no one wanted her to leave Cooper & Co, Clarissa had spoken true earlier.

She needed a change.

Maybe Spence is the change you need, she thought. *Maybe the chance you need to take isn't in San Antonio, but right here in Sweet Water Falls.*

She opened her eyes and looked into his. "I'm sorry about your dad. I remember that summer with you as being magical and fun." She gave him a smile, and it felt real and whole on her face.

"I remember you loving deep-dish pepperoni pizza."

"Guilty," she said with a laugh.

He grinned too, his hand sliding down her shoulder to

claim her fingers. "I remember you looking up into the night sky and making a wish on all the pricks of light, even the planets."

Clarissa smiled, that memory as clear in her mind as if it had happened last night. "I love the stars and planets and heavens."

"I remember the conversation that night being real serious," he added, the moment turning just as sober. "I remember how sad you were that your grandmother had died, and I remember you saying now she was up in the stars, watching over you."

He reached past her to open the door, but he slid his hand into hers as she lowered her arm from the crook of his elbow. The strength in his grip made her pause, and she looked up at him.

Mistake, her mind screamed at her. Not her first mistake today either. In a tender moment like this, with his eyes sparking with attraction like that...

Clarissa was in serious trouble with this cowboy.

"I remember you being an amazing kisser," he whispered, lowering his head toward hers. He paused only a few inches away, giving her a chance to deny him. "Can I kiss you, Clarissa?"

She'd never been able to tell him yes, though "all right" and "okay" were forms of the word.

Tonight, she reached up with her free hand and ran her fingers along the side of his face, guiding his mouth straight to hers, and said, "Yes."

Her heartbeat stayed in a nice, steady rhythm, because kissing Spencer Rust had always felt like the most natural thing in the world. It felt like coming home.

It felt like exactly the risk she'd needed to take to get what she'd always wanted.

CHAPTER THIRTEEN

Spencer couldn't believe what he was doing, but an old flame had been reignited the moment he'd entered the same space as Clarissa, over two weeks ago. It burned brightly within him, and she'd been stoking it with her presence, her acceptance of his confessions, and letting him hold her hand.

At the same time, he knew he didn't want to go too fast. He forced himself to go slow, to really experience kissing her again. This was the first woman he'd kissed in a good, long while, and he sure did like the way she melted into him. The way she ran her fingers up through his hair, dislodging his hat. The way he finally relaxed, feeling comfortable with himself and with her, also something that hadn't happened in a long time.

She smelled like a hint of orange and a bit of vanilla,

mixed with that delicious steak she'd grilled up for those tacos, and he simply could not get enough of her.

He pulled away first, his heart booming in his chest, and his fingers tingling slightly from the chemistry in that kiss.

Clarissa ducked her head so he couldn't see her face, but Spencer couldn't contain his smile. "I think that's the first time you've told me yes," he said quietly.

She tucked herself into his arms, and they swayed slightly. He remembered her going silent after their last first kiss, and he didn't mind it so much. The breeze kicked up a little, and the sky continued to darken.

After another big breath, he said, "I got some of those frozen chocolate lava cakes. Do you maybe want to come over and try them with me?"

She pulled back and looked up at him, so many emotions swimming in her eyes. "Frozen lava cakes?" she asked in the most disgusted voice ever.

Spencer chuckled, the sound growing inside him until it became a true laugh. "They might be good." He threaded his fingers through hers and tugged her to get her to come with him. "Says they only take a few minutes in the microwave."

"I am not eating a cake that came out of the microwave," she said, but her feet moved with him.

"Okay," he said. "I'll eat it and tell you how it tastes." He just wanted her to come with him. She did, and they crossed the lawn between their houses to his.

"How's the bed in here?" she asked. "You said you needed to get a mattress pad."

"I did," he said. "One of those big, four-inch-thick memory foam pads." He grinned at her as he entered the cabin. "It's better." A lot better, but he didn't want her to feel bad about the bed. He shouldn't have brought it up on the Sunday-afternoon horseback riding session.

"And the cabin?" She looked around as she entered, and Spencer wasn't sure what she expected to find. If she thought he might put out family photos or mementos, she's be sorely mistaken. He did have a print of a mustang he'd found at a farmer's market several years ago, that one of his friends from Hope Eternal had painted, but that was it.

He'd hung the horse on the wall above the television, which he'd barely used since moving in over the weekend.

"The cabin is great," he said. "The coffee maker works, and it's just me, so there's not much fuss." He'd shared a house with three other men, and sometimes more, so having a place all to himself was actually a little bit like heaven. "It's clean. I love the back porch."

"Good." Clarissa met his gaze then, a smile on her face and reflecting in her eyes. "You're not going to be seeing much of that new, comfortable bed, I'm afraid. We have *so* much to do before you take over."

They did, but Spencer wasn't worried about it. He was a quick study, and with the pretty, strawberry-blonde at his side, even a long day wouldn't feel like it.

"All right," he said, opening his freezer. He'd gone to

the grocery store on Sunday evening, and he hadn't been able to figure out how to sleep without a bit of chocolate in his stomach. Lord help him, he'd tried over the past thirty-seven years, but he didn't think it was possible. "Let's see how these shape up in the microwave."

"I'm so grossed out by this," she said, entering the kitchen with him. "Cherry loves this kind of stuff, though."

"She didn't get the cooking gene?" he asked, taking out the two frozen cakes. They looked good to him, and he did what the package instructed him to do.

"Not really," Clarissa said. "She once started a fire with butter and onions." She giggled, and Spencer liked the sound of that.

"Where is she?" he asked, needing her to fill the silence with talk this time. He'd said so much that evening already, and he knew he was going to have to address his father at some point. He wanted to go talk to Nate, who always gave him great advice, and he pulled out his phone to text the man.

"Cherry? She's a counselor over veterinarian technicians as SATC."

"Wow," Spencer said. "So she'll be in San Antonio when you get there." He looked up from his partial text.

"Yes," Clarissa said in a tone that told him she really didn't want to talk about her sister.

He forged on anyway, dropping his gaze back to his phone. "Are you going to stay with her while you figure out a job?"

"I don't know." Clarissa retreated from him in more ways than one, but he quickly sent his text to Nate about maybe getting together for dinner soon.

Come anytime, Nate sent back. *Slate was just asking about you.*

Slate stuck in Spencer's vision. He'd had to reconcile with his family too, and it had been extremely difficult for him. *Maybe we could grill here at Sweet Water Falls*, Spencer said. *Or I'll bring some hamburgers to you.*

Ted's the one with the grilling skills to pay the bills, Nate said, and that made Spencer smile.

Friday night barbecue? he asked.

It's on, Nate confirmed.

Spencer looked up from his phone to find Clarissa standing at the window that looked toward her house. He took a moment to drink her in, wondering if he was brave enough to ask her about the job in the city. At dinner, she'd already filled in everyone about the applications she'd put out.

Now I just have to wait, she'd said.

Spencer looked at the microwave. Three more minutes, and then the cakes were supposed to sit inside for five. He wandered closer to Clarissa, taking his time so he didn't scare her away. "Will you go to San Antonio if you don't get a job?" he asked as he stepped next to her.

She turned to look at him. "I'm going to get a job."

He nodded, not sure what to say next. He didn't want

to argue with her, and she wasn't stupid. She knew what it meant when no one called about her application.

"We're having a barbecue at Hope Eternal on Friday," he said. "Would you like to go with me?"

The blazing energy in her eyes went down a notch, and she said, "Sure, that sounds fun."

Spencer wasn't sure if it did or not. The grumbling in his chest told him it wouldn't be fun. But intellectually, he knew he'd have a good time. He always did with the Mulbury boys.

"Great," he said. "Then you can meet all those cowboys you spied on over the weekend."

"I can't believe this was milk," Spencer said, looking down into the huge saucepan Clarissa had poured a gallon of milk into. She'd heated it until it boiled, then she'd reduced the heat and added lemon juice.

The milk had curdled, making cheese. Some green liquid remained on the bottom, and she currently laid some appropriately named cheesecloth over the top of a big bowl.

"Bring it over here, Mister Muscles."

He liked working with her in the kitchen, and warmth spread through him at the nickname. He picked up the big pan and poured the remaining milk and cheese over the bowl while she held the cloth steady.

She bundled it all up as she said, "Now we let it cool while we make our flavorings for the spread."

"That's going to be cream cheese," he said, almost asking but not quite.

"Yes," she said again, smiling. "We'll add some salt to it and blend it up until it's creamy. It'll be cream cheese." She tapped the binder as she moved down the counter. "Now, that made four cups of cream cheese, which is enough to make about two cups of four different spreads. We sell those in four ounce containers, so that will be four tubs of each." She indicated the food service containers, which were made of white plastic and had a clear lid.

She looked at him, and he looked down the counter to the other ingredients they'd assembled. Spices, herbs, garlic, shredded cheese, mayonnaise, butter, and more.

"You don't want to use a food processor with the spreads," she said, lifting up another kitchen appliance. "A simple hand-mixer is your best friend."

He nodded, his heartbeat doing weird things in his chest.

"This one is garlic and herb," she said. "It's one of our bestsellers, and we're completely out."

"So four containers isn't going to be enough," he said.

"No." She smiled at him. "You're going to do two more gallons of milk and repeat these recipes after I show them to you." Oh, so it was a predatory smile, and Spencer could only blink at her.

She giggled and then got down to business. She

chopped garlic at the first station and brought over all the herbs she'd taken from the pantry—dill, parsley, basil, and thyme. She measured everything out into a bowl in front of the small cutting board, talking as she went.

The recipe had been taken from the binder and sat right beside the board, so Spencer focused on what she was doing, not how much of each ingredient she put in the bowl.

"You'll triple this next time," she said, glancing at him. "Okay?"

"Okay," he said.

"Then it's butter in this one, some mozzarella cheese to make it nice and melty if people want to heat it up, and then we'll add in a cup of that cream cheese when it's ready." She moved down to the next station and started talking about the pimento cheese that their shoppe had become famous for.

"So when you do these two recipes," she said. "You'll triple them both. That way, you'll have sixteen containers of each to sell for a while. These last two, you'll just do as normal, and we'll end up with eight of each."

"Okay," he said, and he picked up a pen and made a note on the notebook she'd given him. *Triple the first two recipes. Single the last two.* "Got it."

"Pimento is wonderful," she said. "Lots of cheddar cheese." She put a couple of heavy handfuls into the bowl. "Mayonnaise." A few tablespoons of that went in, followed by the pimentos, and then, "Spices," she said. "Garlic and onion powder. Salt and pepper." She glanced down to the clothed cream cheese. "Then a cup of that. Three when you make it."

"Yes, ma'am," he said.

She continued with the bacon and cheddar spread, and finally the lemon-mustard-dill combination that actually had Spencer's mouth watering.

"Okay," she said, moving around him to the cream cheese. "This should be ready by now. You give it a squeeze." She did, and a few more drops of liquid came out. "And one-fourth of this ball goes in each one." She didn't measure, and she got the job done as if she'd done it countless times before. Which, of course, she had.

"Then we mix," she said. She picked up the hand-mixer and got blending, and Spencer watched as each spreadable cheese came to life.

He set out the containers, and Clarissa weighed them as she split the mixtures into fourths again. She showed him how to print the labels, and when they had sixteen containers of spreadable cheese in four different flavors sitting on the counter, Spencer had never felt such satisfaction.

Clarissa likewise beamed at them as if they were her children, and he suddenly understood why she liked cooking so much.

"Doable?" she asked, switching her gaze to his.

"Yes," he said. "I can do this."

"Okay, cowboy," she drawled. "Your turn. Two gallons

of milk this time. Make the cream cheese." She backed up until she was out of the way, and Spencer drew in a deep breath.

His confidence took a dive, but he pulled it right back into place. He could do this. He could, and he would, even with Clarissa watching.

Please help me not to butcher her recipes, he thought as he set a clean pot on the stove top and opened the fridge to get out the first half-gallon bottle of milk.

CHAPTER FOURTEEN

W atching Spencer make cream cheese and then Cooper & Co's most popular spreads made Clarissa realize two things: He was an incredibly sexy man, and she could easily be replaced by anyone.

One didn't need a culinary degree to do what she did around the farm, obviously. Spencer could read a recipe and follow it, and though it took him longer to chop the garlic and his big cowboy hands fumbled over measuring the delicate herbs, he got the job done right.

Her chest felt like someone had placed her in a vice and was slowly squeezing the life from her. Had the last eight years been a waste of her time? Her life? Why had she come back here to the farm when she could've followed Leslie to the city to get the experience everyone seemed to require?

She was so sick of that line—*needs more experience.* How was she supposed to get that experience if no one would hire her?

"Done," Spencer said, and he carried the sun in his expression. He beamed at the spreads he'd made and then her. "I did it, Riss."

"Yes," she said, her voice choked. "You did." She reached for the first stack of garlic and herb spread containers, which she'd labeled during the demo. "Let's get them out into the front fridge." She led the way, because she couldn't bear to look at Spencer. No one had come into the shop in the past hour or two, which was typical for Thursday afternoon. It would be tomorrow when customers would pick up.

"The shelves are labeled," she said, sliding the older container to the front. "Old product goes up front. Newer behind it."

"Got it," Spencer said, and she had no doubt he did.

She marveled that three gallons of milk could make thirty-six containers, just as she always did. It didn't take as long to move them as it did to make them, and Spencer put the last of the smoked cheddar and bacon spread into the fridge only a few minutes later.

"So you do that twice a week?" he asked, looking at one of the older containers. "You made this on Monday."

"Yes," she said. "Mondays and Thursdays, usually. Depends on how busy the week is. Sometimes I make the weekend products on Friday morning, but you probably won't have time for that."

He nodded and slid the refrigeration unit closed. "Do you know who your dad is going to hire for the morning shoppe time?"

"I don't think he is," she said, turning away from Spencer again. "They're just not going to open until noon, when you come over from the farm."

"Oh." He didn't say anything else, and that was exactly how Clarissa felt. Honestly, it felt like the two hours she spent there in the morning—which was really more like three, after she finished her dairy product pick-ups and came straight here—weren't necessary. That *she* wasn't necessary.

She suddenly needed to be outside, away from walls, ice cream boards, labeled cheese spreads, and Spencer Rust. She said nothing as she strode toward the door of the shoppe, which she'd painted a bright, cheery blue, and practically exploded outside.

"Riss?" Spencer asked behind her, but she kept on going. A car pulled into the lot when she was halfway across it, and she recognized Phillipa Grove, who came to buy milk and cheese curds at least once a week.

Clarissa didn't turn back; Spencer knew how to use the tablet to check someone out. He could find milk and cheese in the small refrigeration units.

No one needed Clarissa. No one here at Sweet Water Falls Farm. No one wanted her in San Antonio. No one, and she barely made it to the back side of the barn, away from the lot, the shoppe, and anyone who might be able to see her, before she burst into tears.

* * *

THE LOUD KNOCK ON HER DOOR LATER THAT NIGHT told her one of her brothers had brought her dinner. Probably Travis.

Clarissa sighed as she got off the couch, where she'd spent most of the afternoon. She'd texted Spencer that she wasn't feeling well, and she'd retreated to her house. She'd found a warm blanket despite the summertime temperatures, put on a romantic comedy, and taken a couple of naps.

She opened the door, expecting to find her youngest brother standing there, a plate of food covered with aluminum foil. They weren't fussy in the Cooper family, that was for sure.

Travis did stand there, but so did Spencer, and they both had something in their hands. Travis grinned at her and said, "Mama sent this for you." He lifted the Tupperware container of what looked like chicken noodle soup. "And I ran into this scoundrel on the way over. He said he had dessert."

"I know she likes dessert first," Spencer said, smiling first at Travis and then switching his gaze to Clarissa. He turned more serious, though the sparkle in his eye didn't die by any means.

Her muscles clenched, and she wondered how easy it would be to get them all replaced. Surely there was someone somewhere who could help her with that. "I'm fine," she said. "I don't need Mama's magic soup."

"Do you really think I'm leaving here with it still?" Travis shook his head and pushed his way past her and into the house. "I'll just leave it on the counter. That way, when Mama quizzes me about it, I can say you have it."

"It's summertime," Clarissa said after him, turning away from Spencer. "It's too hot for soup."

"Mama doesn't believe there's anything that doesn't call for soup," Travis said, grinning as he faced her. "Eat it or don't. I just know I'm not going to be taking the heat for not dropping it off as I was asked to do."

"Mama shouldn't even be cooking," Clarissa said, collapsing back onto the couch. Guilt flowed through her that she'd caused her mother grief with a fake illness. She closed her eyes as the scent of chocolate went past, though that almost made her perk up.

"I brought double chocolate chip cookies," Spencer said. "I made them myself, so you'll probably not want to eat them."

"I'm sure they're better than that disgusting lava cake the other night."

"Hey, that was good," Spencer said. "I think I will put

them under the broiler next time, like you said. They'll be hot *and* crispy then."

"All right, well you two kids have a good night." Travis's boots came toward her, and he bent over her. "Love you, Rissy. Feel better fast." He grinned at her, a gesture that said he knew she was faking but he wasn't going to call her on it in front of Spencer. He pressed a kiss to her forehead and left in a flash, before she could even say good-bye to him.

"I won't stay," Spencer said, coming into her line of sight at the end of the couch. "You've built yourself a little nest here, and there's food. You know where to find me if you need something." He gave her a plastic smile, touched the top of his cowboy hat, and started for the door at a slower clip than Travis had.

"Do you ever just feel useless?" she asked, and he paused. "That's how I feel today. Useless, and like everything I've done here over the past eight years doesn't mean anything."

Spencer walked over to the recliner and eased into it. "Yeah, I think I know what that feels like." He didn't smile this time. "Did I make you feel like that?"

"No," she said miserably. She sat up and ran her hands through her hair. She'd washed it that morning, but it felt greasy and limp to her. She exhaled and lifted her head again. "Watching you make the spreadable cheeses was amazing. You're very good at it, and I suppose it just made me realize...I'm not needed here."

"I'm sorry," he said. "I didn't mean to make you feel that way."

"It's not you," she said. "It's just...this. Everything. Daddy doesn't need me to pull the product pick-ups. He and the boys can do it. He doesn't need me to open the shoppe at ten. You'll do it at noon. He doesn't need me to make the cheeses or the ice cream. I'm just...useless."

"You are not," Spencer said, his voice quiet but powerful. "You've developed all of those recipes, Clarissa. Without you, there is not shoppe. There are no cheeses getting made. Heck, I didn't even know cream cheese was something a person could make. I thought it just came in those little bricks at the store."

She appreciated the sentiments, as well as the intensity in his eyes, but she looked away anyway. "I just need... I don't know what I need. It's not soup, though. Not when it's so hot outside."

"You do have your blanket out," he said, and she caught a grin on his face when she looked at him again.

"It comforts me." She didn't want to tell him what else comforted her, though she had a whole freezer full of chocolate chip cookies that usually did the trick.

He met her gaze. "Maybe the soup will too."

"I like dessert first."

Without a word, he got up and collected the plate of cookies he'd brought. He joined her on the couch this time, and he held the paper plate toward her. She picked up a cookie and sniffed it. "Smells normal."

"Well, arsenic is odorless."

Clarissa blinked at him, and he burst out laughing. He picked up one of the cookies and took a bite of it. Half the cookie disappeared, and he held up the other half in a sort of toast before eating it too. "That was a joke, obviously," he said, still chuckling.

She took a dainty bite of the fresh cookie he'd brought, expecting to find it extremely salty or something. But it tasted...amazing, with milk and semi-sweet chocolate chips in the same dough. "This is good," she said.

"I never cease to amaze," he quipped, and Clarissa felt herself slipping a little further in love with him.

Perhaps her third mistake of the week when it came to Spencer Rust. After this afternoon's think session on the couch, she was more determined than ever to leave Sweet Water Falls Farm in her rearview mirror and strike out into the restaurant business in Texas.

She had to. Her life would not be defined by pimento cheese spread that anyone could make. Oh, no, it would not.

THE SCENT OF SMOKE AND MEAT GRILLING FILLED Clarissa's nose as she got out of Spencer's white truck. The vehicle had seen better days, but the engine purred like a kitten and the seats inside didn't have a scratch on them. It couldn't go over fifty-five, but Spencer didn't seem to care. He drove with one hand on the wheel and the other in hers, about five under the speed limit the whole way from Sweet Water Falls to Hope Eternal.

He said nothing to her as he met her at the hood and took her hand in his. He led her through an opening in the fence that didn't have a gate, and down the sidewalk toward a house that had been connected to another one by a three-car garage.

"I used to live over in the Annex," he said, nodding to the right. "That's where all the cowboys live. Ginger, the owner and boss, lived over here in the West Wing." He spoke with fondness, and Clarissa was glad he had these friends here. Maybe when she left, he wouldn't completely alone.

If you're still leaving, why are you even here?

The question ran through her mind, and she needed to address it sooner rather than later. Right now wouldn't work, so she filed it away, just like she'd been doing every day this week.

Spencer took them through the garage to a long, big back yard, where several more cabins took up the space in front of the back fence. People had started to gather around an enormous cauldron of fire, where a man worked with long leather gloves on and the biggest pair of tongs Clarissa had ever seen.

Her heartbeat jumped and filled her whole chest, especially when seemingly everyone turned toward them at the same time. Spencer's hand in hers tightened, and he said, "I may or may not have told them you were coming," under his breath.

"What?" she asked. "You didn't tell them?'

"Spence," a man bellowed, and she recognized him from the moving crew. He pulled Spencer away whether he wanted to go or not and hugged him tight. "How are things? Going okay? You can come back here any time."

"You don't own this ranch," an auburn-haired woman drawled, grinning at the two men. She muscled the big bear of a man out of the way and hugged Spencer. "He's right, though," she said under her breath. "If they're not treating you right over there, you come on back."

"They're treating me right," he said as he stepped back. He glanced at Clarissa, and she got the message that he wanted her at his side. "In fact," he added as she stepped into that role. "This is Clarissa Cooper." He took her hand in his, the rest of his sentence unsaid but implied.

The woman's eyes opened wide, and her mouth rounded.

"Clarissa," Spencer said. "My old boss, Ginger Talbot. Mulbury. She's Ginger Mulbury now." He grinned at her. "Ginger and I go way back. Her husband Nate is at the grill. This oaf here is Ted."

Ted grinned at her through this bushy, black beard. "So great to meet you," he gushed. "My wife is around somewhere. Probably putting together the tray for s'mores."

"Yes, she's in the West Wing," another woman said, this one blonde with a little boy on her hip.

"This is Jill," Spencer said. "I went out with her a time or two." He smiled at her easily now, but Clarissa wondered if he had gashes on his heart from the women at this ranch. "Same with Jess." He looked around. "I'm not sure where she is."

"They're not here yet," Jill said. "Slate said for you to go help him with the onions and eggs when you got here." She looked at Spencer, and so much more was said. Clarissa didn't know what though, as she wasn't as well-versed in Spencer-speak as Jill obviously was.

Or maybe he was well-versed in Jill-talk. Either way, he released her hand and said, "I'll be back in a few minutes. You'll be okay?"

"She'll be fine," Ginger said, linking her arm through Clarissa's and guiding her closer to the fire. "We'll just be gossiping about you."

"Ginger," Spencer warned, but the fellow redhead just laughed. Clarissa liked her instantly then, and she grinned at Spencer as she went with Jill and Ginger.

"So," Jill said. "Are you two dating?"

"Oh, I...don't know," Clarissa said, her first contribution to the conversation. She hadn't been able to sneak a word in otherwise. She thought about the kiss she and Spencer had shared earlier that week, as well as the one he'd left her with last night after bringing those cookies.

Yes, she was most likely dating him. "Is it called dating

anymore?" she asked, which only made Jill's smile grow two sizes.

"Probably not," she said. "He'll probably say he's 'seeing you' or 'hanging out' or something equally as lame."

"Nah," Ginger said. "Spencer doesn't do casual."

That made Clarissa look into her eyes, a spark of fear igniting in her belly. "He doesn't?"

"Not usually." Ginger shrugged and released her arm. "Do you want a hamburger or a hot dog? We're cooking to order, since our cowboys and cowgirls work in shifts." She smiled at her husband and bent to pick up a toddler too. He had wispy reddish-brown hair that shone in the golden evening light, and everything Clarissa wanted for herself had manifested itself in the flesh right in front of her.

This redhead had found her happily-ever-after. Maybe there was hope that Clarissa could too.

"Hamburger," she said. "Please."

"Are you the one who's leaving to work in San Antonio?" Nate asked, and Clarissa's attention flew from the mother and child to the man at the grill.

"Oh, uh, yes," she said, though that wasn't entirely true. According to her original plan, she'd be moving tomorrow.

Tomorrow.

The word hit her like a punch in the gut.

She still hadn't packed a box or even done a simple search online for an apartment.

"So you'll date Spencer long-distance," Jill said, as if the solution to their relationship was so obvious.

"Yes," Clarissa said, because it was easier than arguing with them or trying to explain a situation she didn't understand herself. "Something like that."

Jill opened her mouth, presumably to ask another question, but a baby's wail filled the air, distracting all of them. Clarissa had never been so thankful to fade into the background, and when Spencer returned, he seemed even more quiet and more reserved than before.

Still, his hand in hers was firm and welcome, and as the food started coming off the grill, he brightened, introduced her around to more of his friends, and perked up once the chocolate came out.

Once they'd eaten far too much, and the fire started to die, she stood out of the way as he hugged his friends goodbye. He took her hand, and they drove back to Sweet Water Falls Farm and their side-by-side cabins.

"Thanks for coming with me," he said as he turned from the highway onto the dirt lane that went down a decline. "Did you have fun?"

"Yes," she said quickly. "I did. Your friends are fun."

"Yes," he said too, nodding. "They are."

"Why did you leave that ranch?" she asked, though he'd told her before. "You seem to really thrive there."

"It was just time," he said, making the right turn to take them toward their houses. His headlights caught on the trees, shrubs, and machinery along the way, and as they came over the rise that then went back down to their little meadow of a community, he jammed on the brakes.

"What?" she asked, throwing her hands out to catch herself against the dashboard.

"There's a truck parked in front of my house," he said. He looked from it to her. "Who could that be?"

Clarissa peered down the road too. She'd been at the farm forever, and she knew every truck, car, and farm vehicle. This was none of those. "I don't know that truck," she said. "Let's go see."

CHAPTER FIFTEEN

outh Carolina license plates, Spencer thought as
he swung his truck in next to the one already
sitting in front of his cabin. His brain screamed a
warning at him, especially since no one sat behind the
wheel, and no one sat on his front steps or front porch.

Where had they gone? Right inside?

His cabin?

He didn't know anyone he was familiar enough with
who would do that, except all of the men and women he'd
just left behind at Hope Eternal Ranch. And none of them
drove a pickup this rusty and this beat up.

He got out of his truck, the darkness nearly complete
now. He put his hand on the hood of the light blue truck
that didn't belong there. Cold. Whoever had driven this
thing here had been here for a while.

Clarissa joined him at the hood, and he squeezed her hand. "Maybe you should just go home."

"So you can go in alone?" she whispered. "No, let's just go see who it is."

"Do you really think they went inside?"

"Did you lock your front door?"

"No," he said. "I never lock my door. Who's going to come in and rob me?" He frowned as he went down the short sidewalk and up the steps. Clarissa moved right with him every step of the way, which only made his heart pound louder and louder in his ears.

He reached to open the door, calling, "Hello?" into the dark and supposedly empty house. He really needed to start leaving a light on when he went out at night. Or install some of those motion lights like Clarissa had next door. Something.

His fingers fumbled along the wall, and then he found the switch. He flipped it, and the house burst to life with light.

A man groaned, and Spencer's eyes flew to the couch. His heart dropped to his feet, then rebounded painfully to the back of his throat. He felt like he'd been kicked in the stomach.

"Who are you?" Clarissa demanded. "This isn't your house, you know. You can't just wander around and enter any old house you want."

Spencer couldn't get his voice to work. He only kept breathing and blinking because those were involuntary bodily functions. His pulse boomed through his whole body, and his chest was nowhere big enough to hold his heart.

The man sat up, and if Spencer had had any doubt, being able to see him more fully would've erased it.

He hadn't seen this man in twenty years, but Spencer knew his father when he saw him. He automatically tried to touch the inch-long scar that slashed diagonally from the base of his thumb up toward the middle of his palm.

An accident, his dad had said, though he'd been swinging the knife that had caused Spencer to get thirteen stitches in his left hand.

"Hello?" Clarissa said, still at his side, the two of them framed in the doorway. "You have to leave."

"He's my dad," Spencer said quietly as Ernest Rust rubbed the sleep from his eyes and squinted through the bright lights toward him and Clarissa.

"Your dad?" Clarissa asked, looking up at him too. "Really?"

Spencer nodded, his throat too tight to speak.

"I thought you said you didn't speak to your dad."

"I don't," Spencer said. "I haven't in a really long time, at least." He wasn't sure how he felt. At the moment, numbness seemed to be the predominant emotion spreading through him, and he couldn't latch onto a single thought to think it.

Ernest got to his feet, where he immediately stumbled into the coffee table in front of the couch.

Spencer's irritation and anger sparked to life. He'd shown up drunk. Spencer wasn't sure why he'd expected anything different from his father, only that he had. "How did you find me?" he asked.

"You've been in the same place for years, son," Ernest said, and Spencer wanted to shove him against the wall and tell him never to come back.

He stepped in front of Clarissa. "Baby, I think you should go home." He had to get her out of there before Ernest said something to her that would embarrass all of them.

She looked at him with fear in her wide, green eyes, but she nodded.

"I'll walk you," he said, still in almost a whisper. He turned back to his dad as Clarissa edged backward. "Stay here. I'll be back in a minute."

"You ain't got nothin' to eat," Ernest said.

Spencer stepped onto the porch, his pulse misfiring now. He'd just been transported back twenty-five years to the month after his momma had died. They'd run out of the food the churchgoers had brought them, and unbeknownst to Spencer, it was his job to go to the grocery store and get more.

"I have plenty to eat," he said. "I'll make you a sandwich when I get back. Just...stay here." He pulled the door closed behind him, quickly twisting the lock on it as he did so to make it that much harder for Ernest to get out.

"Come on." He hurried Clarissa down the steps and

across the lawn to her house. "I want you to go inside and lock the doors, okay?"

"Spencer," she said, out of breath though he'd seen her lift plenty of glass milk bottles. "Will you be okay?"

"I'll be fine," he said, and he believed himself—if he didn't revert back to the passive teenager he'd once been with his father. "He just says inappropriate things, and he's obviously drunk. So...just stay here and lock the doors. I'll text you when he's asleep again so you know I'm okay."

"Okay." She spun to face him before going into her house. "I'm worried about you."

He couldn't even flirt or appreciate her feelings at the moment. "I'm okay," he whispered.

She took his face in her hands and kissed him, and Spencer felt the fear and urgency in the touch. He broke off the kiss by ducking his head. "I'll text you in a bit." With that, he left, pausing at the bottom of the steps to make sure she went inside and locked the door.

Then he faced his cabin again.

Light poured from it now, and he jogged to the back steps and went inside.

His father sat on the couch now, his head down as he looked at something. Because he was intoxicated, his reaction time was much slower than a normal person's, and it took him a second to look up once he heard Spencer's footsteps.

"What do you want, Dad?" he asked, staying in the kitchen as his dad got wobbily to his feet again. "Ham and cheese? Peanut butter and jelly?" He could ask the same question to find out why his father was even here. He had to want something—and it wasn't just food.

Money, probably, Spencer thought, though his father had never contacted him for money in the past. Of course, Spencer had never had much money in the past.

"Ham's too salty," Ernest said, and Spencer bent to get the bread out of the drawer. He collected the jar of peanut butter and one of jelly, all while keeping one eye on his father.

As he slathered a thick layer of peanut butter on a slice of bread, he asked, "What are you doing here in Sweet Water Falls?"

"Lookin' for you." His dad pulled out a barstool and sat down.

Spencer flicked a glance at him. "Well, you found me."

Ernest wore a goofy grin, and it only annoyed Spencer further. He kept his eyes down as he put on the strawberry jam, put the two halves of the sandwich together, and tossed it in front of his father.

He backed up until he hit the stove behind him, and he folded his arms. "You can't stay here."

His father picked up his sandwich, some of the cloudiness clearing from his eyes with the first bite. "Why not?'

"Why not?" Spencer asked, incredulous. "I work here, Dad. This is my place of employment. The house isn't mine. I haven't spoken to you in twenty years. Take your pick of why not."

His chest heaved, and this wasn't going how his reunification with his father had in his mind. He'd spent ten minutes talking to Slate in his cabin while the man fried eggs for hamburgers about how to approach his dad.

Slate had given him some good advice. *See if you can find him. My parents hadn't left Austin, so that was easy. Then I called my mom. She really helped ease things for my dad.*

When Spencer had then told Slate his mother was dead and gone, Slate had said, *Well, you call him then. Tell him you've been thinking about him, and you'd like to see him if he's open to it.*

Now, faced with the man, Spencer was the one who wasn't open to spending any time with him. He hadn't changed at all in the past two decades, and he couldn't comprehend that.

Spencer felt like he'd walked through fire, been reborn, and wasn't anything like the seventeen-year-old who'd left town ten minutes after his graduation ceremony had ended.

A ceremony his father hadn't attended, because he'd been so fall-down drunk, just like he was now.

With every bite he took, his eyes became clearer and clearer. Either way, his dad was a mean old man, and Spencer didn't want him around. He'd just end up with another scar, probably both physically and emotionally. No, he had to go.

"It'll just be for a few days," Ernest said. "I'll never

even leave the house. I'll park the truck around back. In fact, I should move it now." He got up from the counter, and his step did seem steadier.

"Ernest," Spencer said, and his dad tried to turn back to him. His feet caught on the barstool legs or maybe each other. He went down, his knees cracking against the hardwood floor. A groan filled the house, and Spencer rushed around the cabinetry to get to him.

Time slowed down, and Spencer could see every nanosecond. His father was a pathetic, elderly man, down on his knees, in some measure of pain. Compassion filled him, and Spencer forgave his father in that single breath of time.

Relief filled him with the release, and while he didn't approve of his father's lifestyle or want him in his life in this condition, all he felt now was...sympathy for the man.

"Come on now," he said gently, helping him back to his feet. "Let's go to the couch." He got him back there, where he'd obviously stumbled inside and collapsed after arriving.

"I should move the truck," his dad said, rubbing his knees. "Then no one will see it and know I'm here."

Cold fear ran through Spencer. "Why does it matter if someone sees it?" he asked.

Ernest seemed to realize what he'd said, because he clamped his mouth shut and shook his head. "No reason."

"Dad, who are you in trouble with?"

"No one."

Spencer sighed, because when his dad didn't want to talk, he didn't talk. "Where are your keys?" He might as well move the truck, because the last thing he needed was trouble coming to Sweet Water Falls Farm because of his father. An image of each Cooper family member flashed through his head. He would not let his father hurt them.

"I don't exactly know…" His father patted down his pockets and came up empty. Spencer held back his grumble and sigh and got up to look for them. They finally found the keys wedged in between the couch cushions, and he went to pull the light blue truck around to the back of the cabin.

He wasn't sure he should let his dad sleep here, not with Clarissa so close, but he didn't see another option. His father wasn't a creeper; Spencer simply didn't want him talking to Clarissa—or anyone else at the farm.

Back inside, he checked to make sure both doors were locked, and then he helped his father limp down the hall to the second bedroom. It had a twin bed in it, and the moment he laid his father in it, Ernest said, "You're a good boy, Spence. Just make sure Momma is all right before you turn in."

Spencer stared down at him as his eyes closed, that silly smile on his mouth and a horribly sweet smell coming with his breath.

"Momma's dead," Spencer whispered as his father snored loudly. "I did take care of her the best I could, Ernest, but even I couldn't hold back the tide of her diseases." He turned away from his father, a lightning storm moving through his whole body.

He locked the door and pulled it closed, then went across the hall and did the same to his door. He sucked at the air as panic rushed in, and he fell to the bed and cradled his head in his hands.

Spencer's hope to be reconciled with his dad had dried up. He acknowledged that he wasn't angry anymore, and he was so grateful for that.

"What do I do now?" he whispered. Over and over, he asked the Lord to help him know what to do about his father. He hadn't changed, and Spencer mourned the loss of him again and again...and again.

CHAPTER SIXTEEN

C larissa watched Spencer move his dad's truck and zip back up the steps. She lost sight of him under the eaves, and that only made her stomach lock down even further. "He said he'd text," she murmured to herself.

She looked down at her phone, but nothing had come in yet. To distract herself, she left the window and went into the bathroom to begin her nightly skincare routine. The same motions she'd done before many times soothed her, and the minutes slipped by.

Still no text.

Her body ached to go to bed, but her mind felt fully awake. *Are you okay over there? Need anything?*

She read and re-read the text before sending it. Spencer answered with, *I'm okay. Got him to bed, and I'm turning in too. See you tomorrow.*

Satisfied, but still worried, Clarissa plugged in her phone, lay down, and switched off the lamp. The house felt too quiet, and she got up again to plug in the fan she used to provide some white noise. She'd never been afraid on the farm, because it was out of the way and people could drive by it in a blink. The only people who came here were those who knew it was here and had a reason to venture this far out of town and down the dirt roads to the milk sheds or hay barns.

With the fan going, she fell asleep quickly, but dark shadows chased her in her dreams. She woke early and went through her morning routine. Brew the coffee. Eat breakfast. Get to the milk parlor to pull that day's orders.

Spencer would have work to do in the stables, fields, and barns, and she'd see him around noon the way she always did. Since they'd been working together in the kitchen the past few days, she didn't have any inventory to keep up with, and she ended up in the shoppe about nine with nothing to do.

A text from Spencer came in, and she read it quickly. *If you wanted to meet my dad properly, he's up now and mostly sober.*

She immediately turned and left the shoppe and got herself over to Spencer's. If she hadn't had time that morning, or if she'd been elbows-deep in cheese, she still would've gone. She knew what a huge thing it was for him to even be talking to his father.

"Twenty years," she muttered to herself. What had

that initial conversation been like? He'd been so nervous last night. Nervous and angry, and for such an even-keeled guy like Spencer, that was saying something.

She pulled up to his cabin, where nothing had changed. His white truck still sat out front where he'd parked it last night. The other one couldn't be seen.

Clarissa slowed down as she got out of her car and walked toward the front of the house. She wasn't sure why her heart beat like a big bass drum, but it was probably just one of its many flaws. She rapped on the door, the sound anxious to her, and Spencer opened the door a few seconds later.

He didn't look happy, but he didn't look scared as a jackrabbit either. "Hey," he said easily, the frown between his eyes smoothing out. "Good morning."

"Morning," she said, torn between looking at him or searching the house for his father.

Spencer stepped back, and the view opened up. His dad sat at the small, two-seat table in the kitchen, and Clarissa entered the house.

"Dad," Spencer said. "This is Clarissa. She lives next door. Riss, this is my dad, Ernest." Spencer didn't move toward his father, and Clarissa stuck to his side too.

"Good morning," she said, her voice as pleasant as she could make it.

"Mornin'," Ernest said, cocking his head. "You look familiar."

"You met her last night," Spencer said, finally taking a step toward the kitchen. "Coffee, Clarissa?"

"No, I have to get over to the shoppe. But thank you." She scampered after him, something...unsettling about the way Ernest watched her. He too had dark, deep eyes like his son's. He hadn't lost a single hair on his head, though his nearly-black locks had started to turn gray.

He tracked her every move as Spencer said, "He's staying through the weekend. He'll be gone on Monday morning." It sounded like he was telling Clarissa—and reminding his dad.

Ernest nodded, finally looked back at the breakfast in front of him. "Yep, that's right. Gone on Monday morning."

Clarissa felt like someone had released her torso from their suffocating grip, and she pulled in a full breath for the first time since entering the cabin. "That's great," she said.

Spencer didn't look like it was great. Ernest didn't either. She wondered what agreement they'd come to, and she sent up a silent prayer for Spencer.

"Will you still be at the shoppe today?" she asked.

"Yes," Spencer said. "I'm just taking a break from my morning chores." He cut a glance over to his father, who was now muttering something to himself under his breath. "He's promised to stay in the house while I'm gone. I'll lock the doors."

Clarissa wanted to tell him the doors locked from the

inside, not the outside. She wanted to ask him what he thought would happen if his father wandered the farm. He couldn't be carrying more than a hundred and eighty pounds on that wiry frame, and his hand shook as he lifted his fork with a bite of egg on it to his mouth. Besides being here after so long, with no explanation and no warning, he didn't look all that threatening to Clarissa.

But she said, "Okay," and stepped toward the back door. "I'll see you in a little bit then."

Spencer nodded, slid his hand down her arm as he blocked his father's view of her with his body, and whispered, "Thanks, Riss."

She nodded too and stepped out onto the back porch. The air out here went down easier, and she pulled in a deep lungful of it while she listened to the door lock behind her.

With a few minutes to spare, she went home and found two more restaurant jobs to apply for in San Antonio. With her résumé ready and so many places doing online applications now, she completed that task in time to get back to the shoppe before the first customer.

With the Fourth of July in the middle of next week, it seemed like everyone wanted to get their cheese, butter, and milk early, and a steady stream of people in the shoppe kept her busy until Spencer showed up.

Clarissa actually had to blink her way out of her tunnel vision to greet him, and then three women entered the shoppe together. Dividing and conquering worked great, and she and Spencer helped the three of them find what they needed.

"I forgot about the holiday," she admitted as she realized the garlic and herb spread was nearly gone. So was all of their shredded medium cheddar, the most popular of shredded cheeses.

"I can go work in the kitchen," he said.

"Let me show you how to bag cheese really quick." No one loitered in the shoppe, so Clarissa led him into the kitchen with purpose. She got out the bag sealer, the roll of bags, and huge bin of cheese from the walk-in refrigerator.

"You just put a bag on the scale. Weigh it out to a pound or two. Eight ounces or sixteen. Type it into the tablet, and print the label."

She gloved her hand and moved cheese by the handful from the tub to the bag. "For me, it's about three handfuls for eight ounces." She watched the numbers on the scale flicker as the weight adjusted. Sure enough, it settled near eight. "It doesn't have to be exact." She did add a few more shreds, and then she used the tablet to print the label.

"The bag sealer is nice," she said, holding the newly made bag of cheese by the top corners. She shook it all down to give herself room at the top. "You just side it in like this." She put both layers of the bag through the front of the sealer. "Hold this lever down to keep it in place, and press the button."

The machine whirred for a moment, and when it

released, Clarissa lifted the now sealed bag of cheese. "Label me, Spence."

He handed her the label and she put it on the bottom third of the bag. "See? Easy."

"How many of these do you want me to make?" He eyed the bin of medium cheddar like it might bite him at any moment.

"Oh, let's see." She blew out her breath. "Let's go with —oh." She cut off as her phone rang. Her eyes widened at the name on the screen, and she swiped for it quickly, a squeal coming from her mouth.

"Oh, stars above," she said, looking from the phone to Spencer. Her excitement soared, and her heart shot right into space, the silly thing. "It's Marco Holmbrook."

"Should I know who that is?" He snapped a pair of gloves on his hands too, and Clarissa reminded herself that he had a reason to be testy and on-edge.

Instead of answering him, Clarissa squealed again and swiped on the call, her voice much calmer and at least half an octave lower as she said, "This is Clarissa Cooper." She turned her back on Spencer and hurried out of the kitchen.

The front of the shoppe was still empty—a miracle, as was this phone call.

"Clarissa," a man said, his voice clearly accented. "It's Marco Holmbrook, from The Hot Italian in San Antonio."

"Oh, hello," she said, as if her phone hadn't already

told her that. She had a hard time standing, so she went behind the ice cream counter and leaned into it.

"I'm calling about your application," he said. "It says you're in Sweet Water Falls?"

"Yes, sir," she said, trying to keep the Texas accent out of her voice. The Hot Italian was a premier Italian restaurant in the river district, and Clarissa's vision blurred. This couldn't be real, could it? Maybe she just needed glasses.

"I'm not sure where that is," he said with a chuckle. "Would you be able to do an interview sometime next week? We could do it over the phone or in person, whichever is easiest for you."

"I can be there," she said, the prospect of going to San Antonio next week almost too nerve-racking for her.

"That would be ideal," he said. "I'd love for you to have something to cook for me too."

"Oh, sure," she said, her voice stilted. "No problem." Her mind blended all the thoughts together, and Clarissa couldn't recall a single recipe she'd ever made.

"What about Thursday?" he asked. "Before we open. Is nine a.m. too early for you?"

"No, sir," she said. "My family owns a dairy farm. Nine o'clock is like noon for us." She trilled out a laugh, glad when Marco joined in with her. She commanded herself to stop, and she confirmed she'd be at The Hot Italian on Thursday morning, ready to cook something for him, at nine a.m.

The call ended, and her phone fell to her lap. Every

cell shook, and she still couldn't get her thoughts to line up.

After only a few moments of stunned silence, she jumped to her feet and went crashing through the door into the kitchen. Spencer jumped a mile if he moved an inch, and he glared at her as shredded cheese went splaying across the counter.

"You're not going to believe what just happened." She danced over to him, her entire being lit from within. "That was Marco Holmbrook, and he owns the best Italian eatery in San Antonio." She giggled, the sound morphing into a full laugh a moment later.

She hung on his arm as he smiled too, the movement stretching across his whole face. Joy had never felt so full before, and Clarissa actually wondered if she'd ever felt this hopeful before.

"And guess who has an interview with him on Thursday?"

"You do," he said, his voice only sounding slightly froggy.

"Yes!" She threw herself into his arms, and Spencer caught her around the waist. They laughed together while Clarissa's mind raced through what she needed to do between now and Thursday morning to be ready for this interview.

She needed clothes. The perfect outfit for an interview.

She needed to call Cherry and ask if she could stay with her.

She needed to call Leslie and ask for some tips.

She needed a recipe to make, and she'd have to practice it at least seven times before the interview.

"I have so much to do," she said, her emotions still gushing everywhere. Should she go to San Antonio the day before?

If she did, she'd miss the fireworks and most of the Fourth of July celebrations here in Sweet Water Falls. He hadn't asked, and she hadn't brought it up either, but in her mind, she'd go to the festival and the craft fair and the fireworks with Spencer.

Her world tore right down the middle, and she saw the smile slip from his face. He turned back to the cheese and she faced the stainless steel counter too, suddenly without anything to say.

The bell rang out in the shoppe, and Clarissa walked that way, saying, "I've got the front of the shoppe. If you could do eight to ten bags of each weight, that would be great. Then we'll need more garlic and herb cheese spread." She paused with her hand on the black plastic door and looked back at him.

"Yes, ma'am," he said, that smile perfectly hung on his face again. She wasn't sure what to make of that, but the door chimed again, and Clarissa had customers to attend to.

And an interview in less than a week, she couldn't help

thinking, and that brought a genuine smile to her face despite the stormy cowboy bagging cheese behind her. They could date long-distance, as his friend Jill had suggested. They had phones and the capability to text, call, and video chat.

San Antonio isn't that far away, she told herself as she beamed out a grin at the first woman she saw. "Is there anything I can help you find?"

CHAPTER SEVENTEEN

A black cloud followed Travis Cooper as he left the milk parlor. He didn't mind helping Rissa in the morning with her milk pulls. He didn't mind interacting with customers. He didn't even mind getting up at the first signs of dawn. Heck, he'd been doing that since the age of five, when he'd first started going to work around the farm with Daddy.

Travis Cooper was *tired*.

He was tired of living with Will, the next oldest Cooper brother, who left his socks all over the house and didn't seem to have a clue how to put a bowl in the dishwasher.

He was tired of eating with his family every night. He loved his brothers, his parents, and Rissa. He did. He was glad he had the relationships with them that he did. He didn't want to be like some of the cowboys that worked at

Sweet Water Falls—alone in the world, without family or a place to belong.

Travis had that, and he was grateful for it.

"Help me be grateful for things," he muttered to himself as he stomped toward his truck.

He was simply tired of trying to find a woman that would fit into the madness of his life. He knew he worked a lot; he didn't need precious Belinda Felton to tell him that.

He knew he'd never leave Sweet Water Falls. She taught at the elementary school in town, for crying out loud. Where did she think she was going?

She wanted to travel the world. He could still see her with her arms open, twirling through the park, as she'd said that. He'd grinned, and he'd wanted to take her on all of those trips.

"You fell too fast," he told himself as he started the engine and got moving for the day. The sun had barely started to light the sky, and he'd already put an hour in at the parlor, making sure the milking for that morning had gotten off to a good start. Or a start at all, as they were operating their massive dairy operation without the usual assistance of two cowboys who'd quit last week.

Daddy pushed his men hard; Travis knew that. They'd argued about it in the past. If he would just back down one degree, they'd be able to keep people at the farm for longer. Lee didn't seem to get it either, and Travis didn't see anything changing.

If it were up to him, he'd pay more and give more time off. His cowboys would stay longer, which would reduce the workload on everyone, cost less over time, and improve performance. Why Daddy and Lee couldn't see that only made Travis that much angrier.

"No," he told himself. "Belinda said cross."

Of course he was cross. She'd been kissing him for a couple of weeks now, but when he'd asked about the festivities on the Fourth, she'd *declined* to go with him to the fairs, the festivals, or the fireworks.

Declined. It was a fancy word for *rejected.*

She'd *rejected* him, and Travis's pulse hopped around like a rabbit on hot coals. He hated this feeling, because he didn't know how to release the nerves. When he was a kid, he'd taken medication to help him focus, but he didn't like the way the world muted with the pills. He hadn't taken them for a long time, and he managed just fine.

He'd be just fine without blasted Belinda Felton too.

Travis made a right turn and kept going. He had plenty of work to do in the corrals and pastures, as he worked directly with the veterinarians that came to Cooper & Co. He himself wasn't a vet, but he'd taken a few classes to be come a vet tech, though he hadn't finished.

As the last son in the family, no one cared if he was educated or not. It was Lee who got to go to college. Lee who needed to stick to Daddy's side and learn everything. Lee who had to carry all of the burden of running the thirty-thousand-acre dairy farm, with the ten thousand cows, the acres and acres of fields, the outbuildings, the cabins, the deliveries and pick-ups, and all the personnel.

Travis was tired just thinking about it.

He made a left turn and headed up the hill to the highway. If he turned right, he'd head toward Sweet Water Falls, where he did his grocery shopping, church attendance, and the way to the beach he liked best.

Today, he went left, because he didn't want to see anyone he knew. He didn't need eggs, and he didn't need to sit on a bench and beg God to help him find someone who could put up with his insane work schedule, grumpy attitude, and the scent of milk mixed with manure that seemed to hover around him all the time.

"My word," he said, his tires running smoothly on the asphalt as he picked up speed. "You're going to die alone."

He thought about Mama and Daddy, and they'd gotten married young. Daddy had joked for decades about how he'd proposed fast so Mama wouldn't know what she was really getting into, but Travis actually thought that was a good idea.

He'd keep what he did for a living a secret until after the wedding.

He shook his head, knowing he'd never do that. He seemed to be in a perpetual bad mood, but he wasn't devious. He drove, because a drive through the Texas countryside did more to soothe his soul than anything. His mind started to quiet, but that only let the desperation and disappointment in, where the anger held those negative emotions at bay.

A sigh flowed from his mouth, and he rounded a corner a bit too fast, so he eased up on the accelerator. It would do no one any good if he drove his truck off the road. Then he'd have to call Will to come get him, and everyone would be behind on the day's work. If possible, Will had a worse attitude about his schedule than Travis did, and Travis was tired of dealing with his brother too.

He realized how slow he was going at the same time he saw a red SUV off the side of the road ahead. The driver's door opened, and Travis applied the brakes to slow even further. A woman stepped out of the vehicle, and she turned toward him, seemingly unconcerned about his approach.

In fact, she lifted both arms above her head and waved them. She wore a pair of shiny black leggings that hugged her legs from ankle to waist, as well as a form-fitting jacket in bright yellow. That color only made her dark-as-night hair stand out to Travis, and he determined he was going to stop.

He eased onto the shoulder too, keeping his gaze on the woman now striding toward him. She wore a pair of hiking boots on her feet, no makeup, and a look of absolute relief on her face. He couldn't look away from her, but something flashed in his peripheral vision.

He managed to look through the windshield at the same time his seat rumbled and bright red lights flashed on the glass. The warning that he was about to collide with something got him to jam his foot on the brake and come to a complete stop.

His breath caught in his chest, trapped there by his hammering heart. "Get it together," he told himself. He'd always been distracted by a pretty face and long, dark hair. "Not this time." He was not interested in this woman, despite her height and the swell of her hips and chest in those tight clothes.

She appeared at his window, startling him again. The emergency flashers she had going on her SUV still pulsed in his vision as he looked at her. He unbuckled his seatbelt with one hand and rolled down his window with the press of a button. "You okay, ma'am?"

"Thank you for stopping," she said. "I've been out here all night, and you're the first person I've seen." Tears gathered in those eyes, and Travis's heart melted. Oh, he was a sucker for a damsel in distress, that was for dang sure.

He opened the door, and she backed up. "My phone is dead, and I could've walked back to town, but I didn't want to leave my dog. She's sick."

A sick animal too? Travis's heartstrings were getting pulled left and right, right and left. That alone made him stop and survey the situation. A pretty woman out in the middle of nowhere. A car with the emergency flashers on. Had those been on when he'd rounded the corner?

He wasn't sure, and he didn't take a single step toward her SUV, though his front bumper nearly kissed her back one. She walked to the back door and opened it, and Travis half-expected a flock of crows to come flying out. Or a grim reaper to emerge. Something.

Scanning the woman again, he told himself he easily weighed twice as much as her. He could overpower her. *Unless she knocks you out*, he thought as she reached inside the vehicle.

Travis opened his door again and stood behind it, giving himself a shield of some sort just in case a rabid pit bull was this woman's choice for incapacitating a man who'd stopped to help her.

Instead of a dog bearing sharp teeth, a kennel emerged in the woman's hand. She faced Travis, concern in her eyes. She frowned when she saw him behind the door, and he had the distinct thought that he watched too many true crime documentaries. Hey, he had to have something to occupy him in the evenings, because Will annoyed him with talk about politics, and the women he went out with never lasted longer than a couple of months.

"Her name is Sweetie. Do you know anything about dogs?"

"Yes," he said. "What's your name?"

"I'm Shayla Nelson," she said easily, taking a tentative step toward her. "You?"

"Travis Cooper." He hooked his thumb over his shoulder without looking away from her. "Got a farm about five miles back." And he'd just blown it by telling her that. Wasn't he going to keep his occupation a secret until after the wedding? He couldn't even focus for longer than ten minutes.

"Why are you hiding behind the door?" she asked.

"I thought you might be a highway kidnapper," he admitted, smiling at her. "But you probably just need a ride to town."

She blinked those long eyelashes at him, and Travis moved out from behind the door. "What's wrong with Sweetie?"

"I don't know. She might just be hungry. My stupid car died about six last night." She glared at the red vehicle, and she'd probably have liked him to rear-end it. Shayla looked back at him. "Could you give us a ride to town? My assistant is probably going nuts about now."

"Okay," he said, moving to take the kennel from her. "Do you have everything you need from the car?"

"No, just a second." She passed him the kennel, and he peered inside it to find a little poodle-like dog laying inside, the most miserable look on her face.

"All right, Sweetie," he said, smiling at the dog. "Let's put you in the back seat." He did, and then he moved to open the passenger door for Shayla, who hadn't wasted any time getting her purse and a box of something. "What's in the box?"

"Our samples for next week's show," she said. "Elaine is going to be livid."

He took the box from her and put it in the back seat beside the kennel. "Is she the assistant?"

"Yes." Shayla got in the truck and Travis closed the door behind her.

"You will not ask her out," he told himself as he went around the back of the truck. "You need a break from women. Plus, that dog is only ten pounds. Not for you."

He got behind the wheel of the truck, his self-speech firmly in his head. "All right," he drawled. "Let's get you back to Sweet Water Falls." He pulled out and made a U-turn before looking at her. "What show are you doing?"

"Oh, we just set up a booth at the Founders Festival," she said. "I own Sweetspot. Have you heard of it?"

Travis dang near choked on his own tongue. "Sweetspot?" he repeated. "The outdoor outfitter?" They made everything a person could need for hiking, camping, backpacking, river trips, all of it. Her hiking boots and leggings made so much more sense now.

"Yes," she said, clearly pleased. "Are you an outdoors-man, Travis?"

"No," he practically barked at her. "Unless milking cows four times a day counts as spending time outside." It didn't, and he knew it. She did too.

Shayla blinked again and looked out the windshield, probably regretting getting in this truck with Travis. He was regretting it too, because he knew exactly what Sweetspot was.

"I thought Kylie Peregrine owned Sweetspot," he said, clearing his throat and hearing his voice come out two degrees too low.

Beside him, Shayla stiffened. She shook her head, a fire dancing in those eyes now. "We co-founded it," she said. "She's not with the company anymore."

"I know that," he said. "You drove her out of her own brand."

"That is *not* true," she said with plenty of displeasure in her voice too. "You have no idea what you're talking about."

"Well, I was dating her at the time, so I have some idea."

"Whatever," Shayla said, folding her arms across her chest and focusing out the window. "I don't have to explain myself to you." She really emphasized the *you*, as if he was so far beneath her, she couldn't even scream down an explanation to where he was.

Travis searched his memories from five years ago, when he'd been dating Kylie. He'd probably met Shayla at some point, but he didn't remember. Kylie had been a gorgeous brunette too—exactly his type. She'd left the state of Texas after losing her company to Shayla and her ruthless pursuit of taking Sweetspot from her friend and co-founder.

The drive continued in silence, and Travis didn't mind a bit. At least he wouldn't be making a bigger fool out of himself by asking this particular woman to dinner, and he couldn't wait to drop her and her silly little dog somewhere.

CHAPTER EIGHTEEN

Spencer leaned closer to the monitor, trying to read the tiny print. He ended up making it bigger so it wasn't such a strain, and the truth sat there in black and white.

Police are looking for a man they only know as Ernest after he fled a casino in Atlantic City last week. If you have any information about the whereabouts of him (picture below), please call...

Spencer's heart raced through his whole body. The picture wasn't great, as it had obviously been taken from a security feed somewhere. But just as Spencer had known his father the moment he'd seen the man lying on the couch in his house, he knew the man in the grainy, almost-green picture was Ernest Rust.

He continued to read about the alleged theft and card-counting at the casino, and his father hadn't paid for his three nights at the hotel either. He wondered if the truck his father had driven away in that morning was stolen too.

Spencer had written down the license plate, because he didn't trust his dad at all. He hated that he didn't, and he hated that this weekend with his father had been the hardest thing he'd done in fifteen years—and he'd lost baby cows in cowbirth, endured a torn rotator cuff, and been dumped by countless women who always chose something or someone else over him.

His father was just one more example of that, actually. He didn't really want to see Spencer again. He'd needed a place to crash after getting drunk and in trouble, and he knew where Spencer was. That alone was enough to make Spencer want to relocate, because he had a feeling that his father was bad news. He had been while Spencer was growing up, and he hadn't changed at all.

His heart hurt, because he'd wanted Ernest to be different. He'd dreamt of tracking down his father and finding him living in a quaint little house somewhere, going to an honest job every day, and staying sober at night. Perhaps he'd have found someone new to spend his remaining days with, and she'd have kids who had kids, and Ernest would get to live out his life as a doting grandfather.

That image couldn't be further from the reality of who Ernest Rust was, and Spencer found it a difficult, bitter, huge pill to swallow.

He scrolled back to the top of the article, the number

to call staring him in the face. Should he turn in his dad? *Could* he even do it?

He reached for his phone, but he didn't dial the authorities in New Jersey. Instead, he called Slate, who answered on the second ring with, "Spence, I was just about to call you," and a laugh.

"Oh?" Spencer asked. "Why's that?" Maybe he didn't need to tell Slate about his father.

"Porky Pig will *not* cooperate during lessons," he said. "Jess said you always knew what to do to get him to behave." Something scraped on his end of the line, and then a loud bang nearly deafened Spencer.

He flinched away from his phone, but he still heard Slate say, "Sorry, I'm just getting to the stables."

"Porky is stubborn," Spencer said. "But he can be bought with two things—freedom and apples."

Slate chuckled, and Spencer smiled. "So he's a typical horse."

"He hates being in the stable," Spencer said. "He likes to strut past the other horses before they're let out, so take him first. Make it a big show. He likes the north pasture best, because it goes all the way to the river."

"Ginger said not to put him in that one, because we'll never get him back."

"Cue the apples," Spencer said. "He can smell them a mile away. You saunter over to the fence with two of 'em. You call his name, and you take a big bite of one of the apples. He'll come."

Spencer smiled just thinking about Porky Pig, the black and white horse whose markings almost looked pale pink, like pigskin. "You eat the whole apple right there at the fence. He'll make it to you about the time you're halfway through. You make him watch you eat the rest of it."

"Oh, that's mean."

"So is him standin' out at the north fence, refusing to come in." Spencer grinned and leaned away from the computer, this call exactly what he needed. "Then, you give him the core of the apple you've just eaten. And then the second apple, whole."

"And he can do this every day?"

"He does lessons, what? Three days a week? He's fine to get three apples a week. At least he never had any health problems or colic when I was doing that."

"All right," Slate said. "Honestly, I think he just misses you. We all do."

"I'm sure that's not it," Spencer said, clearing his throat. He didn't want to think about what his departure had done to the horses he'd once cared for. He knew horses had personalities, and they did recognize and get attached to people.

"I called, because I wanted to follow-up about my dad."

"Is he gone?" Slate asked.

"Yes, praise the Lord," Spencer said, sighing. He'd been texting Slate all weekend for advice. "I found out why he's on the run." He gave Slate the quick version of the article—which itself was a quick version of what had likely happened in Atlantic City.

"What would you do?" he asked. "Call the police in New Jersey? Do nothing? Pray you never see him again?" Spencer felt torn in a half-dozen directions, but those were the biggest ones.

Slate exhaled, and Spencer could just picture him running his hand up the back of his neck and through his hair. "Wow, Spence, this is tough."

Spencer didn't like that Slate didn't just tell him what to do. "Yeah," he said. It was a tough situation, and he didn't want to reason through it on his own.

"You have to go with your gut," Slate said. "What's it saying?"

"It's saying that if I don't call the police, Ernest could end up here again, and I don't want that." He got to his feet and paced away from the kitchen table where he'd eaten a few meals with his dad. They'd talked about very little, as Spencer had found he had nothing to say to his father. And his dad had never really had any use for Spencer.

That had stung and reopened several stitches in Spencer's life that he'd thought he'd closed permanently. He just wanted someone to want him so badly, and without his momma, that desire had fallen on his dad.

But his dad *didn't* want him, at least not for more than a few nights of shelter so he could hide from the authorities. Spencer had given him a couple hundred dollars too, and he wondered if he could get in trouble for that.

"Maybe you should call then," Slate said.

"Yeah." Spencer sighed. Not calling made breathing difficult, and his next thoughts turned to Clarissa, her brothers, and her parents. Everyone else working on the ranch could be in danger or trouble because of Ernest. Spencer wouldn't be the reason for that. "I think I'll call."

"I'm sorry," Slate said. "I was hoping this would have a happy ending, but it might not."

"It's okay," Spencer said, the smile flashing across his face almost painful. "We each have our own path to trod."

"Stay strong, brother," Slate said. "Let me know what happens."

Spencer promised he would, and the call ended. The clock told him he needed to get over to the shoppe, as he'd agreed to meet Clarissa a half an hour early so she could demo her recipe for him. Her interview at The Hot Italian was on Thursday, only a few days from now, and she still hadn't decided for sure what she'd be cooking.

Before he left, he leaned closer to the computer and tapped in the number for the hotline in New Jersey. A woman answered only a moment later with, "Atlantic City Police Department, how many I direct your call?"

"My name is Spencer Rust," he said, and then he inhaled deeply. "My father is Ernest Rust, the man your cops are looking for. He stayed at my cabin in Texas over the weekend, and I know what vehicle he's driving."

Silence came through the line, and then the woman said, "Hold, please. I'm transferring you to Deputy Chief O'Connell."

———

"YOU'RE THE MACARONI TO MY CHEESE," SPENCER said, grinning at Clarissa as she put a bowl of the creamy, steamy macaroni and cheese in front of him. She didn't even crack a smile, and Spencer shook his head. "Come on. That was funny."

"Just try it," she said. "I can't watch." She turned away from him, her nerves as palpable as the joy had been when Marco Holmbrook had first called over the weekend.

Spencer picked up his fork and dug right through the breadcrumbs and parmesan cheese topping to the savory noodles beneath. "Smells good," he said. "Looks good. I think you're checking all the boxes."

"Mac and cheese is so trite," she said, pacing over to the counter where a binder lay.

"It's Italian," he said. "It's going to be perfect."

"It's Kraft," she said, turning to face him again. "It's Southern. I don't know if it's Italian in the truest sense of the food culture."

"It's pasta," he said. "Which you made from scratch and then refrigerated until your demo. That's going to win him over for sure."

Her green eyes widened and watched him take the

first bite. The creamy milk and tangy cheddar, combined with a flavorful noodle, made him roll his eyes back in his head and moan. "Oh, yeah," he said. "This is amazing." He took another bite, almost wishing there weren't any breadcrumbs or topping. He wasn't going to say that though.

He hadn't told her he didn't want her to go to San Antonio. He wouldn't crush her plans and dreams by saying or doing anything stupid this time. His role here was of support, and he was determined to be her biggest cheerleader as she set off for San Antonio and the restaurant career she so wanted.

They hadn't talked about what might happen to them once she left Sweet Water Falls, but Spencer was viewing it as a bridge he'd cross when he had to. Right now, they were just circling it, trying to find another way across the gulf to each other.

"I think this is really *grate*," he said, grinning at her. She finally gave him a smile in return, and he was going to need to look up more cheesy puns to make it through this week. "Seriously," he said. "It doesn't get any *cheddar* than this."

Clarissa burst out laughing then, and Spencer joined her. *Finally*, he thought. She joined him with a bowl of mac and cheese, and they enjoyed lunch together without any interruption from the bell out front.

Spencer washed their bowls while she put the mac

and cheese into the same containers they used for spread-able cheese. "Mama will love this," she said.

He turned and put his arms around her, glad when she leaned back into his embrace. "I'm going to miss you while you're gone this weekend," he murmured, his lips right at her ear. The scent of cheddar, orange, and vanilla filled his nose, and he closed his eyes as the moment lengthened and softened.

"It's only a few days," she said.

"For now."

She turned in his arms, and their eyes met. "What are we doing?" he asked. "Are we kidding ourselves?"

"I don't know," she whispered. "There's long-distance. We have computers and phones. We both have cars. It's two hours." She sounded desperate, but also like she'd thought about maintaining their relationship after she moved to San Antonio.

"I'm not going to say anything stupid," he said, smiling at her and enjoying the presence of her in his arms. "I think you're going to rock the interview, and I think you're going to have a job in one of the best restaurants in the city soon enough."

She smiled at him, and she was angelic and wonderful. He'd definitely started to fall in love with her, and he hadn't even tried to apply the brakes to slow down or stop himself. He was ready for a good woman in his life, and Clarissa was a fantastic woman. She was kind, she worked hard, she was innovative. She paid attention to details, she was gorgeous, and she put up with his sense of humor. He wanted to be the man to make her laugh, hold her when she cried, and bring her cookies when she felt like no one saw her.

He saw her.

"Thank you for believing in me," she said, pulling him down for a kiss. "It means a lot to me." She pressed her lips to his, and Spencer took it from there, kissing her in a way that he hoped would convey all of the things he hadn't been able to put into words yet.

Things like, *I'm falling in love with you.*

Please choose me.

Come home after this interview.

And *I think you're amazing, and you can nail this interview* too. He didn't want to see her fail, even if he did want her to choose him over a new, fancy job in the city. He had no idea if she'd do that or not, but right now, it didn't matter. Right now, he could just keep kissing her.

CHAPTER NINETEEN

"You're here," Cherry said when she'd opened the door. She grabbed onto Clarissa and laughed, bouncing up and down while she tried to hug her. "You look so good. Look at your hair. You've let your bangs grow out." She held Clarissa at arm's length, and she should've known her older sister would fuss over her.

"The traffic here is terrible," she complained, reaching for her suitcase. She tugged it inside Cherry's house from the front porch, noting that the place smelled like fresh fruit and crisp linens. That was Cherry's favorite air freshener, and she'd obviously been cleaning today.

"It's a holiday," Cherry said. "There's a lot going on in the city in the summer." She closed the door behind Clarissa, shutting the heat outdoors where it belonged.

"Yeah." Clarissa had felt the vibe of the city, and she'd loved it. She craved a pulsating, vibrant atmosphere, and

San Antonio clicked that box for her. Cherry's house ticked all of Clarissa's boxes except for one—the organization of it.

Cherry had her own system, that was for sure. She did normally keep a pretty tidy house, not that Clarissa cared, but today, one of her cats had knocked over his food bowl, and kibble lay everywhere in the kitchen.

She turned back to her sister and smiled, drawing in a deep breath. "It's okay that I invited Leslie to come with us, right?"

"Of course," Cherry said easily. She worked as a counselor at a college here, which meant she'd had today off. In fact, she had the rest of the week off, as July wasn't a huge counseling season.

She stepped past Clarissa and collected her purse. "I'm ready whenever you guys are."

Clarissa sat on the couch, a sigh leaking from her mouth.

"Uh oh," Cherry said, perching on the edge of the recliner. "I know that sound. What's going on?" She trained her deep, dark green eyes on Clarissa. Her hair was long, and straight, without the bubbly crimps Clarissa's got in the heat and humidity. She had a real job, so she could afford cute clothes, and tonight, she wore a black and white striped skirt with a bright blue tank top. It made her auburn hair shine like red gold, and Clarissa smiled at her older sister's beauty.

"I may or may not have started a relationship in Sweet Water Falls."

Cherry's eyes widened, as she'd always been so good at providing the drama Clarissa wanted when she told a story. "Who is it?" She hadn't lived in Sweet Water Falls for a while, but she still knew a lot of people there.

"Spencer Rust," Clarissa said, studying her nails.

Cherry gasped louder than necessary, which somehow annoyed Clarissa. She looked up and rolled her eyes.

"It's not that bad."

"He broke your heart once already," Cherry said. "It's *that* bad."

"Yes, well, I'll have you know that we're going to actually do the long-distance thing this time," Clarissa said. "We've already talked about it and everything."

"I...okay," Cherry said, plenty of disbelief in her tone. She didn't need to say anything else, because the real question hung in the air between them. *And then what?*

What would happen after that? They'd chat via call or text or video, and then...?

They'd drive back and forth to see each other in downtimes, and then...?

Would he move to San Antonio so she could continue her chef career? Would she go back to Sweet Water Falls for him?

So many questions swam through her mind, but Clarissa had been really good at damming them up. The doorbell rang, and she looked away from her sister's still-shocked face. She probably needed to see a plastic surgeon to get that taken care of.

"That's probably Leslie." Excitement built beneath Clarissa's breastbone as she got to her feet and went to answer her sister's front door. Sure enough, Leslie Hanson stood there, and she flung her arms wide.

"Clarissa Cooper," she said, immediately launching into a laugh.

Clarissa hugged her, also laughing while trying to say her first and last name. Oh, it was so good to be with someone who thought more about what to make from milk than where it came from, and Clarissa held her best friend from culinary school tightly for several long seconds.

"All right, girl," Leslie said, tucking her brown hair behind her ear. "We've only got one night to go over your plan for tomorrow morning." She stepped into the house, where Cherry had gotten to her feet.

"My sister," Clarissa said, moving to stand next to her sister. She linked her arm through Cherry's. "Cherry. Cherry, my best friend from school, Leslie. She works at Overlook."

"And you're not on tonight?" Cherry asked, her eyebrows riding high on her forehead.

"Thankfully, no," she said. "I worked the last holiday, so I got this one off by some stroke of luck." She smiled at the pair of them. "Good thing too, because we're open an hour later and have sold all these fireworks packages for our wall of windows." She sighed as she sat on the couch where Clarissa had been.

She immediately jumped to her feet, as if she'd recharged in the half-second she'd touched the couch. "Are you going to do the demo here?"

"I can," Clarissa said, shooting a glance at Cherry. "I think my sister wants to go to dinner though."

"We can do both," Cherry said. "Do you want to demo first or dinner first?"

"Let's dinner first," Leslie said, her face full of life and energy, as usual. Clarissa had known her for months, and she never took naps, never ran out of go-go-go. She was the perfect personality for chefing, as a cook had to be on their toes all the time.

"I know this great place for ribs that will blow your mind," Leslie said, grinning for all she was worth. "Y'all in?"

"Yes, ma'am," Clarissa said, noting that Cherry's response was slightly less enthusiastic.

———

Clarissa peered out of her sister's windshield at the restaurant, the clicking of the blinker irritating her. "This is it."

"Yes," Cherry said. "I can't stay here long, Riss."

"Okay." She got out of the car and collected her plastic bin from the back seat. "I'll call you when I'm done."

"I'm going to go put the car in a garage and go to the mall. Text me, and I'll tell you where I parked. Then you can come meet me."

"Okay." Clarissa didn't think wandering the outdoor mall sounded fun at all, but she didn't want to cause problems for Cherry. Her sister had let her stay at her house last night, and she'd been nothing but kind and respectful when Clarissa said she didn't want to talk about her boyfriend. She'd clapped at the end of Clarissa's demo last night, and she'd let Leslie stay until almost midnight, even though it was clear Cherry had been bushed by ten p.m.

They'd watched the fireworks over the San Antonio sky from Cherry's balcony, where she'd served sweet tea and lemonade, as well as chocolate chip cookies. She'd used Mama's recipe, and Clarissa could still taste the cinnamon in the back of her throat.

Or maybe that was the pure fear she felt at walking into this restaurant before it opened and cooking for the head chef and owner.

Or maybe she needed a new throat.

"Don't be ridiculous," she whispered to herself. "They don't give people throat transplants."

She hefted her bin onto her hip and started toward the double-wide glass doors with the words THE HOT ITALIAN above them. She'd brought along the nicest thing she had to wear, which had been a black pencil skirt and a peach-colored blouse with tiny, brightly-colored hummingbirds on it.

Cherry had deemed the two pieces together "inappro-priate," and she and Leslie had spent forty-five minutes last night going over Cherry's wardrobe and the limited things Clarissa had brought for her weekend stay in the city.

They'd decided on a pair of black slacks, a sensible if a little tipsy pair of white heels, and a the blouse. Cherry had deemed her professional and "cute," while Leslie said no chefs would ever wear a skirt that narrowed at the knees in the kitchen.

"What if you have to lunge for a burning pot?" she'd asked, her blue eyes wide.

Clarissa had never lunged for anything in the kitchen at the shoppe, burning or otherwise. She felt miles out of her league, and when she went to open the door, it didn't budge.

Of course it wouldn't. The restaurant didn't open for another two hours. She gripped her bin with one hand and peered through the tinted glass with the other. Cupping her hand helped her see deeper into the restaurant, but it looked abandoned and vacant.

She looked left and then right, as the foot traffic on this downtown street wasn't much...yet. More and more people would come out as the day wore on, and she didn't want to be standing here like a doofus. Or worse, a criminal.

She'd just stepped back to call Marco when the door opened. It hit her bin, which she promptly dropped.

"Oh, sorry," a man said, the accent familiar. Marco hurried to pick up her bin and straighten, and their eyes met. "You must be Clarissa."

"Yes," she said. "And you're Marco."

"Guilty." He shook her hand and stepped back so she could enter the restaurant. "What are you making today?"

"Mac and cheese," she said ahead of him. She wished she could turn and see his face, but her ankles already felt a little iffy in these heels. He directed her back into the kitchen and set her bin on a wide stainless steel counter.

This one was just like the one in the kitchen at the shoppe, and a boost of confidence filled Clarissa. She looked around and found a stove, a flat top, big prep bowls, and a walk-in refrigerator. She had all of those things too.

She exhaled and turned toward Marco. "So I just dive in, or...?"

"Dive in," he said with a smile.

She took the lid off her bin and started pulling ingredients from it. "I made the pasta last night so it would be a quick demo." She set the plastic container of it on the counter. "So first, I'll get the water set to boil."

She pulled a pot from beneath the counter and started filling it with water. She glanced at Marco, who simply stared back at her.

"How would you make the pasta?" he asked.

"Oh, it's easy," she said. "Semolina flour is my favorite, a little course sea salt, a couple of eggs, and some olive oil. Really good olive oil." She grinned at him and set the pot on the stove. She lit the flame on the burner and stepped back over to the counter.

"Now, my family owns a dairy farm down in the Coastal Bend of Texas, and we know cheese, milk, and butter. All of these are products from that farm. You can't get fresher." She laid out the sharp cheddar, the parmesan —"for some added saltiness"—and the Monterey jack she liked to use in a good, comforting mac and cheese.

"I'm going to melt some butter." She dropped a couple of tablespoons into the pan on the stove, noting the sizzle. The fire was too high, and she quickly turned it down. "Then we'll whisk together some cream cheese, cream, milk, and regular all-purpose flour." She did that, slopping it over the side of the bowl as she tried to mix the harder cream cheese into the softer ingredients.

Embarrassment squirreled through her, but she just wiped up the mess with her towel and kept going. She wasn't sure if she was supposed to talk through every step, and she needed to focus, so she fell silent as she chopped an onion, a couple of cloves of garlic, and measured out a dash of tabasco. She put it all in the butter and got the onion working.

"That'll sweat for a few minutes," she said, realizing she'd put the garlic in too soon. *It's fine*, she told herself, though she'd made this recipe at least ten times in the past five days, and she'd never made that mistake before.

"I'm going to strain that so we don't have large chunks of onion," she said, glancing at Marco, who was busy typing on his phone. *Dear Lord*, she prayed. *Is he making notes about me?*

She forged on, whisking the onions through the hot butter. They had color on them, and horror struck her right in the back of the throat. She turned the flame down even more, saying, "Wow, this cooks hot," with a little laugh.

She hadn't dropped her pasta yet, nor had she measured her cheese. She tried to quell the panic rising through her, but her hands shook as she turned to reach for the pasta so she could get it going. With the rate that burner was cooking the onions, the sauce would be done in mere moments.

"This goes in here." She opened the plastic container and turned it over to put the homemade pasta into the water. "I made the pasta last night, like I said. Then I formed it into these cute little shells with a press." It had taken forever too, and she hoped Marco would know and understand how labor-intensive pasta-making was.

Of course he would; he was an Italian chef who owned an Italian restaurant.

"Then in here goes the milk mixture." Clarissa very nearly tripped over her heels on the way back to the stove with the huge bowl of cream and flour, and it hissed and sent a huge puff of white smoke up into the air when she poured it in.

She tossed the bowl to the back of the stovetop, the

steel clattering against the metal grates in a way that set her teeth vibrating. But she needed to be stirring, and now.

Her heart beat out of control in her chest, and tears pressed behind her eyes. Nothing was going right, and there was no way she was going to get this job. Marco had said nothing for so long, and Clarissa didn't dare look at him as she whisked and whisked, the pan still way too hot for cream and milk.

"Then the cheese," she said anyway, because she'd come this far. She hurried to grab the cheeses she'd brought, forgetting completely that she usually strained the mixture before adding the cheeses to get the onions out.

In the dairy went, and when she remembered, she froze.

Everything in the kitchen froze, and she sniffled as life roared back to full speed. She turned off the burner, sure it was scorching the bottom of her sauce. Her pasta was floating, and she quickly removed it with a slotted spoon, putting it straight into the cheese sauce.

"Then we mix it all up," she said as cheerfully as she could. She finally got the pan off the burner and took it to the counter. She located some serving bowls along the far wall and started toward them.

"This is fine," Marco said, and she spun back to him. Her heel caught on the rubber mat in front of the sink, and her knee buckled. Down she went, and Clarissa couldn't stifle the cry of pain or humiliation—or both—as it flew from her mouth.

"Are you okay?" Marco had abandoned his phone at some point during the disastrous demo, and he arrived in front of her quickly.

"I'm fine," she said, using his hand to get to her feet. "Really." She released him, the hot heat of horror and embarrassment enough to make her want to flee. "You don't want me to plate it?"

"No, I like to taste straight from the pot." He smiled at her, but Clarissa knew she wasn't getting this job.

The onions weren't cooked down enough. They weren't even diced properly. She was using them only for flavor. She'd cooked the garlic too long, and the cream had probably been burnt.

She almost knocked the fork right out of Marco's hand once he'd speared a few shells. He put them in his mouth, his eyes closing a moment later. She wasn't sure if that was in bliss, because everything tasted so wonderfully amazing, or so he wouldn't show her how disgusting this pot of macaroni and cheese was.

"Thank you," he said, not going for a second bite. That wasn't encouraging, and Clarissa couldn't wait to get out of there. "It's a little simple, don't you think?" he asked, nailing the final dagger into her heart.

"It's my grandmother's recipe," she said. "She usually adds some spicy brown mustard." She took the condiment bottle out of her bin. "But I forgot." She started putting everything back into the bin, not caring where it landed. That was such a difference from this morning, when she'd packed and then repacked the ingredients into the bin.

"Thank you," she said, fitting the lid on and lifting the bin. She wanted to pick up the pot of mac and cheese and throw it in the trashcan—which was what Marco would do anyway—but she didn't.

She kept her head high as she marched out of The Hot Italian, and she texted Cherry to find out where the car was. Her sister had given her a key that morning, and Clarissa managed to find the vehicle and put her bin in the back seat. Then she got behind the wheel and started the car so the air conditioning would start to blow.

Then she broke down and sobbed.

CHAPTER TWENTY

Spencer lay on Clarissa's couch and stroked her hair as she finished the story of her "disastrous demo" in San Antonio.

"I'm so sorry, baby," he whispered. Her tears had wetted the front of his shirt, and his heart bled for this good woman. She had a dream, and she'd gone after it. She'd come up short, and that hurt, no matter who it was. He'd had things like that happen to him too, and he understood.

Outside, a summer thunderstorm rolled through the sky, where thunder could break and grumble and groan through the clouds for over a minute. The rain hadn't actually started yet, but all the cowboys had been out early on this Monday morning to get every cow, horse, pig, and chicken fed and sheltered before the storm hit.

Clarissa had arrived home last night, but she hadn't answered her phone or her door when Spencer had texted and dropped by. Now he knew why. Her humiliation felt like a bottomless pit to him, and he wanted to tell her she'd never see Marco Holmbrook again anyway.

He wasn't going to tell her that though. He was just going to hold her and let her know he supported her. He closed his eyes as her breathing evened, and he didn't mind the gray light coming through the windows so much if he could hold this woman in his arms.

"I'm going to go anyway," Clarissa said several minutes later. She sat up, and he shifted with her. He stay laying down, his spine pressed into the back of the couch while she perched on the edge of it.

"What do you mean?"

"I mean, if I stay here, I'm never going to go to San Antonio," she said, pushing her hands through her hair. She combed it with her fingers, trying to get it to lie flat. "I'm just going to pack and go. I'm not going to wait until I have a job." She got to her feet, the energy in her house completely different now. "I can stay with Cherry while I figure out an apartment. I can be there, applying in person for jobs at cafés, coffee shops, those little kiosks in the mall."

Spencer sat up too, sure Clarissa had no idea what she was saying. "I'm pretty sure they don't cook at those kiosks," he said. "That's called frying churro dough and sprinkling on cinnamon sugar."

"Someone has to make the dough," she snapped back at him.

He didn't think so; they came frozen in boxes. But he said nothing as he got to his feet. "I'm going to head home and get my laundry done."

Clarissa acted like she hadn't heard him, and she probably hadn't. He reached for his cowboy hat, which he'd hung on the hook by her back door, and turned to kiss her good-bye. "Who's cookin' tonight at the farmhouse?" he asked.

He only went if Wayne or Clarissa invited him, though Chrissy had a few times too. Spencer had dodged those, because they felt like attempts to set him up with Clarissa. He supposed they were dating now, and the setting up had already happened.

"Daddy cooks on Mondays," Clarissa said, her heart not in the kiss at all. Spencer had kissed her enough to know the difference.

"Okay, I'll see you later." He stepped out onto the porch and looked west to the rest of the farm and then east toward his house. He took a deep breath, not sure which way to go right now. Should he and could he follow Clarissa to San Antonio? Should he and could he call the New Jersey police and find out if they'd found his father?

The Deputy Chief had assured him that the tip could remain anonymous to the perpetrator, though Spencer had given his name. Only the cops would know; they wouldn't tell anyone else, and it wouldn't be reported in the news.

Spencer had been checking every day, and so far, he'd seen nothing. No mention of him, but there was no mention that the cops had caught up to Ernest either. He honestly wasn't sure he wanted them to, though he had called in the tip and given the make, model, and license plate number of the light blue truck to the detective.

His conscience pricked at him constantly, and he told himself he had to be an upright, law-abiding citizen. He'd seen too many men make silly or innocent mistake and end up in prison. Heck, some of his best friends at Hope Eternal had stories just like that.

The thunder broke the sky again, and that got him to move. He hurried down Clarissa's back steps, jogged across the lawn as a wind picked up, and had just arrived on his back porch when the sky opened and the rains fell.

The sound of the water drops against the rooftop was deafening—and also one of his favorite noises. He closed his eyes and took a deep breath of the earth getting cleansed and renewed by the rain.

He went inside his house, the whole afternoon in front of him. There would be a lot of work to do tomorrow to clean up around the farm, but for right now, he just wanted chocolate, an old western on TV, and a pillow so he could take a nap.

JUST AS PREDICTED, THE FOLLOWING MORNING, Spencer found himself working through his second pair of soaked and muddy gloves as he helped Gary and Lee reset a fence.

"A little higher on that side," Lee said, plenty of pressure in his voice. "Got it, Gary?"

Spencer and Gary lifted the heavy metal gate a little higher, though Spencer's muscles felt like they could snap at any moment. His patience felt the same way, actually. Clarissa had ignored his texts for another evening, and he really thought they'd matured past such a thing.

Lee grunted, and Spencer groaned, and together, the three of them got the gate seated on the pins. The weight released as the posts bore it, and Spencer stepped back, his chest heaving.

Lee dropped the bolt in place and started tightening it while they all breathed a sigh of relief. "That's it for the dairy herd," he said. "How are things lookin' on the agri-side?"

"Not great," Gary admitted. "We lost a door on the stable to the wind overnight. A couple of chickens are missing, but they usually turn up. I've got Chris and Mack out casing all the fences in the pastures before we let any animals out. And our equipment shed guys are checking any vehicles left out in fields during the storm."

"So we don't know everything yet," Lee said.

"No, sir," Gary said.

Spencer was glad he wasn't in charge like Gary or Lee. He could be bossed around to lift gates, chase down cows, or repaint a stable. He didn't want to be responsible for thousands of dollars of equipment, and he stayed silent while the other two men talked. Gary would give him another assignment, and then Spencer would race home, shower, and get over to the shoppe just after noon.

Wayne had closed everything yesterday when he'd realized how severe the storm would be, and he'd ordered everyone to go home and to stay there. Clarissa hadn't made her usual Monday cheeses or ice creams, and he wasn't sure he would today either.

He was supposed to be running the shoppe solo today, as a trial run. Clarissa had definitely decided to leave Sweet Water Falls despite not having a job or a place to live in San Antonio.

He found her utterly maddening, but he'd kept his thoughts to himself. She felt frantic and out of control to him, and no one made their best decisions in that state of mind. At the same time, a person in that frame of mind also didn't hear reason very well, and he didn't want to say or do anything that would end his relationship with Clarissa prematurely. Not again.

Not when he'd started to fall for her all over again.

Wayne's big, black truck came down the single-lane road that went between the dairy cow pastures. Spencer watched it approach as Lee said, "My daddy must need one of us for something."

"Good work, boys," Wayne said as he got out of the truck. "Lee, we need to get over to the bullpen. We've got that buyer comin'."

"Yep."

They left, and Spencer watched them go. Then he turned toward Gary and said, "I'm too old to lift gates like that," with a grin.

"You and me both." Gary smiled and bent to pick up the gloves he'd discarded. The remnants of clouds hung on the horizon as he and Gary loaded into a farm truck and started down the road. Mud puddles dotted parts of the path ahead of them, but Gary steered the two of them around them easily.

They checked in with Chris, but all of the jobs were far too big for Spencer to work on before he needed to get to the shoppe, so he took his shower early and arrived at the shoppe thirty minutes earlier than planned.

Clarissa worked in the kitchen, peeling labels from the label-maker and putting them on plastic containers as fast as the machine would spit them out.

He stood and watched her, a smile forming in his soul and on his face.

She glanced at him and offered a small smile too. "What's on your mind?"

He ducked his head, his cowboy hat still on though he stood in the kitchen. "You still know when something's bothering me."

"Apparently," she said.

"I think that says something."

"What does it say?"

Spencer lifted his head and slowed his step. "This is going to sound crazy, but..." He wasn't sure he could say it. At the same time, he didn't want her to drive away next Monday without him having said everything on his mind and in his heart.

She looked at him, her eyebrows up.

"I don't want you to go to San Antonio," he blurted out.

Clarissa wouldn't look at him now, and surely every beat of his heart would crack his now frozen and brittle ribs.

"I—" she started, but then she cut off.

Honestly, what did he expect her to say?

His chest and attitude felt as stormy as the sky had been last night. He felt like the thunder that took so long to grumble and growl through the clouds. Then, the next clap would come, and the world would blaze with bright fire as lightning struck.

"Maybe we need to take a chance," he said next, his voice almost like sandpaper. "A leap of faith." Desperate hope filled him from top to bottom now. "Maybe this is our second chance to find what we both want."

He moved toward her, desperate to make her feel what he felt. Clarissa faced him, but she didn't have the hopeful expression like he did. Rather, one of resignation. "It's been a few weeks," she said.

The lightning struck, and all of Spencer's emotions hardened right where they were. "Okay, got it." He spun to leave the kitchen. He had to get out of here. He couldn't be in the same room with her, not when she'd rejected him.

Part of his heart told him to go back and make sure they were okay. He could do the long-distance thing. He could.

"Spencer," she called after him.

"Go," he said over his shoulder. "It's fine. Go home and pack. I've got the shop today." He left the shoppe through the blue door and headed across the parking lot, the humidity today enough to drown a man who simply dared to breathe.

"What should I do?" he asked the fenceposts, the blue sky, and the Lord above.

None of them answered him.

Foolishness and Spencer Rust were great friends. They spent so much time together that he knew instantly when he'd done or said something he shouldn't.

"Shouldn't have said anything about her leaving town," he muttered to himself as he stared at the ceiling the following Monday morning. The sun hadn't quite lightened the day, and his alarm hadn't gone off. "Just like you shouldn't have kissed her. Shouldn't have taken her to dinner. Shouldn't have started talking to her and flirting with her and thinking you might have a future with Clarissa Cooper."

His alarm rang, and he reached over to silence it. With a sigh, he swung his legs over the edge of the bed, wishing he had a dog to keep him company in this new, strange house. It wasn't quite a cabin, but it wasn't the cottage Clarissa had called it either. The truth was, Spencer didn't know what much of anything was right now.

They'd had a few great weeks together. That didn't mean they'd fallen in love, though Spencer tended to know early on in a relationship if it was going to work or not. He'd had a good feeling about Clarissa, and he'd spent a lot of time while she'd been in San Antonio for six days thinking about their last attempt at a relationship.

He'd been far younger and completely incapable of having a real, committed relationship with a woman. He was ready now. He thought she was too. He wanted them to at least *try*, and if he hadn't said anything, maybe they could've at least had a long-distance relationship where they flirted over chats and texts and he got to see her on weekends when she came back to the farm.

Foolishness accompanied him through his shower, through getting dressed, drinking coffee, and making the ten-second walk from his back door to her front one.

Chefs worked weekends, after all. Once she left, she wasn't coming back.

Clarissa bent over the trunk of her car, with at least

half a dozen boxes on the ground next to her. "There's no way you're getting all of that in your car," he said, and foolishness flooded him again.

Clarissa gasped and spun toward him, her eyes wide. "Oh. Spencer."

"Sorry," he said, still walking toward her. He saw the full back seat and the depth of the trunk, and he'd definitely spoken true.

"Daddy's going to bring some stuff," she said. "I'm just deciding what I have to have right now and what I can leave."

Spencer looked toward the house, but he didn't see her father or any of her brothers. His heart pounded, but he had to take the risk. He'd never gotten anywhere by sitting quietly on the sidelines.

"Some of this is going back inside," she said, toeing the nearest box. "Maybe you could use some of those pretty muscles to haul it away?" She grinned at him in such a flirty way that fed Spencer's bravery.

Instead of bending to pick up a box, he closed the distance between him and Clarissa, took her face in his hands, and kissed her. He poured absolutely everything into each stroke, almost desperate for her to feel what he'd felt these past few days.

"Don't go," he whispered, his lips catching against hers he lingered so close. He pulled away fully and met her eye. "Give us a chance. Let's just take a chance."

Clarissa at least had the decency to wear an apologetic

look, and Spencer backed up fast. She didn't even have to say a word for him to know what was on her mind, and he dropped his chin to his chest so he could use his cowboy hat to hide his humiliation.

Without another word, he bent, picked up one of her boxes, and went inside her house.

Thirty minutes later, she clung to her father while he watched from the corner of his cabin. He didn't need to say good-bye—that kiss had said everything.

And it still wasn't good enough. *He* still wasn't good enough to get a woman to choose him over something else. He'd never lost to a job, though, and he'd now reached a new low in his life.

A dairy farm didn't care about his personal life, though, and he still had chickens to feed and stalls to shovel out. He needed to make all the spreadable cheeses that morning too, and as he went about his tasks, he could hear Clarissa's sweet voice accompanying him every step of the way.

Women had affected him like this at Hope Eternal Ranch too, and he really just wanted to get in his truck and drive until he crossed the Texas state line.

Instead, he finished his chores and stepped into the shoppe, which screamed Clarissa to him, right down to the hand-lettered menu board behind the ice cream counter.

"You tried," he said to the empty shop. He was proud of himself for that, and he wasn't going to hang his head because this second summer fling hadn't turned out to be as much as he'd hoped it would be. He just wished his heart wouldn't hurt quite so much and that the negative voices in his head weren't quite so loud.

CHAPTER TWENTY-ONE

Clarissa once again rolled her suitcase toward Cherry's front door. Her heart thumped heavily in her chest for some reason. "She's your sister. She has two extra bedrooms. You can stay here for a while."

She could, yes. She just didn't want to. She was thirty-five years old, and she felt like she'd gone backward a couple of decades. She didn't have anywhere to live, and this past week had been such a whirlwind of packing, trying to continue running the shoppe, and dealing with Daddy and Lee, that she hadn't even been able to put out more applications or look for an apartment.

"You're here now," she said, putting her foot on the first step that led to the porch. "You'll have time." Right now, in fact, as Cherry was at work on this Monday, and the house should be empty except for her cats.

Clarissa reached the top of the steps, sweating as she heaved her bag up every bump. She found the front door open, and she went right inside as if she owned this house. Her chest felt so tight, and she knew it was because of what she'd left behind in Sweet Water Falls. Not what. Who.

Spencer.

She sighed as she closed the door behind her, and she towed her suitcase down the hall to the bedroom she'd stayed in a couple of weeks ago. No evidence of felines existed, besides the food and water bowls in the kitchen, but Cherry had three cats.

Clarissa called their names as she went into the office, where Cherry had a couple of cat towers. She saw a pair of eyes inside one of the compartments, but she didn't approach the cat. She knew better than that.

"Okay," she said. "I'm here, and you can come sit by me if you'd like." She lifted her laptop slightly. "I'm going to be looking for a job." If there was anything more demoralizing than that, she didn't want to know about it.

She settled on the couch and went to her job boards, searching for the new listings. In the past, she'd searched for chef positions, at restaurants. But now, she expanded the search to include anything in any kitchen. She'd work at a fast casual place to get experience. A diner. A café. She couldn't expect to go from spreadable cheese to filet mignon overnight—and that was exactly what she'd been trying to do.

An image of that disgusting macaroni and cheese infil-trated her mind, and she pushed it away. "Not dwelling on negative today," she muttered. The two-hour drive from Sweet Water Falls had been the time for that, and she was ready for a break.

She applied for job after job for hours, all the way until Cherry walked in wearing a pair of cute black and white heels, the pencil skirt Clarissa had wanted to wear to her interview, and a stunning dark purple blouse that made the outfit. Her sister was so good with clothes and fashion.

"Hey," she said with a big smile. She put her oversized purse on the table beside the front door. "How was the drive?" She glanced around. "No feline friends?"

"I think they think I'm a cat killer," Clarissa said, closing her laptop and standing. "I'll get dinner started."

"Oh, we had lunch in the department today," Cherry said. "I'm still stuffed." She reached down and took off one heel and then the next. "Let me change, and then you can tell me how it went this morning."

Clarissa simply nodded, though she didn't particularly want to talk about the good-byes from that morning. Daddy had been stoic, and Clarissa had realized that he hadn't actually thought she'd leave. She'd told him she was, but when her moving date had got pushed back, and she didn't have a job...

She swallowed against the sting in her throat. He hadn't truly believed she'd leave the farm.

"But you did," she whispered to herself, and that gave her a sense of pride and accomplishment she hadn't felt in such a long time. In the back of her mind, a voice whispered, *Yes, but at what cost?*

———

Four days later, with a few applications out for single-bedroom apartments and an interview at a fast-casual restaurant that needed a cook, Clarissa rolled out of bed.

A cook. The listing had specifically said *cook*, not *chef*.

She tried not to get all tangled in the semantics, but deep down, they mattered to her. She still didn't know if she'd made a mistake by leaving Sweet Water Falls Farm or not. She knew Spencer had awakened something inside her that had been missing all these years. Maybe something he'd put inside her heart nine summers ago and had brought back to life.

As she stuffed her hair dryer back into her suitcase, she frowned. "Why couldn't he have shown up a year ago?" Why did everything seem to happen at once, when she least expected it?

With everything finally out of the bathroom and back in the guest bedroom so as to not further clutter Cherry's house, she headed out the door. This was her first interview, despite the many applications she'd put out. She had yet to hear on an apartment, and Cherry said the rental market in San Antonio was crazy right now.

Dozens of applicants for every place, within hours, she'd said.

Helplessness crowded Clarissa's throat, and she couldn't help feeling like she'd done something wrong. But she could only tackle one problem at a time.

"Interview first," she muttered to herself as she got into her car. "Apartment second." She couldn't afford much, and that was why she had so much competition with others looking to rent.

And Spencer? The voice in her head had been plaguing her for four days now, and all it seemed to be able to say was *Spencer, Spencer, Spencer. When are you going to deal with Spencer?*

She didn't know how to deal with him. So she'd felt the earth move every time he kissed her. It didn't mean she should change her plans to see if they could make a real relationship work this time around.

Take a chance, he'd said. Wasn't that what she was doing right here in San Antonio?

Frustration filled her as she buckled her seatbelt and adjusted the air so it was blowing in her face. She needed a wake-up call, and the chilly blast of air conditioning did the trick. She *was* taking a chance here, but on her career. Not on getting the two things she'd literally been dreaming about for decades.

A job at a restaurant—or SaltFish, the fast casual fish

taco joint where she was interviewing this morning—wouldn't make her a wife or a mother.

As she drove across the city for her interview, another battle began in her brain. "Focus," she told herself as she got out of her car and tugged on the bottom of her crisp, white blouse. She put that fake smile on her face and squared her shoulders. This was a "restaurant" that served fish tacos in under five minutes. The job was as good as hers.

A WEEK LATER, CLARISSA WAS STILL LIVING OUT OF A half-packed bag, in her sister's cute little house on the outer ring of downtown San Antonio. She hadn't heard back from SaltFish yet, and at this point, she knew she wouldn't. The fact that she couldn't get a job where someone literally assembled tacos from ingredients in bins brought her to tears every time she thought about it.

Cherry had been trying to cheer her up for days, but Clarissa suspected it was only to get her to shower and keep making dinner. If it killed her—and it might—Clarissa vowed to do both today.

She hadn't spoken to Spencer in almost two weeks, and that made her throat dry up. She hadn't been able to get an apartment, though she'd looked at four now. They hadn't been great, and they were expensive. The one she'd tried to get, she'd been too slow on.

In short, nothing was going her way, and she almost pulled on her well-loved sweats and camped on the couch before she remembered her vow. While she was in the shower, Cherry called into the bathroom that she was leaving.

"Okay," Clarissa said, but it didn't really matter if it wasn't okay. Cherry had a job—a good one. She even had a boyfriend, and she was leagues ahead of Clarissa.

She'd put out at least fifteen more applications at various eateries all over the city, and it seemed no one was hiring women with dark green eyes and strawberry blonde hair. She didn't want to call her father and admit defeat, but he'd asked again if he should bring her boxes and leave them at Cherry's. He asked every day about the apartment hunt and how the job search was going, and her desperation had reached a new high.

In moments like these, which had been coming more and more often lately, she thought about simply packing up and going home. If she did that, Clarissa would have to admit to things she didn't want to acknowledge, and she gritted her teeth to prevent herself from letting that train of thought continue.

After getting dressed, she wandered into the kitchen and poured herself a cup of cooling coffee. "Is this your way of saying I should just go home?" she asked, folding her legs underneath her body as she curled into the recliner in Cherry's living room and looking up toward heaven. The space held the slight scent of toast, as her sister loved the stuff and ate it every morning. Her bravest cat, Feathers, jumped up onto the armrest of the couch, and Clarissa stroked her absently.

She sighed and looked at the TV she'd turned on, some cooking show flickering on the screen. "We're back with Gray Bell, and he's here to show us how to make his momma's Southern pimento cheese."

Clarissa found herself getting to her feet, her eyes stuck to the TV now. A tall man wearing a cowboy hat filled the screen, and everyone in Texas knew Gray Bell, the country music star.

And he was making a flavored, spreadable cheese like it was the greatest thing that had ever happened to him. A family recipe, no less.

"So your mom would make this every week?" the hostess asked. She was a flawless woman, without a hair out of place and wearing so much makeup on that her skin looked plastic.

"That's right," Gray said. "Every Sabbath Day. My momma believed in two things: goin' to church on Sunday and serving crackers with pimento cheese afterward." His grin could've filled the Mississippi River, and the hostess laughed.

"All right," she said, adding plenty of drawl to her voice now. "Tell us what goes in this." She peered into the bowl, but Clarissa knew the ingredients to pimento cheese.

Cream cheese, she checked off as Gray put it in the bowl. *Sharp cheddar. Pimentos*—obviously, he said.

He added a few spices too—far too much salt in Clarissa's professional opinion—and the country music star started to beat together all that dairy to make the "most delicious thing you'll ever eat."

"Sometimes," he said. "My momma would heat it up, and hoo boy. That was a real treat." He seemed so happy, and Clarissa wanted to reach through the screen and grab onto that joy. Harness it and saddle it and ride it.

What makes you happy?

The thought entered her mind, and Clarissa didn't have to think very long to identify a few key things: the shoppe, creating new recipes, and...Spencer Rust.

"I've made a huge mistake," she said as the heavens opened above her, flooding her mind and heart with light. "I have to get back to Sweet Water Falls."

She had to return to Sweet Water Falls *right now*.

CHAPTER TWENTY-TWO

Spencer ran his fingertip along the scar on his left hand, reminding himself that he didn't want his father in his life. Not the version who'd caused that scar, and not the man who'd shown up uninvited in his house a few weeks ago. They were the same person, and while he'd hoped the man had changed, he hadn't.

He groaned as he stood, and he took a moment to stretch his arms above his head. His back was so tight from lifting all the crates of milk yesterday morning. Lee had just hired two more men to work in the milk parlor, so he wouldn't be packing milk for pick-ups for much longer. Two or three more days, at the most.

Today was one of them, so Spencer showered, caffeinated himself, and got over to the milk parlor. The scent of dirt and warm dairy mixed together, and he didn't particularly like it. It lessened inside the refrigeration unit, and while Texas was plenty hot in the middle of July, he didn't much like spending time in the fridge either.

It was quiet, however, and he did like that. He filled the crates and stacked them by the door until their buyers arrived. When they did, he helped them carry out their orders. This progressed normally for this Friday morning, and Spencer didn't see Lee, Will, or Travis in the office, though he sometimes did.

With only one more order to go, Spencer got the job done and stepped out of the fridge just as someone else darted down the hall and outside from the office. He froze, because it hadn't been one of the Coopers. They all had big, broad shoulders, and that man had been...skinny.

With no cowboy hat.

Spencer's pulse rioted in his chest, in the veins in the his throat, and up into his head. *Go!* his mind screamed at him, and he got his feet moving quickly down the hall and past the office.

"Hello?" he called, jogging as he burst out of the building.

A light blue truck peeled out, the back end fishtailing —but not so badly that Spencer couldn't see the South Carolina license plates on it.

"No," came out of his mouth. His father had returned —and he'd been coming out of the office. Not just coming out—running out.

He'd likely taken something, and while Spencer didn't know the extent of what Wayne and Lee Cooper kept in the office here in the milk parlor, he suspected there might be some money.

Fumbling now, he quickly pulled out his phone and dialed Wayne.

"Morning, son," he said easily. "Pick-ups go okay?"

"I think someone just robbed you," Spencer blurted out. "There's a light blue truck leaving, and he doesn't belong here." He couldn't believe what he was saying. Why had he called Wayne? He should've called the police.

"A light blue truck?" Wayne asked. "I'll send Lee over."

"He's leaving," Spencer said, watching his dad make the right turn onto the road that would take him back to the main highway. "He's headed up past the cowboy cabins."

"Will's over there," Wayne said. "I'll call 'im."

"I'll call the cops." Spencer took a deep breath. "Sir, it's my dad."

Wayne said nothing for a few seconds—which actually felt like years—and then he said, "I'll call you back," and ended the call.

Spencer let his hand drop to his side, pure adrenaline rushing through him. He couldn't think. He couldn't move.

He absolutely couldn't let Ernest hurt the Coopers. They seemed to have plenty of money, but that didn't mean his dad was entitled to it.

The extra buzz inside him prompted him to move, and he ran toward his rickety white truck. He got behind the wheel and got it moving in the same direction his father had gone. He dialed nine-one-one as he rounded the corner, and he nearly lost the phone in the turn.

"State your emergency," a woman said.

"Hi, yeah, this is Spencer Rust. I'm out at Sweet Water Falls Farm, and there's been a robbery. Ernest Rust is here. He's wanted by the police in New Jersey."

The sky started to fall, but Spencer pressed against it, holding it up piece by piece. He couldn't look at everything fast enough. Which way had his father gone? Surely to the right again to get off the farm. He wouldn't know all the back exits.

"Slow down, sir."

"He's going to get away again," Spencer said, making the turn and gunning the engine. The truck lurched forward, and Spencer dropped the phone. He cursed under his breath, but the world was moving too fast for him to retrieve the device.

He left it on the floor over on the passenger side of the truck and gripped the wheel with two hands. The cowboy cabins came into view—and so did a mess of vehicles.

Trucks in all colors and sizes blocked the road—all of them converging around a light blue one. As Spencer applied the brake so he wouldn't go crashing into the trucks, the driver's door on the blue truck opened, and his father came tumbling out.

He sprinted away from the truck, and Spencer jammed his into park. He leapt from his truck too, already running after his dad.

Other men yelled, but Spencer didn't devote any brain cells to figuring out what they'd said. He focused on the thin figure darting between two cabins. He carried something with him, and Spencer had to get it back.

Will and Lee were in pursuit too, and along with Spencer, the three of them each took a different route around the cabins. "There's nowhere to go back here," Lee shouted, and as Spencer cleared the cabin, he saw how right Lee was.

A grassy area took up the space between the cabins and an eight-foot fence. Spencer would've had a hard time scaling it, and that meant his father had no chance.

Ernest spun back toward the three men, each of them advancing slower now, on a different trajectory. He looked wild and unkept, like perhaps he'd been sleeping in the light blue truck for a few days. Or longer.

"Dad," Spencer said, holding up both hands as he took a step. His chest vibrated with the need to take a breath. He had sprinted quite a ways, after all. "There's nowhere to go, Dad. Just calm down."

He felt Lee and Will looking at him, probably because of the *dad* reveals.

Now that Spencer was closer, and things had slowed down, he could see that Ernest held a money bag in his hand. He reached into his pocket and withdrew a knife with a flourish.

"Stay back," he commanded, his voice surprisingly rough for how frail he seemed physically. Spencer had been impressed by the running too. His eyes swept the three men, all of whom had frozen. They locked onto Spencer's. "I don't want to hurt you."

"Just come on back to the cabin," Spencer said, his voice loud and clear. A shocking level of clarity filled his mind. His father was very, very ill. He needed help, and not just for a day or two. Not just a meal or two. But real, professional help.

"I'll make you a sandwich, Dad. It's okay." Spencer took another step, waving for Lee and Will to stay back. At least Wayne wasn't here. Or Clarissa.

Humiliation crept into Spencer's throat, but he swallowed against it. This was not his fault. He was *not* his father.

You brought him here, ran through his mind, but he silenced it.

"Give me the knife," Spencer said, having a flashback to the last time he'd faced his father while he held a weapon. The scar on his left hand seemed to pulse with heat. "And we'll go have breakfast."

His father looked gaunt, hungry, desperate. He backed up another step, his gaze wild as he looked from Spencer to the Cooper men.

"Look at me, Dad," Spencer commanded, still

advancing slowly. His father complied, and Spencer smiled at him. "I can make those over-easy eggs just how you like them. I even have English muffins, and you love those."

Help, he prayed. *Help him. Help the Coopers. Please make sure no one gets hurt.*

Another step, and his father let the knife droop a little. Spencer still had several yards between him and Ernest, and he didn't dare rush him. The man could turn mean with the flip of a switch, and being backed into a corner brought out a rage in him which Spencer had only witnessed one other time.

A sense of calm overcame him. He wasn't going to get cut this time. No one was.

He lowered his hands and increased his pace. "Do you want coffee or hot chocolate?" He reached his dad in a few strides, and he could've reached out and touched him. Taken the bag. Knocked the knife from his fingers.

He simply looked at him. "Dad," he whispered.

In one swift breath, the malice in Ernest's eyes turned on. Spencer threw his hands up, knocking the knife to the side with one of them as his dad swiped it toward him. He turned his face away instinctively, and his other hand caught his father in the chest.

He went flying backward, and Spencer continued his forward motion, something roaring through him he hadn't even known he possessed. Shouts sounded around him. A siren wailed. Pain emanated in his left forearm.

None of it mattered.

Ernest hit the fence, and Spencer had one arm across his chest, pinning him in place in the very next moment. They both breathed hard, and Spencer stared into the watery gray eyes of the one person who was supposed to be good in this world. The one person who should've been there for him, no matter what. The one person who should've taught him how to be a man, how to grieve after the loss of a loved one, and how to treat women right.

"Spencer," his dad begged, and Spencer realized he had one fist cocked back, as if he'd hit his father.

He dropped his hand, but he didn't give Ernest an inch. Lee and Will arrived, and a whole bunch more footsteps sounded behind them.

Spencer couldn't move, though he heard someone say the knife had been cleared and someone else said they had the money bag. It wasn't until Wayne Cooper touched Spencer's shoulder and said, "It's okay, son. You can let him go," that Spencer was able to remove his arm from his dad's chest and let him straighten from the fence.

He fell back a step and then two, feeling like the ground beneath his feet would vanish at any moment. He actually prayed that it would, so he could be taken from this situation. He didn't want to be here. He didn't want to explain anything to the family who'd taken him in, fed him at their dinner table, and given him so much.

He walked away as the cops arrived and began arresting Ernest. Someone called his name, but he couldn't

turn back to see who. He made it to his truck, plenty of
eyes on him, and even though the road was blocked, he
just went over the grass and around.

He drove right off the ranch, needing to get away and
get away now.

An hour later, he knocked on Ginger's door. At
mid-morning, he wasn't sure where she was. He hadn't
cried. He hadn't raged at God. He'd simply driven around
town, then through it. Down the beach a little bit, and
then to Hope Eternal, where he could sometimes hear the
ocean roaring if he went right to the southern edge of the
ranch.

He wanted to go to the beach right now. He could lay
in the water and drown out all the earthly noise
around him.

The door opened, and Connor stood there. "Uncle
Spence!" He launched himself into Spencer's arms, who
gripped the child tightly as every emotion he'd kept caged
for the past couple of hours emerged.

"Hey, bud," he whispered into the boy's cornsilk hair,
his eyes pressed closed. This was how fathers felt about
their sons. Connor wasn't even his son, and Spencer loved
him so much. He couldn't imagine hurting the boy in any
way, and everything jumbled inside him.

"Is your momma here?"

"Right here," Ginger said, and Spencer's eyes flew open. Connor stepped back, and Spencer grabbed onto Ginger, his chest heaving as his eyes burned with tears. "Hey, hey," she said gently, holding him as tightly as he was her. "What happened? Are you okay?"

He couldn't answer her, and she said, "Connor, go get your dad. Tell him we need him and all the boys here as quickly as possible. Hurry up now."

Spencer didn't want to cause a problem. He didn't want eyes on him at all. And yet, when he thought of Nate and Ted, Luke and Dallas, and Slate, he decided it would be okay. They'd understand, as they'd all dealt with difficult family situations over the past couple of years. They'd handled stressful times, where their pasts had come back to haunt them.

"Spencer," Ginger said. "You're scaring me."

He stepped back and swiped at his eyes. "It's my dad, Ginger. He came back, and he stole money from the Coopers." He hung his head and stepped into the house. Ursula, Ginger's trusty, loyal German shepherd whined and nosed his hand. He crouched down in front of her and scrubbed his fingers along her ears. "I think I might be bleeding. He had a knife."

"I'll get the first aid kit," Ginger said, closing the door and walking into the kitchen. Spencer couldn't look away from the dog, and Ursula rested her head against his shoulder, somehow telling him everything would be okay.

"Come on over here," she said from the kitchen. He

straightened and did what she said. He couldn't look her in the eye, but Ginger added, "It's going to be fine, Spence. We'll get you cleaned up, and Nate will be here, and it's all going to be just fine."

He nodded, because he wanted to believe her. He lifted his left arm, where the dull pain had started to throb. "I think he got me on the back of my forearm there."

She sucked in a breath, and that caused Spencer to look at her. With eyes as round as dinner plates, she said, "Yes, he sure did." She met his gaze. "This might need stitches, Spencer."

"Wouldn't be the first time," Spencer said.

The front door opened, and Nate said, "Ginger?" in a panicked voice. He ran toward them, taking in the situation. "Slate's right behind me. The others are coming in."

Ginger looked at Spencer, and Nate met Spencer's eyes, his sliding down to the wound on his arm.

Without another word, Nate stepped closer and grabbed onto Spencer and held him right against his chest. "It's okay," he whispered. "It's all okay."

Spencer's composure broke again, because he really wanted Nate to be right, and he was really tired of holding everything together.

Slate arrived next, then Ted and Dallas. Luke entered the house last, with Connor in tow, and while Ginger doctored up the wound as best as she could, Spencer told them what had happened.

Finally done and completely exhausted, he accepted

the cup of coffee Ginger offered him. The five men he'd met and learned to know and love over the past few years simply looked at him. They'd each taken a barstool, and at the curved counter, he could see all of them.

"I'm going to have to go talk to the cops," Spencer said, bending his arm back to look at the gauze pad Ginger had put over his cut.

"Yes," Slate said. "But you did the right thing."

"No one got hurt," Ted said. "I mean, besides you. The Coopers are all okay."

Spencer nodded, because that was one great miracle. He loved Wayne and Chrissy Cooper, their loud, grumpy sons—and their youngest daughter. Misery drove through him again, because he hadn't heard from Clarissa in weeks. They weren't long-distance dating at all, and that hurt almost as much as the slice his father had put in his flesh.

"He can get the help he needs now," Luke said quietly.

"Maybe this will be his second chance," Dallas said. "People only know what they know, right? He'll learn something new, and he might come out different."

Spencer nodded, because the living proof of that sat at the counter with him. Times five.

Nate slung his arm around Spencer, and they looked at one another. "Don't give up on him yet," he said. "You don't have to have him in your life, but Dallas is right.

Maybe he'll go to prison for a little bit, and maybe when he comes out, he'll be someone new and different."

"People change," Spencer whispered.

"Yes, they do," Nate and Ted said together.

Ginger turned from the oven, a sheet tray of chocolate lava cakes in her hand. "People do change," she said. "But chocolate stays the same." She grinned at Spencer, who smiled right on back.

Even though he'd left Hope Eternal Ranch, he'd come here for the comfort he needed. They'd welcomed him back with open arms—and chocolate cake.

He wondered if Clarissa would do the same, and he knew she would. He took a lava cake and said, "Okay, now I need help with my girlfriend too... She sort of left town and went silent, and I need to figure out how to get her back."

CHAPTER TWENTY-THREE

W hen she passed the sign announcing her return to Sweet Water Falls, Clarissa's emotions surged again. She'd made it. She'd returned home.

There was still so far to go, and she gripped the steering wheel, her resolve firm. She was going to apologize. She'd get down on her knees and beg if she had to. Spencer simply had to take her back, and he was absolutely more important that any career she could ever have.

She'd just been so laser-focused on that dream, because she had wanted it for a long time. She'd reached a pivotal moment in her life, and when he'd come back into it, she'd never course-corrected.

A sigh passed through her body as she turned onto the dirt road and the farm, only to have every muscle seize up again a few seconds later when she saw the police vehicles.

"What is going on?" she murmured, trying to peer through all the windows in her car to take in the whole situation. Many, many vehicles had congregated on the road leading toward the milkshed, the milk parlor, and her house.

She pulled off the road when she saw her brothers grouped together in a triangular huddle, and as she stood from the car, they all turned toward her simultaneously. "What happened?"

Travis reached her first, and he enveloped her into a hug. "Spencer's dad was here. He took the money bag from the office and tried to run."

"They've taken him to the station," Lee added, arriving and making a group hug.

"No one got hurt," Will said.

"That's not true," Travis said. "Spencer got hurt."

"But he left," Will said. "I just meant none of us got hurt. Daddy's fine. Mama's okay. Even Ernest didn't get hurt."

"Where's Spencer?" Clarissa asked, but her brothers didn't even hear her.

"It sure looked like he might," Lee said. "Spencer had him pinned to that fence. Hard."

"But he didn't swing at him." Will frowned at Lee.

Clarissa squirmed away from Travis, trying to make sense of their argument. "Where's Spencer now?" she asked again.

"I think he might have," Lee said. "I said three sentences to him, and he didn't even hear me."

"I was there," Will bickered back. "I did the same. What I'm saying is, he didn't hit his dad. Ernest didn't get cut. The knife was kicked clear."

"Whoa, knife?" Clarissa asked. "What is going on?"

Travis shook his head. "Good thing Daddy was there. He always seems to know just what to say to get through the fog."

"Where is Spencer?" She glanced around, thinking she might find him with the other cowboys, who stood in small groups beside cabins and trucks. No one seemed in any hurry to clear the blockade keeping her from her house, or to get back to work.

She found Daddy talking to a small bunch of cowboys —two or three—and Gary nodding like his neck had turned to rubber. They broke up a few moments later, and Daddy turned toward her. He came straight at her, but with his limp, he wasn't fast.

She met him halfway, and he clutched her tightly in his arms. "What are you doin' here?" he asked. "I didn't think you were coming home this weekend."

"I'm coming home permanently," Clarissa said, her emotions riding the roller coaster up again. Her throat narrowed to the size of a straw, making it hard to swallow or breathe. "Are you okay?"

They parted, and Daddy met her eyes. "We're all fine, baby."

Lee, Will, and Travis joined them, all four of them talking now. Daddy said, "Gary's gonna get the boys back to work. I've talked to everyone, and so have the cops. They're finishing up with the fence back there, and then they'll go."

"And that's it?" Will asked.

"We got the money back, so." Daddy blew out his breath.

"Where's Spencer?" Clarissa asked, very much like a broken record.

"I want to have everyone for dinner tonight," Daddy said. "Trav, will you call over to Truck Ranch and see if they can put together our usual catering order on short notice? Tell them I'll pay extra for it."

She thought of Spencer, bleeding somewhere. Maybe he'd had to go to the hospital, and her heart took a dive toward her toes.

"Sure, Daddy," Travis said.

"Okay, then we—"

"Everyone stop talking!" Clarissa yelled. All four men looked at her, Lee blinking quite rapidly. She drew in a frustrated breath. "Someone better tell me where Spencer is right now." Her chest heaved, and her fingers curled into fists. "Right. Now."

The four of them exchanged a group glance, and then Travis put his arm around her shoulders. "Rissy, we don't know where he is."

"What do you mean, you don't know where he is?" She looked up at her brother, one of her best friends. He wouldn't lie to her, would he?

"He left, almost immediately after the fight. The cops want to talk to him too, but we don't know where he is. He's not answering his phone."

Desperation rose through her, and she quickly pulled out her phone. Though she hadn't talked to him in almost two weeks, she dialed his number without hesitation. "Maybe he'll answer me," she said, her voice the only thing shaking, and only a little bit.

His line rang and rang, with his voice finally saying, "Clarissa?"

"Spencer," she said, relief rushing through her with the power of a herd of stampeding bulls. "Where are you?"

He did hesitate before asking, "Why? Where are you?"

"I'm at the farm," she said, though she didn't want to get into why. She met Daddy's eyes and turned her back on the men in front of her. "My brothers told me what happened. Sort of."

He sighed, and she could hear the unrest in his very soul. "The cops want to talk to me, I'm sure."

"They did say that, yes."

"I'm at Hope Eternal Ranch," he said. "Ginger is going to feed me lunch, and I'll call the cops right now."

She nodded, her own hope spiraling up and down and

around. After giving herself a few more feet of space to have a more private conversation, she said, "Would Ginger be able to handle another mouth for lunch?"

"I don't see why not," he said, his voice guarded.

"Can I come?" she asked outright. "I want to talk to you."

He sighed, and maybe she should just tell him right now how she felt about him. "It's fine with me," he said.

She looked over her shoulder, where all the men in her family still watched her, silently. It might have been the first time they'd done that, and she gave them a small smile.

"Are you okay, Spencer?" she asked, her voice tender to her own ears.

"Ginger fixed me up for now," he said, and if Clarissa hadn't seen the friendship between him and Ginger, she might have been jealous. "I might have to go get stitches. We'll see after lunch."

Clarissa had no idea what time it was. She'd driven from San Antonio on a seat of pinpricks and anxiety. "I'm on my way."

"You remember where the house is?"

"Yes, sir," she said. "See you soon." She ended the call and faced her family. "He's going to call the police station. He's at Hope Eternal. I'm going to go eat lunch with him." She hugged her father again, so many more things to say that stayed in the back of her throat.

"Bring him home," Daddy said, as if he'd heard all the

things of Clarissa's heart and understood them. "Dinner tonight. Six o'clock at the pavilion. Everyone—especially him—is invited. Bring the cowboys from Hope Eternal too." He stepped back and smiled at her, and Clarissa tucked his confidence into her pocket and headed for Hope Eternal Ranch.

Twenty minutes later, her sedan bumped over the dirt road that went across the river. The big double-house came into view, with all that sparkling green grass around it. Spencer's beat-up, white truck sat in the drive-way, and Clarissa's pulse went wild.

She drew in a deep breath and pressed her palms together. She only needed to do one thing at a time, and the first item was to get out of the car. After managing that, she looked toward the porch only to find Spencer already standing there.

She froze as their eyes met across the distance. With her pulse booming in her ears, she practically yelled, "I made a mistake. I want to take the leap of faith."

He came down the steps, his cowboy boots making plenty of noise on the wood. "You don't have to yell, sweet-heart. I'm right here." He smiled at her, and that only caused tears to prick her eyes.

He was so sweet, and so good. "I'm sorry," she said, still unable to move toward him. "Maybe it's too late.

Maybe you've already found someone else to take to dinner and send cheese puns to. I don't know." She swallowed, her throat so dry. "I just know that there's no shame in making spreadable cheeses and ice cream."

"No, there is not," he said, still coming toward her, that perfect cowboy hat perched on his head.

"I also know that I'm not supposed to be in San Antonio," she said. "And while I'm kind of mad at the Lord for re-introducing you into my life at a most inconvenient time, maybe it's those times when you least expect to find your soul mate that you find them." She caught sight of the large bandage on his forearm, and she wanted that whole story right now. She wanted to check and make sure he was okay. Really okay, and not just physically.

"Soul mate?" Spencer asked, his voice half the volume of hers as he reached her and slid his hands up her arms.

"Potentially," she whispered. "That's what I want, Spencer. Not just a husband. A soul mate. Maybe it's you, and I don't want to throw away this chance without knowing."

"Then let's find out," he said, leaning down and pausing only a breath away from her. "Just so I'm clear, you're choosing to come back to the farm, right? Permanently?"

She grinned and wrapped her hands around the back of his neck. "That's right, cowboy. See, I saw Gray Bell making pimento cheese on TV, and it was his momma's recipe. And I thought, oh my word, I'm not above making spreadable cheeses. What if one of my sons is a famous country music star, and he's on TV one day, making one of my recipes?"

Spencer's eyes softened as he heard what she was really saying. "Can't have a famous country music star son without a hot cowboy husband."

Clarissa wondered how he always knew exactly what to say to heal her heart. She laughed with him and then pressed her forehead to his. "I'm sorry, Spence. Can we try again?"

"I'm not sure if I just lost my job or got myself a girl-friend," he said, and he closed the gap between them. He kissed her like he'd gladly be unemployed as long as he got to see her and kiss her every day.

He pulled away too soon, and she pressed her cheek against his. "You're choosing *me*, right, Clarissa?"

"Yes, Spencer. I'm choosing you."

He smiled, the movement in his mouth subtle against her face. "I'm choosing you too," he whispered, and then he kissed her again.

Applause filled her ears and told Clarissa to stop making out with the hot cowboy not-her-husband-yet. She pulled back to find his friends coming through the garage, all of them wearing smiles and cowboy hats. Since she'd been here a few weeks ago, she recognized all of them.

"Looks like you won't need that plan," Nate said, clapping Spencer on the shoulder. Then he scooped Clarissa into a hug, which sent a bolt of surprise through her. "He loves you so much."

"I haven't actually told her that yet," Spencer said, and Nate pulled away, quite the look of alarm on his face.

"You blew it," Ted teased him, and he slung his arm around Spencer's shoulders. "I think the turkey's out of the bag, Spence. You might as well tell her." He grinned like no one Clarissa had ever met, and his spirit was so *big*.

"Yeah," Slate said, also smiling like the Cheshire Cat. "Tell 'er. We won't listen."

"My ears are plugged," Dallas said, his eyes shining with bright light.

"You guys are impossible," Luke said. "They did this to me at Dallas's wedding too. Totally ganged up on me, and I had to put them all in their place." He stepped next to Clarissa's side. "Come on, you idiots. Let's leave them alone." He started herding cowboys, which turned out to be as hard to do as trying to do the same to cats.

Spencer watched them go, a glow on his face too. He faced her again and lifted one shoulder as if to say, *What can I say? They're kind of crazy, but I love 'em.*

Clarissa wanted to tell him she loved him too, because she did. "I'm in love with you," she blurted out, the words practically a shout. She cursed her Cooper genes and dialed back the intensity of her red hair. "I mean, I love you, Spencer."

"Even after what happened today?" He dropped his

chin toward his chest, clearly distressed by that morning's activities.

"Nothing that happened sounds like it was your fault."

"Even though my family is so dysfunctional and yours is so great?"

"Are you kidding me right now?" she asked, folding her arms. "I had to scream at them to get them to stop talking long enough to tell me where you were. I asked five or six times. They're maddening, and loud, and so grouchy all the time."

"But you love them."

She sighed and dropped her arms back to her sides. "Yes," she said. "I love them."

"They don't steal from you."

Her heart bled for him, and she reached up and cradled his face. "You're not your father."

His eyes shone like black gold, and he leaned into her touch. "I love you, Clarissa." He didn't say anything more. No qualifiers. No follow-up.

She felt his love flow through her, pure and simple and oh-so-good. A smile filled her face, then her soul, and she knew there would be nothing better than this man in her life. No restaurant job would hold a candle to being his wife, and she laughed as he took her into his arms again and spun her around.

He set her on her feet again and swayed side-to-side with her. "I love you, I love you, I love you," he whispered as he lowered his head toward hers. When he finally kissed her, Clarissa experienced peace, light, and love in their purest form.

She'd finally gotten what she wanted, and it had happened on a ranch in the middle of some small town in Texas no one had heard of.

CHAPTER TWENTY-FOUR

B y the time Spencer returned to his cabin at Sweet Water Falls Farm, the sky had settled into complete blackness. After lunch at Ginger's, he'd gone to the police station. They wanted to talk to him in person, despite the phone call he'd made before Clarissa's arrival.

He'd been there for hours, and Clarissa hadn't left his side once. His gratitude for her had doubled and then tripled.

Then, they'd had dinner at a pavilion behind the farmhouse he hadn't even known existed. Everyone who worked at the farm had come, and he'd invited everyone at Hope Eternal too. Nate and his family had come, as had Ted and his, Slate and his, and Luke and his. Dallas had been late, because Jess was dealing with a sick baby, and she and the little girl hadn't come.

Spencer appreciated the outpouring of love from those around him, as it did help to lessen the humiliation and embarrassment continually tugging at the corners of his mind.

As he climbed his steps now, he'd be entering the house alone. If he'd have known how pivotal today would be for him, he might have chosen to stay in bed. He'd truly let go of his father; he'd told Clarissa he loved her; he'd faced the demons within him, their fists cocked above their heads, ready to strike, and he'd chosen *not* to be that man.

He'd hugged Wayne as tightly as he could for a good long while once dinner had ended, because the man had saved him from himself. The police said they'd be holding his dad in the county jail there in Texas until the authorities could arrive from New Jersey. He could receive visitors between six and eight p.m., and Spencer hadn't decided if he'd go see his dad or not.

He wouldn't have any alcohol in jail. No drugs. Three square meals and some time outside. Spencer had never been to jail, but he knew men who had, and they'd survived. They'd come out better than they'd been before. All he could do now was as Nate had said—he wouldn't give up on his father. He'd choose to believe that people could change, and that his father would be one of them.

Inside the house, Spencer found something amiss immediately. He switched on the lights, his nose working to identify the smell.

Chocolate.

He spotted the plate of cookies on the counter, and his smile lit up the house as he crossed through the living room. Clarissa had been here, though she'd left the family dinner only five minutes before him.

The cookies were frozen solid, and he started to laugh. Of course the woman would have cookies in her freezer. She was nothing if not prepared for every type of emergency.

FOUR MONTHS LATER:

Spencer whipped the cream while Clarissa poured the sugar into the pot he'd set over low heat. Watching it dissolve brought him such satisfaction, much like watching his girlfriend lean over her notes for a new recipe.

"Last time," she mused, studying the page where she'd written all of her notes. Watching the woman brainstorm a recipe had been a fascinating experience for Spencer. "We put in two teaspoons of maple extract, and it was far too much."

"We should try syrup." He adjusted the flame under the burner, the thought of his dad never very far from his mind. He'd gone to visit him the night before he'd been taken to New Jersey, and Spencer had experienced the same calming, forgiving, peaceful feeling as he had when his father had fallen in his house, months ago.

There was nothing more Spencer could do. He

couldn't go to Atlantic City to visit in person, so he and Clarissa had been sending emails over the past few months as they'd continued to date. Pictures from the top of Enchanted Rock. Pictures of Spencer with Mighty Mouse, his horse. Pictures of the two of them, grinning at the camera.

"I'm worried it'll turn back into a congealed mess." She straightened and looked at him. He smiled at her and shrugged, because he was just the sounding board. He'd mentioned syrup before, and she'd written it somewhere in her organized, yet chaotic, mess of notes.

"Let's try it," she said, lifting a bottle of amber liquid from beneath the counter, a teasing glint in her pretty eyes.

He left the whisk in the pot and took her into his arms. "You're sneaky." He swayed with her, a sense of love and peace enveloping them. He'd felt the same way when he emailed his dad every week, without fail. His father had been responding too, even if the messages were short and stilted. Spencer had shown them to the boys at Hope Eternal Ranch, and they'd all agreed that Ernest was trying.

He doesn't know how to be a good father, Nate had said.

He doesn't know what to say, Slate had added.

He only gets fifteen minutes a few times a week on the computer, Ted had reminded him.

Be patient with him, Luke had said. *Sometimes the biggest change comes after someone gets out of prison.*

Be patient with yourself too, Dallas had told him. *You'll both get there, one step at a time.*

"You're smart," she said. "And sexy stirring that ice cream base."

"You should see yourself bending over that binder." He leaned down and kissed her, thinking about the diamond he'd hidden in the drawer next to the sink. She'd come back to the farm, and she did the same tasks she'd done previous to her departure. "Talk about smart and sexy."

He didn't really need to work in the shoppe too, and it wasn't part of his official duties anymore. Wayne had been steadily increasing Spencer's duties at Cooper & Co—the dairy operation on the farm—and decreasing his involvement in the agriculture side.

He'd been learning the ropes from Lee, Will, and Travis, and he had to work hard in a new way. He liked it, and he genuinely liked Clarissa's brothers. He knew for certain he was happier now than he'd ever been, all because he'd taken a risk and embraced this unexpected relationship. He'd opened his mouth and said something, even when it was hard, in all the relationships in his life.

He grinned at her and went back to the ice cream, the diamond engagement ring on his mind. She'd pulled out that syrup bottle, her message clear. She listened to him. His opinion mattered to her.

The base bubbled merrily, and he had a few minutes before she'd be ready to add the flavorings. He walked over to the sink and turned on the water, his heart pounding like the fence-post setter he'd used last week. He opened the drawer and took out the black box, drawing a deep breath. He'd only asked the one woman to marry him, and he'd been young and foolish.

He was ready now.

He so was, especially with this woman.

He cracked open the box, the crinkling sound as loud as gunshot to him. His voice suddenly went on vacation as he turned toward the woman he loved.

"I think if we—" Clarissa stopped talking as she lifted her widening eyes to Spencer and that ring.

"I love you," he said, not daring to get down on his knees in the kitchen. The floor here was dirty, and he knew, because he'd spent hours here with Clarissa. Hours talking to her. Hours falling more and more in love with her. "Will you do me the great honor of becoming my wife?"

Clarissa blinked, her smile slow as it filled her face. She nodded, her eyes glassy. "Yes," she finally said, squealing immediately afterward. "Yes, I'll marry you."

He laughed as she threw herself into his arms. "I love you too, Spence," Clarissa said, and Spencer let his fiancée kiss him and kiss him...while the ice cream base boiled over.

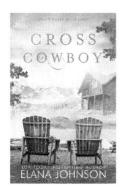

KEEP READING FOR A SNEAK PEEK at the first book in the Sweet Water Falls Farm series, **CROSS COWBOY**, which features Clarissa's brother, Travis!

T ravis Cooper whistled through his teeth, his irritation spiking. "Get up!" he yelled, though the dairy cows he herded only lowed in return. Some of them gave him the stink-eye, though he supposed he'd started the somewhat volatile relationship with the cattle by muscling them around, telling them not to stop in doorways, and perhaps even calling them a name or two when they disobeyed.

People thought the big black-and-white dairy cows were "just so cute" on social media, but to Travis, they were nothing but trouble. They loved to break down fences to get to the grasses and other tasty vittles in fields they weren't supposed to be in. They made a huge mess of their pastures, day in and day out. Diseases spread like wildfire, and they never waited nicely in line for their turn to be milked.

"Come on, Bertha," he said, shoving his shoulder against one of the huge beasts. Every dairy cow was named Bertha to Travis, and he actually smiled at his private joke. "To the right, girl," he said, digging in with his boots and *pushing*. See? Stubborn things, cows were.

He got Bertha #1 in the chute, and by some miracle, the girls after her followed suit—at least for a few cows. He and the veterinarian had been playing this game of chutes and udders for four days, and Travis was so done with it.

But the cows had to be checked every so often, and it was up to Travis to get that job done around Sweet Water Falls Farm. His older brother, Lee, took care of so many other things that Travis had gladly accepted the health of the herd as his responsibility. He just wished it came with less mud and less lowing.

Sometimes his ears heard the sound cows made when he was all alone, and that noise followed him into his dreams too.

He finally got the last Bertha into the chute, and she lumbered along until she reached Finley Rappont, the veterinarian that came out to the farm to check eyes, ears, tongues, and udders. He made a report for Travis, though he'd have separated any cows that had a problem.

Today, there were none, and Travis thanked his lucky stars above for that. Five or six of their newest milkers had shown sores, and Finn had pulled them. That hadn't been a good day for Travis, and the conversation around the family dinner table at the farmhouse had included a lot of rolled eyes and pointed questions.

The energy between Travis and his brothers always ran high, and he blamed all the redhead genes in the family. Lee could go from frowning to raging in less time than it took to breathe, and the worst part was that Travis never knew what would set him off.

Truth be told, he never really knew what would set him off either. Sometimes, he just couldn't carry one more thing, and something simple like a broken fence—something he'd dealt with countless times over the years he'd worked the farm—would irritate him to the point of snapping.

Not that it really mattered. He didn't rant to anyone but Daddy, Lee, or Will. He treated his cowboys well. He didn't have a girlfriend to speak of, and even when he did, those relationships barely made it out of the dugout. He might get to first base, but he might not, as he hadn't had a girlfriend who'd lasted longer than two months in at least a decade.

"Lookin' good?" he asked Finn.

"Yeah, today was easy." He glanced up from his clipboard, which had a tablet attached to it. He tapped and swiped, and then he added, "All sent. You'll get the report in your email."

"Thanks." Lee shook his hand, and they started toward the milkshed, where the small, dirt parking lot held their trucks. He had no idea what Finn got to go do now, but Travis had to get over a thousand cows into and then out of milking stalls in the next couple of hours. The work at Cooper & Company, the milking side of their family farm, could consume a man, and Travis had seen the with his very own eyes.

Lee had been married and divorced, and while his ex-wife had never said their marriage had dissolved because of Lee's dedication to fences, milk, and cows, Travis had a suspicion it did. All of the women he'd dated over the years had said some form of the same thing to Travis—he worked too much. He was never available when they wanted to go to dinner. Sometimes he had to text during their dates.

Blah, blah, *blah*. He'd heard it all, and he'd decided Lee had things figured out now—he didn't date at all. After Travis's last attempt at a relationship had ended after only a few dates, he'd put himself on a female-free diet too.

He bid farewell to Finn and turned to enter the milkshed, where the brothers kept the administrative office for Cooper & Co. The moment he did, shouting met his ears. Oh, boy. Lee wasn't happy this morning.

"...that just won't work," he said.

"Why are you yelling at me?" Will fired back, and he was definitely the grumpiest of the trio of brothers. "I know it won't work. That's why I came to talk to you about it."

Travis strode the few steps to the office and found Lee

sitting at the desk while Will hovered near the window. There were no clenched fists or red faces. The brothers just had loud voices, growly barks, and short fuses.

"What won't work?" he asked, and both Lee and Will looked at him. Will was the lightest of the gingers, with almost blond hair, and eyes between blue and green. He was the middle brother, and his eyes definitely came half from Mama and half from Daddy. When he grew out his beard, the red really came in then.

Lee was the darkest of the brothers, in attitude and physical appearance. His hair shone like red gold, a deep auburn that matched their oldest sister's. Cherry didn't live on the farm, but she and Lee could've been twins with their auburn hair. His green-black eyes only glinted with darkness when he was angry, as he was right now.

Travis sat somewhere in the middle of the two of them, with tons of the typical red hair people pictured when someone said, "he's the redhead." His eyes came straight from Mama, as did his hair, and they glinted like emeralds when he laughed. Or so Mama said.

He was the youngest son, and he was very close to his mother. He didn't deny it when everyone in the family told him he was a mama's boy. He was, and he wasn't embarrassed about it.

Lee stood. "What are you doing?"

"Milking three," Travis said, glancing at Will. "Why?"

"We've got a shipment of essential parts coming for

the threshers," he said. "And Leonard can't get them to us until next week."

Travis didn't work much on the agriculture side of the farm, but he knew so much of the nutrition of the dairy cows relied on the grain they grew over there. "That won't work," Travis said. "Why can't he deliver it?"

"I don't know," Lee said, sighing as he sat back down, that permanent frown etched between his eyebrows. "Will?"

"He's got one guy who broke his leg or something, and another one quit. Bottom line, he's behind on deliveries, and we're so far out that he won't come until Wednesday."

Lee shuffled some papers. "I could maybe send Chris."

"Yeah, and I'll hear about it for months," Will said. "He'll want every Sunday off to make a trip to town."

"It's a trip to town," Travis said, not getting the problem. "We'll just go pick up the parts ourselves." Sure, the farm sat about thirty minutes from the town of Sweet Water Falls, but it was a half-hour, not a half-day. They went once a month for groceries and to run errands, and Travis himself definitely left the farm more than his brothers. He could go. In fact, an after-noon off the ranch suddenly held great possibilities for him.

"If we send Brad, we won't see him until evening," Lee mused.

"I'll go," Travis said, looking from Lee to Will. "Send Brad over to help with the milking, and I'll go right now." He dug in his pocket for his truck keys.

Lee looked up from his papers. "While you're there, you'll have to load up the fertilizer too."

Travis almost backed out. No wonder they weren't happy about not getting the delivery. No one wanted to load up the fertilizer, as they bought it from the farm supply store, and it was all-natural and organic. That made their milk organic, which meant they could make more money for the dairy products. It also came with a certain...smell.

"So I can't drive my own truck," Travis said.

"You'd take the dump truck." Lee looked up, his eyes filled with questions.

Travis didn't really want to drive the dump truck. It had no radio, and while he didn't usually mind the silence, right now, it had a way of screaming the truth at him. And the truth hurt at the moment.

"Please?" Will asked. "If you go, I'll take care of all the milking today and tomorrow."

"Tomorrow too?" Travis couldn't remember the last time he'd had a day off. They all paid for it when men took full days off on the farm.

"Yes," Will said. "We need those parts, and the fertilizer is just on the way."

Travis didn't really need to think too hard about it. He'd get off the farm today and he'd get to sleep in tomorrow. "Fine," he said, folding his arms. "I'll go."

Will grinned, his face lighting up from within.

"Thanks, Trav." He looked at Lee. "Let's call Leonard right now."

"I'll get the receipt printed for the fertilizer too," Lee said. "Thanks, Travis. This is really going to help us."

"We're okay for me to be gone for the rest of today and tomorrow?" he asked.

Lee frowned again. "We'll see about tomorrow. We're on the last harvest here, Trav."

"As if I didn't know," Travis said sarcastically, smiling at his older brother. Lee didn't return the gesture, and Travis wondered what it would take to get him to loosen up a little. Probably a miracle from the Lord above.

From there, things happened quickly, and the next thing he knew, he climbed into the dump truck and started her moving down the dirt road from the equipment shed to the highway. Everything bounced in the old truck, and Travis had loved riding in it as a child. He hadn't had the opportunity very often, but when he did, it was just him and Daddy. He got to go to town with Daddy, and they always got ice cream in Sweet Water Falls before Daddy returned to the farm.

They were good times, and Travis felt some of the tension he carried everywhere with him finally start to seep away.

The drive to town passed in a blink, and Travis wasn't even sure what he'd thought about. He pulled up the back of the farm supply store, and he showed the attendant there his receipt for the fertilizer.

The man handed Travis a pair of gloves and put on a pair too. Travis pulled around to the fertilizer bin, the scent of it permeating the inside of the dump truck already. It had been mighty hot in Texas lately.

"Oh, boy," Travis said, noting the attendant had put a bandana around his nose and mouth. He handed Travis a shovel, and they faced the dark brown stuff spilling from the bin. Neither of them moved.

"Let's dig in," Travis finally said. "It's not going to shovel itself." He took the first shovel full, and the other man got to work too. Dislodging the fertilizer only made the smell intensify, and it was impossible to stay clean. Travis swore the fertilizer—which contained manure and bat guano that had been baking in the sun—covered him from head to toe by the time they got the truck filled.

"Thanks," he said to the attendant, who waved to him as he pulled back up to the loading dock. Someone brought out the mechanical parts they needed, and Travis signed the invoice and accepted the receipt.

A flyer flapped in the breeze, announcing the Fall Ball, which the farm supply store was sponsoring that year. They often sponsored events and happenings around the town of Sweet Water Falls. Looking at the cartoon rendition of a man and a woman, both dressed in their finest clothes, dancing under the stars, Travis's heart bumped out a couple of short, stilted beats.

He wanted to go to this ball.

"Nope," he told himself, tossing the invoice and

attached flyer onto the seat beside him. "That would not be a female-free date." Plus, he probably didn't have time anyway.

He backed away from the dock and got the truck moving toward the exit. He slowed as a large F-350 appeared, slowing to obviously turn into the back lot behind the farm supply store. The truck had a sleek, sophisticated logo on the side that said Sweetspot, with a hiker hanging off the long end of the P.

His heart tapped strangely again, because he knew this company. And he knew the woman behind the big truck now turning toward him. Shayla Nelson.

He'd picked her up on the side of the road a few months ago, and he hadn't exactly been nice to her. His mouth had a way of running away from him, and he only seemed to be able to realize it after the fact.

She made the left turn, but he hadn't stopped the truck, and he'd crowded the entrance. When she realized it, he clearly saw the displeasure on her face. Her disgusted and frustrated look screamed at him through two windshields, but he couldn't move.

She really was pretty, and his mind started thinking about what Shayla Nelson would look like in a ball gown... all that dark hair piled on her head in some elegant updo...

She honked her horn and gestured for him to back up, and Travis jumped to action to do just that. He eased the truck backward, giving her room to get into the lot, which she did.

His phone chimed, and he pushed on the brake to check it, as that was Daddy's specific sound. *Lee says you're in town. Can you stop and get Mama's medicine at the pharmacy?*

Sure thing, Travis said, his heart heavy in his chest now. He thought of his mother and the constant medications she needed. He pressed his eyes closed and said a prayer for her health, and that if she had to suffer, maybe the Lord could just take her home already.

His eyes jerked open when someone rapped on his window with sharp knuckles.

He flinched away from the sound, his gaze locking onto Shayla's through the glass to his left. Adrenaline ran from his toes to his scalp in half a second, and his heart dropped to his stomach, rebounding back to its rightful spot a moment later.

He reached to roll down his window. "What the devil are you doing? You scared me."

She'd climbed right up on the runners of the dump truck, and she didn't look happy. Snaps, crackles, and pops filled the air between them, and Travis wondered if he was the only one who could feel them.

"What the devil am *I* doing? You're blocking everyone coming in and out of the parking lot." Her eyes narrowed, and she pinched her fingers over her nose. "And you stink."

He looked in his rearview mirror, and sure enough, he

had three or four other people behind him, waiting for him to move so they could get out too.

"I'll move," he said, releasing the brake pedal where his foot sat. The truck started backward, and Shayla yelped.

"I'm on the truck," she said. "Stop. Stop it!"

He jammed on the brake again, and Shayla grunted and groaned as if he'd been going fifty miles per hour and had slammed on the brakes. She glared at him. "My goodness, Travis Cooper. What is wrong with you?" She peered at him as if she was really trying to figure him out. Could see feel that electricity now zinging from the ends of his fingertips? Or was that all him?

"Well, get off the runner," he said, not looking away from her. "I need to move."

Shayla Nelson thanked every star in the universe that she had a good grip on the metal arms holding the rearview mirror out to the side of Travis Cooper's stinky dump truck. The man himself smelled like he'd rolled in manure and then old, wet grass, but those eyes...

She drew in a breath and hopped to the ground, repeating her prayer of thanksgiving for the trail boots she wore. She'd just introduced these boots into the market, and they were selling really well. Better than even she'd expected, despite the marketing money she'd put behind their launch.

Travis's truck groaned and the brakes released as he put the behemoth in park. At least he'd moved it out of the way, and Shayla turned as a truck towing a horse trailer with three equines in the back of it edged around her and the truck. She had to press pretty close to the big vehicle, and that only seemed to smell worse than before.

The stunningly handsome cowboy got out of the truck, and Shayla tried not to scan him from those delicious cowboy boots up to that delectable cowboy hat. Tried, and failed.

Wow, he was good-looking. And boy, did he know it, if the dark glint in his eye said anything. He lasered that gaze on her and said, "Sorry about that."

Surprise filled her from head to toe, rendering her mute. He wore a baby blue T-shirt with the outline of Texas on it in faded white, with big, blocky letters through the state that said STRONG.

Mm hm, he was Texas strong, if the way his shirt-sleeves clung to his biceps was any indication. She'd found him downright mouthwatering a few months ago when he'd happened past her on the highway out by his farm. He'd been right gentlemanly by helping her with Sweetie, her dog, and giving her a ride all the way back to town.

It was just the conversation that had been terrible. He'd accused her of stealing Sweetspot from Kylie, which so wasn't true. Shayla pushed against the memories of what had really happened between her and her former best friend. They still caused bitterness to surge in her throat and her stomach to tighten.

She hadn't explained anything to Travis, and while she'd thought she'd like to get his number when he'd first picked her up, that thought had fled pretty fast. Now, though, faced with him in the blazing hot September sun, with those long legs clad in jeans... She could admit she'd like the man's phone number, if only to text him all the funny horse videos she saw on her social media.

He owns a dairy farm, she told herself as another truck went past them and left the parking lot. *And you should say something instead of staring at him silently.*

"Thank you," she said, not even sure what she was thanking him for.

His brow furrowed in an adorably sexy way, and he was obviously wondering the same thing. "For what?" he asked, his voice stuck somewhere in the back of his throat.

She waved toward the pickup going by them now. "For moving." She wanted to press her eyes closed and disappear. Teleporting to another location sounded amazing about now, but when she opened her eyes again, she still stood six feet from Travis Cooper. Her heart still boomed strangely in her chest when she thought about holding his hand. Her mind still went a bit blank when talking to him.

"It was like you didn't realize there were other people in the world," she said. "I realize you probably don't get off the farm much, but still."

"You're right," he said, folding his arms and cocking a hip, which was a fairly challenging stance. "I don't get off the farm much." He didn't say why he'd been taking up the whole driveway, and Shayla wasn't going to ask. She just needed to get her feed and get back to the showroom.

"The traffic is cleared out," she said.

"You don't work here," he said, glancing toward the farm supply store. "In fact, what are you doing here?" He looked at her again, his eyes traveling down the length of her body.

Shayla felt every inch of that look, and she was glad she'd put on the lightweight trail shorts to go with her new boots. She ran the trails in the morning, and she'd simply put on a fresh pair of shorts and the matching tank once she'd gotten to the showroom floor. She wore the complete trail running package that day, and the way Travis licked his lips made a current run through her veins.

"I don't have to tell you why I'm at the farm supply store," she said dryly, glad her wit had returned. "It's none of your business." She turned away from him to go get her wallet and go get the chicken feed she needed for her hens. Everyone in Sweet Water Falls had chickens now, as it was the trendy thing to do. Travis would likely make fun of her for it, and she really didn't need the cowboy's attitude today.

Shayla bore the weight of Travis's gaze on her back as she walked away from him, and she checked discreetly over her shoulder as she opened her truck door. Yes, he was still watching her, that frown frozen between his eyes. She collected her wallet and went in the back door of the supply store, running through ways she could get his number.

You don't want his number, she told herself as she

grabbed a flatbed cart and started for the outdoor animals section. A shade had been erected over this part of the store, as it was outdoors, and she found the chicken feed without incident. Her hens seemed to be going through quite a lot of it, and she found someone wearing the bright green vests, and asked them about it.

"They should be getting out too," the man said. "To root for bugs and the like. Do you let them out into the yard?"

"Well, sort of," Shayla said, thinking of her coop "I don't have a farm or anything. They're backyard hens."

The man smiled, and it felt a little placating to Shayla. "They still need to be out in the grass or weeds. A garden even."

"I've got a garden," she said, brightening. "I can put them in that."

"Try that," he said. "Then they won't eat as much feed. You'll probably get better egg production too."

"Thanks," she said. She paid for the feed, tossed the flyer about the Fall Ball into the trashcan, and drew a deep breath as she headed toward the exit. Her breath whooshed out of her body the moment she stepped into the parking lot.

Travis's dump truck was gone. That was that.

She lowered the tailgate of her truck—a huge, white vehicle she'd bought with business money since she hauled so many boxes to and from festivals and shows. Not only that, but she spent as much time outdoors as she possibly could, and she loved throwing a tent and a back-pack in the bed of the truck and heading into the wilds of Texas.

She returned the flatbed cart to the store and hurried back to the truck. One couldn't abide this heat for long, and she muttered, "It would be nice if it could cool off a little," under her breath.

She reached for her door handle at the same time she saw the paper stuck to her window. Her hand froze halfway there, as the handwriting looked sloppy and like it had been hastily scrawled.

Did you get a receipt?

She read the sentence again, not sure she'd gotten it right the first time. "What?" she asked herself. Below that nonsensical question, he'd written *Trav*—and his phone number.

Shayla pulled the note from the window, the edge of it ripping from where it had been stuck between the window and the metal on the truck. She sucked in a breath as the bottom of the eight on the last digit of his phone number tore off, quickly glancing around to see if anyone had seen or heard her.

Everyone seemed to be going about their business as usual, and Shayla told herself she better do the same. She'd left her assistant, Elaine, and her junior partner, Jadyn, alone in the showroom, and it could be a lot to handle if more than a few customers came in.

Shayla told herself that they didn't get extremely busy

in the afternoon on Wednesdays, and she didn't go a mile over the speed limit on the way back to the showroom. She needed the extra space and time to think about Travis's note. Or rather, *Trav's* note.

"Trav," she said, rolling the single-syllable name around in her mouth. "Sure, Trav," she added. "I'd love to go out with you. Have you been to The Bluebell Café?" Of course he wouldn't have been there. It was total frou-frou food, and a man with muscles like that ate red meat for every meal. Probably *raw* red meat.

She made the turn to get on Main Street, as Sweetspot had just secured a prime, downtown location for their new showroom. Their foot traffic had increased over three hundred percent since they'd moved into the light, airy storefront three weeks ago. All the spots out front had cars in them, and Shayla navigated around to the back.

The feed could stay in the truck, and she leapt from it and jogged inside to make sure Elaine and Jadyn were okay. Several people milled about in the store, and sure enough, when Elaine turned and saw her, the entire story spilled from her eyes. She didn't have to say a word, because Shayla had been working with her long enough to communicate telepathically.

The blonde nodded toward a couple perusing the lightweight jackets, and Shayla put on her game face. "Can I help you two find something?" she asked, adopting her professional voice. She could gush about Trav later and ask Jadyn and Elaine how she was supposed to answer such a weird question.

Right now, she wanted to sell one of these jackets, and as she looked from the man to the woman, she thought she could probably get two sales out of this couple.

***

SHAYLA PEERED AT THE COMPUTER SCREEN, wondering when things had become so hard to see. She squinted at the comment on social media, trying to make sense of it so she could answer it. She personally manned their social media accounts, posting pictures of herself using their equipment, or collecting photos from her customers that she then reposted or shared to their main account.

Sweetspot had quite the following, and their online sales had ticked up another five percent last quarter.

Her eyes hurt, and she answered the question and then leaned away from the computer, pressing her palms to her eye sockets. Maybe she needed glasses, but they were a pain in the neck. She didn't want to deal with contact lenses while camping, or glasses sliding down her nose while rock-climbing. Fine, she wasn't that into rock-climbing, but she did like hiking, picnicking, hammocking, and camping. Her favorite part was a campfire, with a tin foil dinner or a charred hot dog, cooked right over hot coals.

"Shayla," Elaine said, and Shayla opened her eyes. Elaine blurred along the edges, but that was because of the bright, flashing lights in Shayla's vision.

"Is it time?" She got to her feet. Her hours in the office could pass with the snap of a finger, and she always had something more to do.

Elaine approached with a couple of folders. "The new accounts for Wiseman's and Mountain Top Outfitters."

"Oh, great," Shayla said, taking the folders and putting them on he desk. Elaine did all the paperwork. She made sure all the contracts got signed. She made sure payments got sent on time and that their accounts payable kept the company thriving. She'd started at Sweetspot as an accountant, but she oversaw that department now. They had another woman running all the money in the company, and Shayla met with her team every other week to make sure everyone was happy, that things were operating the way they should be, and that the communication stayed open.

If they'd have done that from the beginning, maybe Kylie would still be with them. Maybe Shayla wouldn't have such a hollow feeling every time she thought of the woman she'd known since childhood—and that she hadn't spoken to in over four years now.

"We have a conference call with Alexander Huffman on Monday morning at seven-thirty in the morning."

"My goodness," Shayla said, locking eyes with Elaine. She had bright blue eyes to go with her blonde hair, and

Shayla couldn't remember a time when she'd seen her assistant wear anything but skirts, blouses, and heels. While Shayla opted to wear the clothing they sold, Elaine was a professional through and through. "Why so early?"

"He's in London," Elaine said. "It'll be two-thirty for him there, and it was the only slot he had."

"All right." Shayla pulled out her phone and made an alarm for the call. "Here? Or can I do it from home?"

"We can all call in from home, if you'd like," Elaine said, clicking her pen into operation mode. That *click-click* triggered something in Shayla, because it was the sound of Elaine about to get stuff done. "Just let me know, so I can set up the online meeting."

"Let's do it from home," Shayla said. "Then I won't have to be showered and here so early." By that time, she'd barely be back from running.

"Okay." Elaine made a note on the clipboard she carried. As she finished up, she cocked her head, which meant their saleswoman was likely talking to her.

She reached up and pressed the button on the wire coming down from her ear. "I'll let her know." She looked at Shayla. "You've got a customer asking specifically for you."

Time to do business. Shayla felt her mask sliding into place, and she actually cracked her neck left and right, as if she were going into a battle. Elaine turned and left the office, with Shayla right behind her.

They went down the hall together, Elaine telling her

about the supplier meeting on Tuesday, and the price comparison sheet she'd put together for the nylon they needed to make their tents. Their agreement was expiring soon, and Shayla needed to lock in a price for the next couple of years. But the prices had gone up over fifty percent, and since she ordered so much, she wanted a better deal than that.

In truth, she'd sign the contract with the higher prices, because finding a new nylon supplier would be a nightmare. Her customers expected a certain quality of product, and she actually had all of the tents Sweetspot sold custom sewn. She didn't skimp on anything, which was why Sweetspot had grown so fast and still did so well.

"I'll be right there." Elaine paused and turned back the way they'd come. "There's a delivery coming to the warehouse," she said. "I want to see if it's those sweat bands."

"I hope so," Shayla said with a smile. "You've been *sweating* about those for a week." She giggled at her own lame joke, glad when Elaine did too.

The two women parted, and Shayla went out into the showroom, wondering who was asking about her. She'd sold outdoor equipment to a lot of people—companies, suppliers, retail stores, as well as the common man taking a biking trip with his family.

She glanced around, the world narrowing to a single man standing in the camping section—Travis Cooper.

"Campers unite," Shayla murmured. The man stood

out like a sore thumb in the store, because he was the only one wearing a cowboy hat.

She'd never texted or called him to answer his question. In truth, she hadn't known how. Every time she'd thought about it, she just felt stupid texting him a yes or no answer. Not to mention the last couple of days had been extraordinarily busy. She hadn't forgotten about Travis Cooper. Such a thing seemed impossible, and he lifted his head as if he could feel her watching him.

Their eyes met, and lightning cracked right through the roof. He grinned at her and walked toward her, every ounce of confidence in the world in those shoulders.

"Hey," he said.

"What are you doing here?" she asked.

"Thinkin' about goin' camping," he said, indicating the gear she had on the shelves.

She blinked, her long eyelashes almost sticking together, and she realized she'd been pressing her palms to her eyes. Had she mashed her false eyelashes? Surely Elaine would've told her if she had.

Still, she reached up and brushed her fingertips along her lashes. "Why does that sound so false?" she asked.

Travis chuckled, and that sound could make a woman swoon. "Guilty, I suppose." He ducked his head, barely lifting it enough to peer up at her from underneath the brim of that big, brown hat. "I was wondering if you got my note. The one I left on your truck at the farm supply store a few days ago?"

Shayla's chest crackled with heat and sparks. "Yeah," she said slowly. "It was confusing."

His expression darkened as he ticked his head up even more. "It was?"

"Did I get a receipt? I don't get it. Why did you want to know that?" She had programmed his number in her phone, but she hadn't used it. Yet.

"Did you get one?"

"Yes," she said.

"It had that flyer for the Fall Ball on it," he said, immediately clearing his throat.

Shayla could only stare at him. "Okay."

Travis laughed lightly, though his feet shifted along the painted concrete floor. "Gonna make me work for it, I see."

"Work for what?" she asked, genuinely confused.

His face turned blank, and Shayla glanced around to see if anyone was watching them. Didn't seem to be. Then Travis blinked, and that familiar fire entered those pretty, emerald-green eyes.

"I was wondering if maybe you'd like to go with me," he said, dropping his chin again. "To the Fall Ball."

Shayla's mouth dropped open, and she quickly snapped it shut. Her brain whirred, taking a long time to come to a three-letter or a two-letter answer. In fact, she still hadn't landed on what to say, and the seconds ticked by, each one like a silent bomb landing in her ears.

BOOKS IN THE HOPE ETERNAL RANCH ROMANCE SERIES

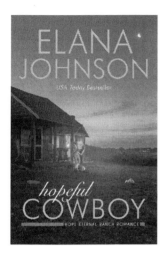

Hopeful Cowboy, Book 1: Can Ginger and Nate find their happily-ever-after, keep up their duties on the ranch, and build a family? Or will the risk be too great for them both?

Overprotective Cowboy, Book 2: Can Ted and Emma face their pasts so they can truly be ready to step into the future together? Or will everything between them fall apart once the truth comes out?

Rugged Cowboy, Book 3:
He's a cowboy mechanic with two kids and an ex-wife on the run. She connects better to horses than humans. Can Dallas and Jess find their way to each other at Hope Eternal Ranch?

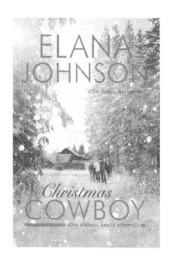

Christmas Cowboy, Book 4: He needs to start a new story for his life. She's dealing with a lot of family issues. This Christmas, can Slate and Jill find solace in each other at Hope Eternal Ranch?

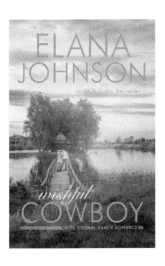

Wishful Cowboy, Book 5:
He needs somewhere to belong. She has a heart as wide as the Texas sky. Can Luke and Hannah find their one true love in each other?

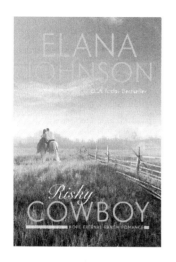

Risky Cowboy, Book 6: She's tired of making cheese and ice cream on her family's dairy farm, but when the cowboy hired to replace her turns out to be an ex-boyfriend, Clarissa suddenly isn't so sure about leaving town... Will Spencer risk it all to convince Clarissa to stay and give him a second chance?

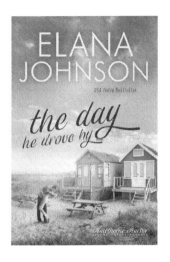

The Day He Drove By (Hawthorne Harbor Second Chance Romance, Book 1): A widowed florist, her ten-year-old daughter, and the para medic who delivered the girl a decade earlier...

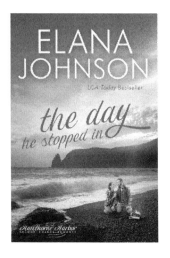

The Day He Stopped In (Hawthorne Harbor Second Chance Romance, Book 2): Janey Germaine is tired of entertaining tourists in Olympic National Park all day and trying to keep her twelve-year-old son occupied at night. When longtime friend and the Chief of Police, Adam Herrin, offers to take the boy on a ride-along one fall evening, Janey starts to see him in a different light. Do they have the courage to take their relationship out of the friend zone?

The Day He Said Hello (Hawthorne Harbor Second Chance Romance, Book 3): Bennett Patterson is content with his boring firefighting job and his big great dane...until he comes face-toface with his high school girlfriend, Jennie Zimmerman, who swore she'd never return to Hawthorne Harbor. Can they rekindle their old flame? Or will their opposite personalities keep them apart?

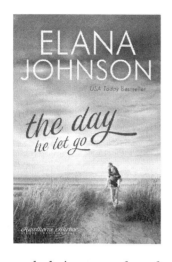

The Day He Let Go (Hawthorne Harbor Second Chance Romance, Book 4): Trent Baker is ready for another relationship, and he's hopeful he can find someone who wants him and to be a mother to his son. Lauren Michaels runs her own general contract company, and she's never thought she has a maternal bone in her body. But when she gets a second chance with the handsome K9 cop who blew her off when she first came to town, she can't say no... Can Trent and Lauren make their differences into strengths and build a family?

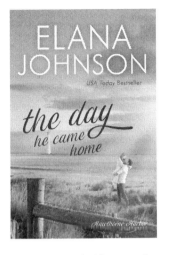

The Day He Came Home (Hawthorne Harbor Second Chance Romance, Book 5): A wounded Marine returns to Hawthorne Harbor years after the woman he was married to for exactly one week before she got an annulment...and then a baby nine months later. Can Hunter and Alice make a family out of past heartache?

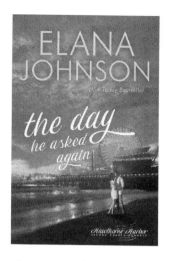

The Day He Asked Again (Hawthorne Harbor Second Chance Romance, Book 6): A Coast Guard captain would rather spend his time on the sea...unless he's with the woman he's been crushing on for months. Can Brooklynn and Dave make their second chance stick?

ABOUT ELANA

Elana Johnson is the USA Today bestselling author of dozens of clean and wholesome contemporary romance novels. She lives in Utah, where she mothers two fur babies, taxis her daughter to theater several times a week, and eats a lot of Ferrero Rocher while writing. Find her on her website at elanajohnson.com.

Made in the USA
Columbia, SC
21 July 2024